LOSING SARAH

by

Jonas Saul

PUBLISHED BY:
Imagine Press Inc.
Ebook ISBN: 978-1-927404-44-7
Paperback ISBN: 978-1-998047-07-9
Hardcover ISBN: 978-1-998047-39-0

Losing Sarah

The Sarah Roberts Series

Dark Visions (One)
The Warning (Two)
The Crypt (Three)
The Hostage (Four)
The Victim (Five)
The Enigma (Six)
The Vigilante (Seven)
The Rogue (Eight)
Killing Sarah (Nine)
The Antagonist (Ten)
The Redeemed (Eleven)
The Haunted (Twelve)
The Unlucky (Thirteen)
The Abandoned (Fourteen)
The Cartel (Fifteen)
Losing Sarah (Sixteen)
The Pact (Seventeen)
The Terror (Eighteen)
The Chase (Nineteen)
The Betrayal (Twenty)
Sarah's Return (Twenty-One)
The Hunt (Twenty-Two)
The Delivery (Twenty-Three)
The Trap (Twenty-Four)
The Ultimatum (Twenty-Five)
The Depraved (Twenty-Six)
The Condemned (Twenty-Seven)
Payback (Twenty-Eight)
The Unknown (Twenty-Nine)
Wrath (Thirty)
The Damned (Thirty-One)
The Game (Thirty-Two)

The Decoy (Thirty-Three)
The Disappearance (Thirty-Four)
The Whole Truth (Thirty-Five)
Alex (Thirty-Six)
Parkman (Thirty-Seven)
Darwin (Thirty-Eight)
Aaron (Thirty-Nine)
Remains To Be Seen (Forty)

The Jake Wood Novels

The Immortal Gene (Book One)
The Immortal Target (Book Two)

Standalone Novels

'Til Death Do Us Part
The Drowning
The Woman in the Woods
The Threat
The Specter
The Mafia Trilogy
A Murder in Time
Frequency of the Dead

Co-Authored Novels

Collision Course (Written with Gary Ponzo)
There Will Be Blood (Written with Rania Stone)
The Soulless (Written with Rania Stone)

Short Story Collections

Twisted Fate (Tales of Horror)

Losing Sarah

Twists of Fate (Tales of Hope)

Chapter 1

Sarah Roberts couldn't handle the pain anymore. No matter what side of the fierce battle she stood on, she was losing. A full-body sweat engulfed her in this war for self-control, clarity, and for resolute calm. The sheets below were soaked, wet clothes clinging to her skin. The drug had an unbearable hold over her. One she was losing.

The recreational vehicle edged closer to the United States-Mexico border. She had just destroyed the Enzo Cartel. Aaron Stevens, her boyfriend, was by her side, holding her hand as she shook from the internal tremors.

Long-time friend and colleague Parkman sat up front with Aaron's dojo teachers who had come to Mexico in her time of need. Everyone had risked their lives to stop the mad cartel.

It was over, and yet it was only beginning for Sarah. Could injuries add up? Could they accrue? Was she wearing down, weakening? She was worn out and needed rest. She needed to heal. Yet, gnawing at her, a sense of understanding, like an innate feeling, overwhelmed any rational thought. A need. A burning desire echoed through her core with every tremor of her hands.

The need for one more fix.

The cost was too high, and the price was not yet set. What would she pay for one more fix? Just one more, then she'd kick thoughts of heroin to the curb. She could do it. She was strong enough. She beat worse in her twenty-six years on this earth. A little substance wasn't stronger than her.

They had kept her high in the short time she was held at the Enzo Cartel's compound. Needle marks on the inside of her arm told the story. Now all she had to do was destroy the ache on the inside and move on with her life drug-free. But the ache intensified by the hour, and she wasn't doing anything to appease it. Kill the ache, or ease it off with one more hit. Kill the ache or ease the ache. Which was easier? Which was feasible?

And the battle raged on.

"Stop the RV," Sarah whispered.

Aaron patted her hand. "We're almost at the border, Sarah."

"Stop it." This time she spoke louder.

"We are stopped. Stopped behind hundreds of vehicles trying to squeeze through customs. Maybe ten minutes left."

"I want off."

"Off? For what? If you need a toilet or you think you might throw up, there's a bathroom on this—"

"Off!" she shouted, her gaze falling on him. "Get me the

hell off this RV now," she said, her voice only loud enough for Aaron to hear. "Our vacation started a half hour ago, and we're already in Mexico. This is where we stay. We're out of danger. Everyone's safe. But I need a vacation and want to be alone with you to start it. And I want to do that now."

He studied her face, eyes roving back and forth. A shadow crossed his face like a cloud passing in front of the sun. At that moment, she knew Aaron had decided to listen to her. Maybe he was excited about the idea of a vacation. Or maybe, just maybe, he saw the desperation in her eyes and understood it for what it was. The withdrawal symptoms were upon her, and as they advanced, she didn't want to be around loved ones or people she cared about. The embarrassment was too much. They saw her one way. This weakness enveloping her from within would show them a side they had never seen before and one they would never see again. She needed out. She needed to be away from everyone.

If that was Aaron's understanding, fine. Whatever made him stand up and talk privately with Parkman didn't matter to her. She just needed off this RV.

She caught Parkman's glance over Aaron's shoulder. Their eyes met. In his, she saw sorrow and immediately wondered what he saw in hers. Her lids dropped, and she knew more than ever that she needed off this RV. Whatever side won, whether she healed the urge or took another hit, she couldn't continue this internal battle surrounded by all the people in the world she loved. If Aaron didn't help her up and get her off this RV before they hit the border, she would do it herself.

She counted her breaths, slowly inhaling, exhaling,

waiting. The RV edged forward again, ever closer to the border. Her stomach clenched as knots tied and then untied. The urge to vomit caused a cool sheen of sweat to ooze over her. Pain in her head pulsed to the beat of her heart.

She'd been through many dangerous situations in her life, and each time faced them with a brave countenance with her dead sister close, on her mind—or in her mind as it were. But this was a new monster. Something heretofore unchallenged, one that had a power of its own and seemed to make decisions for her, whether consequences played a role or not.

She would overcome this. There were too many things to do in her life yet. Too many battles to be won. And she'd start with this battle. One day at a time, one step, one inch.

But first, a fix. Then she'd fight. One fix. Just one.

She opened her eyes, got her hand under her, and pushed up off the bed. Once her feet were on the carpeted floor of the RV, elbows on her thighs, her head spun. She waited for the spins to ease.

A hand rested gently on her shoulder.

"I got our passports from Parkman," Aaron said softly. "He gave me a cell phone to stay in touch. No one will follow us. They will consider us on vacation."

She met his eyes. "Thank you. Now, can we go?"

He helped her to her feet. She surprised herself that she didn't stumble as they walked through the narrow RV until they reached the door to the outside. Aaron must've prepared everyone for their departure because his three teachers stayed seated, each one nodding her way as she looked at them and offered a silent thank you and goodbye, one by one.

"Where's Casper?" she asked. "Darwin?"

"They ran ahead of the line of vehicles ten minutes ago to ensure everything will run smoothly through customs."

Parkman was close enough to touch. She rested a hand on his forearm.

"Thank you," she whispered. "For everything."

He tapped her hand with his in a calming gesture. She was going to miss him. It had been many years and struggles, but somehow they had managed it together. This one she had to do on her own. "I love you, Parkman, but this is personal. Personal for me. I need this right now."

"Of course. Whatever you need."

"Aaron and I will disappear for a couple of weeks. Then we'll come stateside. Be ready for a get-together. We'll have dinner. Drink. And be merry. Deal?"

"Deal."

She let her hand slip from his arm. The RV edged forward. She turned her eyes to the door.

"Please, don't follow us. This is a vacation, not work. There are no bad guys here. Let Casper and Darwin know, too. Cool?"

"Cool."

She opened the door and stepped onto Mexican soil. A warm breeze chilled her as it hit her sweat-soaked body. She felt stronger since she'd gotten out of the bed in the back of the RV. It must be the adrenaline in her veins, her will to be strong. Maybe the strength came from the first traces of beating the addiction. She was confident that every trace of heroin in her body would be gone within a week, even the ache gone, too. She would never touch the stuff again. Ever.

After the next hit.

Just one more, and she'd be fine.

Chapter 2

EDDIE COLEMAN, A BLACKJACK dealer at the Rosarito Hotel and Casino, wiped crumbs off his uniform as Mark Struben, one of the poker dealers, entered the lunchroom. They nodded to one another as if they were mere acquaintances. But Eddie Coleman and Mark Struben weren't just friends; they were partners.

Partners in crime.

And within a few hours, they would be free and clear, ready to change their ID, hairstyles, and clothes for a new life of beach, sun, and rum and Cokes because rum and Coke was the only drink for Eddie.

"Hey," he said.

Mark acknowledged him with a nod as he undid the top button of his uniform shirt. "Busy day on the floor," Mark said. He cast a glance downward toward his shoes. After a moment's hesitation, he smiled. "But nothing we can't handle, eh Eddie?"

"No, nothing we can't handle."

Planning for six months had brought them to this day, this moment. Usually, before a robbery, people would be nervous. So nervous in some cases to consider backing out. There was still time. They hadn't hit the point of no return yet. But for Eddie, and he was sure Mark, too, getting the deed done couldn't come fast enough. He had been waiting a long time. The waiting, the calculating, the planning, and the timing had all come down to this moment, this evening, when they would take what was theirs, and no one would be the wiser. And as soon as casino officials discovered their crime, it would be too late to find them, even though Eddie and Mark were leaving behind a clue as to who perpetrated the crime.

"Is Wallace ready?" Eddie asked. "You still believe in him?"

Mark pulled the fridge door wide enough to grab a can of Coke, cracked it open, and drank some back. After swallowing, he wiped his mouth with the back of his hand.

"Wallace is ready. He covers in the cashier's cage for an hour this evening. He knows what needs to be done." Mark pulled on the Coke again. "He'll do his part. Then I'll do mine." He cupped a hand over his mouth and whispered, "What's a little murder between friends, eh?"

Eddie swiveled in his chair and stared down at the word search book in front of him. Looking for words in a jumble of letters kept his mind off things and eased his nerves. His excitement for the new life he was about to embark on was getting the better of him. It was like he'd won the lottery and was sitting out the final few hours before the lottery corporation paid him his due.

The Rosarita Hotel and Casino had shitty uniforms, and this was the last few hours he ever had to wear one. He was a thinking man, an enterprising man. At thirty-two, he would be richer than his parents ever were in their miserable life. He had the smarts to make it happen.

If someone says it can't be done, they need to stop interrupting the person doing it. That was exactly why Mark Struben was along for the ride. Eddie's belief was if they couldn't find a way, they would make one, and by golly, they'd made one.

A cool million in cash would disappear from the cashier cage without anyone being the wiser for at least twenty-four hours. It would happen tonight with the help of their favorite pit boss, Wallace Stern. Then Wallace would have an unfortunate accident. But Wallace didn't know that part yet.

Too bad for him.

Eddie glanced across the lunchroom as Mark tossed his empty can in the trash and wondered for the hundredth time if Mark would go through with murder. It was one thing to talk about it and plan it while knowing it was necessary for their survival, but quite another thing to actually do the deed. They needed Wallace gone so they could split the money fifty-fifty. There would be no thirty-three percent bullshit. No way. This was Eddie's idea from the start. Bringing Mark in was Eddie's choice. So he'd give up money for that. But bringing Wallace in was Mark's doing. Sure, they needed him inside that cage, but it had nothing to do with Eddie. Once Eddie explained that in detail to Mark, he agreed that not only would Wallace Stern be killed, he would be left behind to take the heat. He would be the one behind the cashier's cage when the money disappeared. He would be the one who robbed the casino and the one who accidentally got run over as he ran into the street. The money would disappear, and people will mourn; the casino will write off the small loss compared to what they make annually, and Eddie and Mark would go on to live fruitful and enjoyable lives as two newly rich folks traveling Europe.

Unless, of course, Mark wouldn't drive the car over the pit boss as he promised. If Wallace didn't die, then Mark would have to take his place. After that, Eddie would kill Wallace. Ultimately, Eddie would make sure the only people who could link him to the money were gone because the only way to keep someone silent was if they were dead.

"You sure about the car accident angle?" Eddie asked as he turned back to his word search.

"You're asking me that now?" Mark asked. "Bit late, isn't it?"

Eddie shrugged and kept his eyes aimed at the puzzle in front of him. "Just checking. Can't have anything go wrong."

Mark trudged over to Eddie's table and placed his hands down, open-palmed. "I'm in," he whispered. "All the way. You don't need to worry about me. I'll be in the car, waiting, as planned. When Wallace comes out, I'll be there to pick him up. Instead, I'll pick him off. I got it. I know how this works. I'll have my gloves and hat on. I won't leave DNA behind. And it's Wallace's own car. No one will ever connect us to this."

Eddie looked up and tapped his pen on the table twice. He searched Mark's eyes and only saw determination behind them.

"Good. By this time tomorrow, we'll be sunning

ourselves on a beach somewhere, trying to decide what to buy first."

"I already know what I want," Mark said as he approached the lunchroom door.

"What's that?"

"A muscle car. Something modified. Like a '68 Camaro with racing stripes."

"For Mexico? You don't think that'll stand out too much?"

Mark stopped at the door and turned back, a frown creasing his brow. "No. It won't stand out. I'll have a new name, a new passport, and a new look. For all anyone knows, my parents are rich and sent me to southern Mexico for a year. Whose business will it be anyway?"

"You're right," Eddie said. "It won't matter." *But it would. Too much attention and all that.*

"It sounds to me like you're worrying too much. You keep asking me if I'll be there, do the right thing when I'm supposed to. Questioning my spending habits before the job is even done. How about you? You nervous? Or worse, considering backing out?"

Eddie couldn't believe what he was hearing. His brainchild. The seed he planted. His idea. Why would *he* back out? He only checked with the troops to see if they were ready for war. And why did he ever agree to split the money fifty-fifty when it was all his idea? When it was over, and they were counting the money, he would explain why this had to be an eighty-twenty deal. All Mark had to do was show up and drive a car. Easily worth two-hundred thousand and not half a million.

Fuck him.

Without answering Mark's questions, Eddie started to work on his word search again. "Just be ready. I'll see you at the end of your shift at eleven tonight."

He searched his puzzle and waited until the door to the lunchroom closed. He looked about the empty lunchroom while tightening his grip on the pen until his knuckles lost color.

Maybe he would kill Mark after all. The newspapers would work it up as a robbery gone wrong, with no honor among thieves. One million missing from the casino, and two dead bodies. They'd never find the money, but that's what made good mysteries. Who else was behind the Rosarito Casino Heist? And like D.B. Cooper, Eddie Coleman would disappear. Maybe he'd make it on the FBI's most-wanted list one day. How cool would that be?

He'd have to think about Mark. Should he stay, or should he go?

Eddie looked at his watch. Break time was coming to an end, as were so many other things. Like working for a living. And Wallace's life.

Eddie knew what was right and what needed to be done. This was his baby, his gig. He knew all the answers if he had just searched deep enough.

Mark Struben needed to be taken out so Eddie could keep all the money. Mark must be kept quiet and stopped from buying flashy cars with his share of stolen money.

What was a little murder between friends, eh Mark?

Eddie laughed to himself and decided to spend the rest of his last blackjack shift trying to decide how to kill his friend Mark Struben. Would he opt for brutal and bloody or push him off a cliff or run him over with a car? What would give him the most pleasure?

He stepped onto the casino floor and started for his table, a euphoric feeling of gratitude and elation enveloping him like never before.

He was starting to like the idea of being a criminal before he actually did the deed. A murderer? That would be the best part.

He rubbed his hands together and said under his breath, "Oh, this is going to be fun."

Chapter 3

Sarah gazed out the back window at the four-door sedan behind the taxi. It had followed them for the last twenty miles or so. She was sure of it.

"He's not following us, Sarah." Aaron patted her lap. "No one knows where we are or where we're going."

Once out of the RV, Sarah turned back and spoke to Parkman one more time.

"Because of what happened recently," she had said, "Aaron and I need time alone. We need a vacation." She averted her eyes from Parkman's, looked at the road, then at the line of cars in front of the RV, and then forward to the small customs shacks eight cars ahead. "We need time alone," she repeated.

"It's okay, Sarah. No one will follow you. You're safe now." He closed the RV's door, then opened its small window to the right of the door. "Call me when you want to come home. If there's any trouble whatsoever, don't hesitate. If I can't help, Casper will."

Sarah nodded, turned, and walked away, with Aaron following close behind. After twenty paces, she glanced back. The RV was three cars from the customs booth. Parkman was still at the RV's window. He waved and pulled away. She lowered her head and kept walking.

A thimble was taller than how she felt at that moment.

What would he think of her if she failed to win the biggest battle of her life, the one raging inside? How could she ever face Parkman again? What about Aaron? She would have to suffer in silence. She could rejoin them and return to work with Vivian when she was healthy and back to normal. Easy work. Like when she was eighteen. Stop a kidnapping. Beat someone up. Small-time, petty crimes. Hunting serial killers, human traffickers, and entire cartels had taken its toll.

Hotel first. Give Aaron the slip. Then tie herself down to a bed somewhere with an ample water supply and wait until the shit was out of her veins and brain.

They had gotten into a taxi, and Sarah told the driver to take them to Rosarito.

"What's in Rosarito?" Aaron asked.

"Our vacation."

She watched the line of cars waiting to cross into the States disappear through the back window of the taxi as it drove away, deeper into Mexico, a sense of loss coming over her. All those people in the RV had come to Mexico for her, and she just walked out on them so she could go on a vacation. What would they think of her? Did they really know what she was going through? Did they read it on her face? If they did, would Parkman follow? Darwin? Who was coming? Or would her friends return to their lives while she suffered alone, waiting for the addiction to subside?

She turned back in her seat. "That car *is* following us. I'm sure of it. My instincts can be trusted. One hundred percent."

Aaron turned back to look. "I can almost see the driver from here. It's not Parkman. It doesn't look like Darwin or anybody from the RV." He turned back to her. "And the cartel business is over."

Sarah fiddled with a fingernail. "It's never over." She licked her dry lips. "Where's Vivian? Huh? Where's all her wisdom in this?"

"What are you saying?" Aaron asked. "You haven't heard from her?" He cast a glance at the driver.

"Don't worry. He's not listening."

Aaron touched her wrist. She withdrew her arm and stared out the window.

"What's going on, Sarah? You can talk to me."

She watched the Mexican countryside race by the window until her stomach couldn't manage it anymore, then closed her eyes.

"Sarah?"

"It's nothing. I'm sick. I feel sick." She lowered her voice. "I don't want this. I didn't ask for this. I'm stronger than this. But the urge comes with a violent appeal, begging me to answer its call. As much as I refuse to, the urge increases." She opened her eyes and stared down into her lap. "The need increases by the hour, Aaron. I'm afraid. For the first time in my life, I fear that I'm unclear if I'll be able to shirk off."

He touched her shoulder. This time she didn't pull away.

"I'm there for you, baby. You're not in this alone. Let it out. Just let it all out. I understand and will fight for you. You're my Sarah, my woman. No one and nothing controls you. You've been there for so many over the years, and I'll be there for you."

A tear slipped from her eye. Her abdomen clenched, and she bent forward. He pulled her his way. She succumbed to his will and leaned into him. His arms wrapped around her like a cocoon, shielding her, protecting her. It felt good to be wanted and loved, but most of all, it felt good to be held and protected. At that moment, Sarah was reminded that Aaron would protect her with his life.

How odd, though, as she was the protector, the fighter, the champion of hope, yet she was being consoled here. She wondered if that was what Maslow talked about in his hierarchy of needs. She needed to watch more Dr. Phil and read a Mars and Venus book on relationships. Had she offered Aaron as much as he offered her? Had she lost a finger because of him? This man said he would be there for her, and then he was. Like she expected. She had forgotten how special that was. How rare. And how unbelievable that was. She had forgotten to be grateful.

And so she let it out and cried in his arms.

Never feeling as weak as she did at that moment.

Never feeling as feminine, as soft. As small.

And then Vivian showed up. She planted a name in Sarah's mind. A dealer. A man in a hotel and casino resort in Rosarito. A dealer. This man could help her. For that one fix. But he wasn't just any dealer. Find him. Make a deal.

According to Vivian, buying heroin from him could mean the difference between saving or killing hundreds of people in one catastrophic event that would take place in Las Vegas soon.

Buy drugs? To save people in Las Vegas?

Sarah hugged Aaron's legs tight as Vivian receded from her consciousness. She realized her own sister didn't support her. Why buy heroin? Why not attack the guy? Shoot him. Beat him. Talk to him. Persuade him to be nice and not kill those people in Vegas. How was it all connected? Or was a part of her brain still high, and she had contorted the facts Vivian offered because none of it made any sense?

What pissed her off the most was her own sister wanted Sarah to buy the drug she yearned for at that very moment.

"How fucking cruel," she grunted, then wiped her runny nose.

Aaron leaned down. "What was that?"

"Just thinking about heroin and how fucking cruel it is to the human body. It's nothing. Just talking to myself. Forget about it."

Another lie. Why didn't she tell him she was pissed at Vivian for what she let the cartel do to them?

It was so unlike her.

But there was a reason she didn't tell him what Vivian said. Because she was going to take the advice. She was going to buy drugs and didn't want Aaron to know any of it.

She wiped her eyes and sat up. After a moment, she found her voice again and told the driver to go to the Rosarito Beach and Casino Hotel. He said he knew the one. They were twenty minutes away.

Of course, she would buy the heroin. She had followed Vivian's will for over seven years. Why stop now?

Heroin. In her hands within hours.

She hated Vivian for the torture she would endure because of the drug. And she hated herself for feeling relief at the idea of buying heroin.

But it was just one fix.

Then all would be well in the world again, and she could quit.

Just one …

Chapter 4

Eddie Coleman checked his watch.

"Hit me," the heavy man, intoxicated from one too many whiskeys, said from spot seven. Mr. Finnegan always played Blackjack and always sat in spot seven. It was his lucky spot. Yet time and time again, the house won, and Mr. Finnegan got drunk. He'd been removed from the casino more than once in the past for being drunk, and tonight was no different.

"Hit me," Finnegan slurred.

Eddie pulled another card and flipped it on the table.

"Busted."

He collected the cards.

"Hey, wait," Finnegan protested. "That was nineteen."

Hank, Eddie's pit boss, eased in closer. "Mr. Finnegan, it was twenty-two. That was a nine, not a six. You were reading it upside down." Hank edged in close enough to bump Eddie's ass cheek before he backed off.

Eddie grunted, happy this was his last night because he didn't know how long he could keep brushing off Hank's advances without getting rude or even hostile.

Mr. Finnegan grunted, too, then pushed away from the table, mumbling something about liars and thieves.

If you only knew, Eddie thought.

"Close up your table, Eddie." Hank noted the time. "Your last shift, eh Eddie? We're going to miss you here."

He placed the cover over the casino's chips and turned back to Hank. "It's been a long month since I put in my notice. But it's time, Hank. I want to travel." He retrieved his cell phone from his back pocket and opened the email, where he flipped to the British Airways quote he had requested. A week ago, he had set up a flight from Los Angeles to London for tomorrow and printed out the emailed quote. It looked like an itinerary as if he'd bought the ticket, but it hadn't cost him a dime. To an unfamiliar eye, it looked like a ticket. He had no intention of leaving Mexico, but he wanted everyone to think he was on a two-month vacation in the UK.

"See. This time tomorrow, I'll be crossing the pond, as it were," he said in his best James Bond accent.

"Don't," Hank said, shaking his head and waving a finger back and forth. "Don't use that accent. You're liable to get your ass handed to you if some of those yobs over there hear you speak like that."

Hank had no idea what he was talking about. There was no UK and no flight in Eddie's future. There was only Eddie with a million dollars of the casino's money. Money he was entitled to. After almost a decade of working at the casino, he still lived paycheck to paycheck.

In contrast, the casino profited hundreds of millions per

year off the likes of the Mr. Finnegans of the world, who they plied with alcohol served by scantily clad, hot women. The average man couldn't resist the casino's charm and wit. A man's wallet—and bank account—was in jeopardy the moment he entered this version of Alice in Wonderland for adult gaming addicts, complete with mind-altering beverages.

No, Eddie had had enough. He would leave it all behind tonight.

He closed his table in record time, punched his time card, and started for the lockers to change into civilian clothes before heading out to meet Mark in the parking lot.

In the rear corridor that led to the employee change room, Hank stepped in front of Eddie, blocking his path.

"Hank?" Eddie said. "Did I forget something?"

Hank studied Eddie, looking him up and down. "What's going on?" he asked. "What are you planning tonight?"

"What?" Eddie stammered, his mind racing. What did he know? What *could* he know? "I'm sorry?"

"I wanted to ask since it was your last night here and tomorrow you'd be gone if you'd wait another half an hour until my shift ends. We could go for a drink. Say goodbye the right way."

Eddie frowned, his stomach twisting. Hank stepped closer, suffocating Eddie's personal space.

What the hell is this?

"I'm tired, Hank. Maybe some other time—"

"Shhh," Hank whispered. "No protest. Just a half hour. You'll not regret it, nor will you forget it."

What the fuck?

There had been rumors that Hank Olsen was gay, but no one knew for sure. Eddie had been single for so long that he hated the heat that rose to his face as an erection started in his pants.

What the fuck is that?

"Sorry, Hank, but I'm heading home to pack." He tried to step around him, but Hank crowded closer, jamming Eddie into the wall.

"I can help you pack," Hank cooed. "You've always been friendly to me, Eddie. *Extra* friendly." Hank's arm moved closer, almost touching Eddie's chest. "If I've misread your friendliness, then I'm sorry. But, you know …" Hank's hand dropped quickly and passed across Eddie's firm crotch.

Eddie jumped. "Gotta run," he said, his voice two octaves higher.

He pushed past Hank and nearly ran headlong into the changing room. Once inside, alone, he debated changing into his clothes. What if Hank walked in and did that touchy-feely thing again?

"Shit," he muttered to himself. "What the hell, man?"

He decided to change anyway, and five minutes later, duffel bag packed, Eddie Coleman was ready to leave the Rosarito Beach and Casino Hotel for the last time.

He started for the back door, waving at colleagues along the way, and hit the bar on the door without seeing Hank again. Relieved, he pushed the door open and nearly bumped into Hank.

"Whoa," Eddie gasped and reared back.

Hank's smiling face gleamed with pleasure as he placed one hand on the open door and one on the doorframe.

"Eddie, last chance. After tonight, you'll be gone." He glanced over his shoulder, then back at Eddie. "If you're nervous, I assure you, no one will ever know. Then you're gone. I'll be kind and considerate. And I give a mean pegging. Or I can receive—whatever works for you." He smiled wide.

Eddie's stomach, already knotted up, twisted another way, weakening his knees.

"Hank, I'm straight. Seriously. Listen, no offense, but I don't swing that way."

"No offense taken," Hank said. He let go of the door and backed off a few steps. "It's just … you know."

Eddie stepped outside and moved sideways so he couldn't be boxed in by Hank again. Hank's behavior surprised him. There had never been a signal, a sign of any kind, that Hank would come onto Eddie so strong tonight. Eddie was sure he couldn't have caused this by condoning Hank's previous behavior.

"What do you mean by, *it's just, you know*?"

Hank appeared preoccupied as he looked around the parking lot. Eddie followed his eyes and saw Wallace's car, but no Mark inside yet. Mark was supposed to be waiting for Wallace to come out this very door in about fifteen minutes with the million dollars from the cage. Time was running out as he stood there talking to Hank about being gay, but he was curious to find out what led Hank to think he'd be into it. And he still had over ten minutes.

"It's just," Hank started. He met Eddie's eyes. "Remember the employee Christmas party?"

"That?" Eddie exclaimed. "I was drunk."

"I know. But you made me feel special. Everyone crashed. You and I stayed up all night drinking. When we finally fell asleep, we woke in each other's arms. You had a leg wrapped around me. I called you a few times after that

—"

"I remember."

"But you didn't want to go out. I don't know. I guess I just thought you were curious."

"Curious?"

"Yeah, like bi-curious or something."

The erection started again. *Shit.*

"No, Hank, I'm not bi-curious. I'm sorry. We were drunk. I'll hug anybody when I'm drunk."

"Then let's go out tonight as work friends, and that's it. We can get drunk if you know what I mean." He giggled, then bit his lower lip.

"I'm not going out to get drunk the night before my flight to England, Hank. I'm going home. And seriously, I'm not curious."

Hank pointed at Eddie's crotch. "It seems he disagrees. You have no idea what I can do with that."

Eddie felt naked in front of Hank. He turned away and started for his car.

"Goodnight, Hank," he said. Then, over his shoulder, he added, "Have a good one. Enjoy your life."

Halfway to his car, the employee door opened and closed behind him. He turned back and saw Hank was gone.

"Holy shit, that was creepy," he muttered.

Once in the darkness between parking lot lights, he turned toward Wallace's car and saw Mark in the driver's seat.

Perfect.

Everything was going as planned. Nothing had derailed the plan. He would get the money and enjoy it on a beach hundreds of miles south by the morning. He could get Hank's ideas out of his head with the first prostitute he hired tomorrow night. Eddie just hoped he didn't make a mistake and get a woman with a dick—a she-male tranny—because, in the end, transsexuals weren't women with dicks; they were men with tits.

He rapped on Wallace's car window. Mark rolled it down an inch.

"You good?" Eddie asked.

Mark nodded. "All set."

Eddie tapped the glass twice with his hand. "We got this," he said and turned away.

"Hey," Mark said.

"Yeah?"

"What did Hank want?"

"You really want to know?"

Mark nodded, not taking his eyes off the employee entrance of the casino.

"My dick."

Mark shot his head sideways. "What? Really?"

Eddie nodded. "He felt since I was leaving, his secret would be safe."

"Oh. Crazy."

"Anyway, let's get our heads back in this. Less than ten minutes left."

Mark laughed a small chuckle.

"What?" Eddie said as he backed away from the car.

"Let's get our *heads* back in this?" Mark repeated.

"You know what I mean."

"Sure I do."

Eddie headed for his car. When Mark was lying dead in the street, he would know exactly what Eddie meant. He would learn in one swift lesson the kind of man Eddie was.

"Laugh all you want at my expense, asshole," he whispered. "Let's see who gets the last laugh."

Chapter 5

The taxi drove close to the ocean, the moon reflecting a ribbon of light across the surface. Hotel lights along the road cast their glare on the shore. Under other circumstances, Sarah would be overjoyed to be in such a gorgeous place with Aaron. But not today. Today, she was weak, tired, sweating profusely, had an upset stomach, and was headed for trouble. The Vivian kind.

Vivian, Sarah's sister, had been dead since Sarah was only a few years old. When Sarah was eighteen, Vivian began talking through her from the other side, channeling messages and ominous notes about future events and crimes. Sarah quickly learned to answer the call and ultimately loved what she did. Vivian had pulled her out of many scrapes and near-death experiences, but she'd also sent her into harm's way several times.

Now, whenever it pleased Vivian, she could drop into

Sarah's consciousness at will. Their hunt for human traffickers led them to Toronto, Amsterdam, and finally, Athens, Greece, where Sarah thought it was over. But by some strange twist of fate, the people Sarah hurt in Toronto were connected to the Enzo Cartel in Mexico. They had kidnapped Aaron to get to Sarah, and it had worked. But now the cartel was dead and gone, Aaron was back—minus the finger they had cut off to send to Sarah as a message—and it was time to move on. But Sarah couldn't move on right away. She needed to deal with the addiction to the stuff they'd shot her up with. Once she got settled in the hotel, she was confident this heroin business would be easy to beat. If anyone could beat it, she could.

The taxi stopped in front of the Rosarito Beach Casino Hotel, and Aaron paid the driver for the forty-five-minute ride. Then he ran around to the other side and helped Sarah out.

She held Aaron's arm on wobbly legs and moved toward the stairs leading to the lobby. Before entering the lobby, she took one last look down the road from where they had come.

The four-door sedan, the one she was sure had followed them, was parked two blocks away on the other side of the street.

"Wait," she said.

Aaron stopped. "What is it?"

"That car." Sarah pointed. "It's the same one. I'm sure of it."

Aaron followed Sarah's pointed finger with his gaze. After a moment, he shook his head. "No, couldn't be. Neither Parkman nor Darwin have cars like that."

"So it isn't them? If not, someone else followed us."

Aaron moved to block her view of the car. "Sarah, it's over. You're on vacation. No one followed us. Either that's not the same car, or it's a rare coincidence that those people were coming to this hotel, too."

"You or me?" Sarah asked.

"You or me, what?"

"One of us is walking to that car. One of us will talk to the driver, or if there's no driver, at least mentally record the make and model and license plate number. One of us will remain on duty even though we're on vacation. One of us will watch our backs. Just in case."

He stared at her a moment too long. "I'll do it. But I know I'm right. Nothing is going on, Sarah. All is well in the world again. You're safe, honey. I'm here. And that's why I will check it out for you." He walked away from her backward. "Be right back." He started for the car at a brisk pace.

He looked good in form-fitting jeans, with a slight swagger of his manly hips, his upper body built tough from years of rigorous training. Aaron was her man, there to protect her. Yet she hadn't fully accepted that yet. *She* was the protector. *She* was the aggressor. What would that look like in their future? Would she have to soften for them to be successful as a couple? Or would he?

As Aaron hit the halfway mark between Sarah and the four-door sedan, its headlights flicked on. The engine roared to life. Aaron broke into a run, but before his feet struck the pavement twice, the car was halfway through a U-turn. It fishtailed, bumped the curb, the trunk lifting a foot, then settled back to the road as the driver gunned the vehicle and sped away.

He waved his arms after the car in a *what the fuck* gesture. After a moment, he walked back to Sarah.

"Looks like you might have been right," he said. He took her arm. "You want a different hotel? I mean, now that he's gone, he won't see us walk up the street."

Sarah thought about it. She considered Vivian's message. Should she stay and look for a heroin dealer as Vivian told her to? Or, actually, be on vacation and hide in another hotel? Would she ever get a vacation where she's one hundred percent away? Could she ever escape Vivian? Did she really want to escape Vivian? She loved what she did. Couldn't wait to right wrongs, fix things, help people who needed it, and dole out consequences wherever required. It offered her a rush unlike anything else.

"No. We stay. We don't change our plans for anyone. Whoever that was will return, and then we'll know why they followed us. Or Vivian will tell me. Doesn't matter. I need the room. I need the bed. I'm exhausted."

"Okay. I'm with you."

With one last look over his shoulder, Aaron led Sarah into the hotel lobby and checked them in for a week. Once they got their room keys and entered the elevator, Vivian came back.

In a rush, she explained to Sarah that a man named Wallace would die tonight. He couldn't die. Another man would die in his place. And yet another man was dead, but he was coming back. But before all that, Sarah needed to buy heroin. The dealer was in the casino.

Vivian, that's too confusing. The dealer is in the casino? What the hell? Aren't casinos filled with dealers? How the hell am I supposed to find the right one? Blackjack? Poker?

It was time to go to work. But how? She had no idea where to start or really what to do except look for a dealer. Aaron would never let her out of his sight. She only had twenty minutes before it was too late.

Hurry, Sarah!

What?

Vivian's message made her woozy and overwhelmed her. Sarah decided that now, on the elevator, was a good enough time to vomit. Although it was coming whether she liked it or not.

Her stomach clenched and shot bile up her throat and out through the fingers she had clamped over her mouth. It hit the carpeted floor of the elevator before she could stop it.

As she dropped to her knees, a hand pressed against the elevator wall, Vivian pleaded for her to hurry.

It's almost too late. Sarah, I need you to act!

Sarah closed her eyes as Aaron grabbed her arms and hauled her off the elevator.

And the ideas began to flow.

And she knew what to do.

And Sarah was back.

Chapter 6

Blair Turner surveyed the crowd. His crowd. His clients. They were the best kind. Transient. Nomadic. Most people gambling in the casino were on holiday. They were here for a good time; he could supply that in spades.

Now eighteen, he had built a small business as a supplier to the wealthy, using this casino and one other as his main distribution focus. Did it matter if he got caught? No. Would he rot in a Mexican jail? No. Because his mother was one of the richest women in this part of the country. Her contributions to the Mexican government virtually assured preferential treatment. He knew that firsthand. He'd been arrested for trafficking drugs twice without a single charge sticking. The most amount of time spent in jail was an overnighter while he waited until the paperwork was filed.

Jane Turner, his mother, didn't like him much. In fact, she professed to hate him without ever telling him why. But she would never remain idle as he suffered, and she'd never leave him in a prison to rot. His father died so many years ago that he already forgot what the man looked like. But none of that mattered now, and neither did his parents. As far as he was concerned, his mother was his get-out-of-jail-free card. Literally.

When he wanted to go to school, she refused. She didn't allow him to buy books when he wanted to read. When he wanted to run away at fourteen, she sent a team of detectives after him and brought him back, locking him in his room for months. She was a cruel woman that would steer him to either madness or drugs. By the time he was sixteen, he was experimenting routinely with drugs. Since she didn't allow him to advance himself intellectually to prepare for the world, he turned his entrepreneurial skills toward the drug market. Now, at eighteen, he was known to several pit bosses and dealers as a friendly. Not to be harassed. To be endured, allowed. Some said selling drugs wasn't up to community standards. But Blair Turner would point out to those naysayers that the community keeps him in business.

He straightened his jacket and started across the casino floor toward the three-card poker tables. He would start with poker, chat up a few guests, zero in on his clientele, and set up a transaction. Because of the cameras throughout the casino, a quick sale would take place out back in his Camaro, in the employee parking area, and everyone would be content.

A smile crossed his lips. Tonight would be a good night. The casino was full. The waitresses looked great. The dealers were nodding at him, and his favorite poker table had a spot available in seat one, where he always sat. If he had a good streak, his cards wouldn't be affected in seat number one by gamblers getting up or sitting down at the table.

"Evening, Jessica," he said to the dealer.

She smiled. "Blair."

"Hot night? Good cards?"

Two players, as white as a Brit in winter, shook their heads. An old couple sat in spots six and seven. They didn't appear too talkative.

He dropped two hundred on the table, got his chips, and played ten on the pair plus and ten on his bet. When Jessica dealt his three cards, he dropped ten on the backs of the cards without looking and sat back to wait, scanning the crowd.

"Playing blind?" Jessica asked.

"Yup. Works best for me. You need the queen or higher to qualify, which doesn't happen all the time. Lately, I've found blind works very well."

"Suit yourself."

Two men across the pit sitting at a Caribbean stud poker table could use some uppers. A woman playing blackjack was in need of a joint. No question, the drunk guy at the Wheel of Fortune machines was good for a couple of grams of hash. He was a regular customer. Even if Blair lost the two hundred playing blind, he'd clear a grand before the night was out.

Jessica flipped the dealer's cards. A queen, king, three, off-suit. She grabbed Blair's cards and turned them one by one. An eight, a nine off suit, then an ace. He won his ante and bet.

"Nice," he said. "See. It works for me."

The white Brits weren't as happy. They'd stayed with a king, ten, and a queen, eight.

Jessica retrieved the cards and prepared to deal another

hand. Near the cashier's cage, the blackjack pit boss Wallace Stern, one of his best customers, fidgeted with something on his jacket. He looked over his shoulder, turned back, checked his watch, and straightened his jacket. Why was Wallace in the cage tonight? Filling in for someone?

"You in?" Jessica asked.

"Oh. Yeah."

Blair placed his bet and looked back at the cage. From thirty feet away, Wallace looked nervous. Scared. Blair prided himself on his ability to read people, their mannerisms, gestures, and twitches. His goal to work in law enforcement when he was younger hadn't faded, only blocked by his mother. Until then, if it ever happened, he would continue to read people to determine who used drugs and who didn't.

Reading Wallace Stern right now gave Blair the creeps. Something was bothering Wallace. Something menacing.

Blair blinked. Maybe he was seeing things. Wallace always wore a smile. He was the man with the one-liners. Everyone thought of him as the resident Jim Carrey. That's why Wallace needed the drugs Blair sold him—because he was so depressed. But tonight, the depression that raged on the inside seemed to have surfaced on Wallace's face.

Blair decided to go see him after another hand or two. See what was bothering him. Maybe he could fix him up with something special. Something to take all the pain away.

"Folding or betting, Blair?"

"Sorry, Jess. Daydreaming."

Blair placed his bet and lost to a pair of nines. When Blair looked back at the cashier's cage, Wallace was gone.

Chapter 7

SARAH EASED DOWN ON the bed and moaned when her head hit the pillow.

"I need help, Aaron."

A moment later, he was at her side.

"I'm here." He caressed her hand.

She placed her free arm across her forehead, blocking the light.

"Advil," she whispered. "In the lobby. There was a gift shop. Can you?"

"On my way. Don't move."

Aaron let go of her hand. She listened to him walk to the door and slip out quietly.

When they had entered the room minutes before, Sarah headed straight to the bathroom, where she cleaned her face and hands in the sink. The bathroom was elegant and gorgeous. Crown molding lined the ceiling. Granite counters that had to be an inch thick with his and her sinks. It even had a bidet. Behind glass doors, the shower was as wide and long as a two-person tub with a stone bench, presumably for a woman to sit and shave her legs.

The hotel room itself was stunning, the furniture something from a magazine. It was the perfect room for a young couple to vacation in. Unfortunately, Sarah wouldn't be in the room long enough to ever know.

Without wasting time, she rolled to the side of the bed, placed her feet on the floor, waited a moment then stood up. She experienced only a slight waver of dizziness, then she was fine. Movement in her stomach had decreased. She'd make it. Everything would be fine. There were more important things than dealing with an unwanted addiction, like saving a man's life. She had work to do.

Vivian had given Sarah a name and an allotted amount of time, but that was it. No description, no location. Just a name. And fifteen minutes to find him in the casino. One of the dealers.

Outside the room, she debated using the stairs. If Aaron came back while she waited for the elevators, she'd be done for. He wouldn't allow her to work for Vivian in this state. But the stairs would make her sick, and since time was short, the elevator would be faster.

She pushed the button and leaned against the wall. The sound of a TV came from one of the rooms. A simpler life. One filled with TV programs and a beer. Maybe an episode of *House of Cards*, *Madmen*, or *The Walking Dead*. Anything would do.

As the elevator door opened and she stepped inside to push the lobby button—grateful Aaron hadn't returned yet and grateful to get the elevator without her vomit in the corner—a thought occurred to her. Was she getting tired of doing this? Was she wearing out? Did she fantasize about quitting? Is that what she was doing? If so, why not just quit then?

Because she was duty-bound. She'd made a pact with Vivian a long time ago, and she meant to keep it. This had to be the withdrawal talking. Otherwise, she wouldn't be having these thoughts. She'd be energized to be on the job again, ready to deal with whatever came her way.

The elevator slowed as it neared the lobby. Hiding to the side in case Aaron stepped on, she waited until the doors were fully open, then peeked into the lobby. Aaron was nowhere to be seen. She didn't have much time, though. He'd get to the room, see she was gone, and come back down here.

She had to find the dealer and get things done, all without Aaron seeing her.

The lobby had a large counter, a huge chandelier over the main check-in area, and plush couches and chairs in waiting areas on either side of the lobby. She stayed close to the wall to avoid being seen by Aaron as she walked toward the double doors that led into the casino.

Halfway to the doors, she saw him. Aaron sat on the end of a leather sofa, staring out the front windows. He was on the phone, talking to someone. Privately. He would have made the call in the room if it weren't meant to be private.

When she returned to the room, he'd tell her who he called and why he chose to do it in the lobby. At least she hoped he'd tell her everything. It was probably just Parkman. If he knew Sarah was in trouble, he'd come running, and she didn't want anyone else here right now.

She stopped at the double doors. Two casino security men stood on either side, watching the faces of people passing them, making sure minors didn't wander into the casino. She took one last look at Aaron on the couch and considered the Advil. He had come to get her headache meds, yet he sat talking to someone on the sofa in the lobby. Was he trying to arrange a rehab clinic for her? Or was he attempting to buy heroin to tide her over? Or something worse?

She leaned back and smacked her head against the wall. She should have never questioned Aaron's integrity after what they just went through at the Enzo Cartel compound.

"You okay, ma'am?" one of the guards asked.

Sarah shot a look at Aaron. He was getting up from the couch. She turned away from him to face the guard.

"Yeah, just not feeling well." She walked past him and into the casino. "I'll be okay."

A bell sounded off in the corner somewhere. A jackpot. Within two steps, another bell went off, then quieted. Someone gasped. The place was full of tourists trying their luck.

She had to find a dealer? No distinction of what kind of dealer. Just a dealer. A man named Blair Turner.

She slowed near the blackjack table, close enough to read the dealer's nametag, then moved on. After five minutes, with Vivian on the edge of her consciousness egging her to go faster, she had cleared the blackjack, the pai gow, and the baccarat tables. Only two rows of poker tables were left, with half of them female dealers.

Vivian, I need help here.

Along a new aisle, she got to the Caribbean stud poker tables and stopped at a man named Blair Thompson.

Got the name wrong, sis?

The feeling of *wrong guy* came over her as if it was an original thought. She kept moving. Near the last table in the aisle, her stomach twisted up. A cool sheen of sweat covered her forehead.

I feel like shit, Vivian. Isn't there something else I could be doing?

A loud, echoing, resounding *NO* reverberated through her mind. She stumbled and reached out to hold onto a table, bumping into a young man in a seat. Four people were playing a version of poker that only used three cards.

"I'm sorry," she said.

"It's no bother," the man said.

He folded his hand, grabbed the chips piled in front of his spot at the table, and got up.

"Looks like you need a drink." He touched her arm above the elbow lightly and guided her away from the table. "Are you okay? In need of something," he paused, "special?"

"I need—" she cut the word short. He wouldn't understand, and she didn't trust many people. This mission seemed to have failed. She was too sick to carry anything on with a reasonable semblance of control. Aaron had been out in the lobby talking privately on the phone and, by now, was probably entering their empty room. Nothing was what it seemed, and everything was fucked.

"I need sleep, is all," she said. She pulled her arm out of his grasp and licked her dry lips. The roof of her mouth felt like it was lined with sand. "Been traveling too much. Need a break. I'm heading upstairs to my room." She backed away and started for the double doors that led back into the lobby.

"Fair enough," he said, then stepped closer as if he meant

to follow her. "But if you *need* something, something special," he held out a card—a fucking business card—with a marijuana plant on the front, "text me. I service this area with the finest products and pardon my rudeness, but you look like you could use a hit of something."

Sarah stopped moving away. She took the card and read the name.

Blair Turner. A dealer. A *drug* dealer.

Oh my shit, Vivian. You could've offered a fucking heads-up. I'm a little under the weather here. Where's the sisterly love?

She met Blair's eyes. "You're right. I am in *need* of something."

"Then you've come to the right place."

"Where?" she asked.

"Where? What?" He stumbled over his words. "This place. You've come to the right place. Like, right here."

"No. I mean, where? As in, where do we do the transaction?"

"Oh, right, that. Never in the casino. Too many cameras. Meet me out back. Employee entrance. Side of the parking lot. My car."

"Sounds a little dangerous for a girl on her own."

"That's why I meet my clients at the car. In that parking lot, you're a scream away from casino security. Also, cameras cover most of the lot, just not where I park. Behind my car, a two-foot jump places you near the front lobby of a neighboring hotel. Not far to run if you sense danger." He raised his hands to his sides. "We good?"

The urge for a fix ratcheted up. It was like her body rebelled against her desire to be rid of the drugs because it knew the man standing before her could fix her up.

"If you have what I need, we're good."

"Five minutes. Back door. It's marked with a capital E for employee." He pointed at the lobby. "Out the front doors, turn left, and follow the wall of the building around until you get to door E."

"Five minutes," Sarah said and turned to walk away. When she looked back, Blair was heading toward the restrooms. The dealer at the table caught her eye. The expression on her face told Sarah everything. The dealer knew who Blair was and what they had just arranged. Anyone seen talking to Blair probably got no benefit of the doubt. She was a user. She looked like a user tonight. She needed a fix, and woman to woman, the dealer was disappointed. It was enough to bolster Sarah away from drugs. In that one look, she determined to do what Vivian wanted her to do, but she wouldn't use the heroin. She wouldn't shoot up. She would flush it down the toilet and beat this thing. She had to because that's who she was. A fighter. A winner. Not the perceived woman in the eyes of the poker dealer.

On the flip side, what the hell was Vivian getting her to buy heroin for as she endured withdrawal? A test? If so, it was a cruel fucking test.

She exited the casino, slowed for a moment to check the lobby for Aaron, didn't see him, and started toward the front doors.

A man by the check-in counter turned toward her. Sarah faltered, leaned down, and stopped, resting against the back of a couch. Her legs got weak. She continued down until she was sitting, her mouth agape, her mind racing.

What the hell was going on? Was she hallucinating? Seeing this man right here, right now, couldn't be possible. There was no way. Absolutely no way.

She gasped when she started breathing again, confident her face had turned as white as snow. The thudding of her heart reminded her she wasn't dead. The man wasn't a ghost. But as far as she knew, this man had died many years ago.

Something Vivian said came back to her.

A man was dead. He was coming back.

Did she mean he was coming back from the dead? Her drug-addled mind threw a crazy mix of nonsense into her consciousness.

Then the man touched her. His hand rested on hers on the edge of the couch. It really was him in the flesh.

"Good evening, Sarah," he said, his voice deep, dark. "It's been a long time."

She thought she would lose consciousness and faint, but then Vivian roared in from nowhere and woke her back up with a start.

Door E! echoed through her mind, her eyes widening.

"It's been a long time," he repeated. "About four years. Thought I'd drop by. See if you needed a hand."

He took her hand and helped her to her feet, and all was right in the world again. He was here. Back from the dead. Her guilt over his loss could dissipate. She had done well. He was alive. It was all okay. They had so much to talk about and catch up on. First thing he needed to tell her was how it was all possible.

Not now! Vivian shouted.

She brought him close, whispered in his ear that she had to do something before they could talk, and walked out of the lobby. When she looked back, he remained where he was, his hand suspended in the air where it had last touched her.

One foot in front of the other, he began to follow her.

Chapter 8

PARKMAN FOUND A ROOM in a hotel one block from the Rosarito Beach and Casino Hotel, where Sarah and Aaron stayed. He settled in, went to the little kiosk in the lobby to obtain a travel-size toothpaste, toothbrush, and other sundries —they were sold out of toothpicks—and went to his room to await Aaron's call.

To watch Sarah suffer tore him in two. They all witnessed her squirming in her restless sleep in the RV, her body shuddering in a full-body sweat, hands shaking. Casper and Darwin had left the RV to clear the way at customs, but Parkman knew it was to avoid seeing Sarah in such a state.

Who would try to stop her when she demanded to be let off the RV? Who dared challenge Sarah? There were always two options, and everyone connected to Sarah knew that. Sarah's way willingly or Sarah's way forced. In the end, it was always Sarah's way. Understanding that as her friend didn't make it easier to endure. It was just the way things were. It was about accepting who she was without judgment or making it about himself. Engaging one's ego around Sarah often got that person hurt.

They'd let her go. Do her thing. Get a fix, or beat the urge. Whatever Sarah needed. But they would never leave her alone. That was why Aaron was with her, and Parkman was close. What came of her decisions today could have a ripple effect that took years to fix, and they needed to be there to support her regardless of what she wanted. The drugs were making most of the decisions at this point.

After half an hour, he couldn't sit and wait any longer without toothpicks. He couldn't call Aaron either. If Sarah got wind he was here, she'd be pissed. This was supposed to be her holiday. She had specially asked not to be followed.

Not all of Sarah's decisions were right. She wasn't a god. If she was capable of making a mistake at any time in her life, it was right now. After what Enzo did to her, he was surprised she still walked upright.

Cell phone in his back pocket, Parkman left the room and headed down to the restaurant. As he approached the open doors, one of the waitresses picked up a menu and addressed him.

"Seating for one?" she asked.

"No, I'm not eating tonight. Just need toothpicks."

She frowned for a brief moment, then her smile returned.

"Of course. Please give me a moment."

Parkman turned and studied the lobby. People came and went, even at this late hour. A well-dressed couple out for dinner. A family of four getting back to the hotel late. Three men in their early twenties talking about college back home and how this beat studying.

The familiar chime of his cell phone interrupted his people-watching. He grabbed it by the second ring.

"Yeah."

"It's Sarah." Aaron cleared his throat. "She's in a bad way."

Parkman moved away from the front of the restaurant. "How so?"

"We got to the hotel, checked in, and made it to the elevator, where she threw up. Back in the room, she got on the bed, covered her eyes, and asked for Advil."

"Did you get her any?"

"Not yet. Parkman, I'm worried for her."

"Me too, Aaron, me too." He looked back at the waitress who had returned to the front of the restaurant. She held out a handful of toothpicks. He motioned that he'd only be a second. "Where are you now?"

"In the lobby. On one of the couches."

"Okay, get her Advil, head back up, and stay with her. Don't let her out of your sight."

"Why? Is there something I should be worried about?"

"Just a hunch."

"What kind of hunch?"

"That she's working something."

"Working something?" Aaron gasped. "Now? How the hell? Vivian wouldn't. Not in Sarah's state."

"Look, I've seen that look in Sarah's eyes before. I think she's onto something. Either that or she really is trying to get another fix, and she knows how much that would disappoint us, so I don't see that as a viable option."

Aaron remained quiet for a moment.

"You still there?" Parkman asked.

"Yeah, just not sure what to think. Sarah's been through a lot. She endures, she takes it in, moves on, and stays strong. This, geez, I just don't know, Parkman. This might beat her. She is human, after all. I think we forget that."

"Yeah, and humans need support. Humans need love, caring, and understanding. Go give it to her. That's your job as the man in her life. Do that, and she'll be eternally grateful. Do it, even when she tells you not to. Sarah only respects people who stand up, and not just stand up, but stand up to her."

"You're right."

"Be Gandhi to her. Do what's right and stand up for what you believe in because you believe in her."

"Got it."

"Now go. Get that Advil. I'll be by my phone if and when you need me."

"Thanks, man. Couldn't do it without you in my corner."

"Always."

Parkman hit end and turned back to the waitress. A pen in hand, she was writing something down on a little wooden stand by the front.

"I'll take those toothpicks now."

She handed him a dozen or so individually wrapped toothpicks. He thanked her, turned to head for the elevators, and unwrapped one. It was already in his mouth when the elevator arrived. On the sixth floor, nearing his hotel room door, he flipped the toothpick to the other side of his mouth at the sound of his phone's ring tone.

"Everything okay?" he asked as Aaron's number appeared on call display.

"No," Aaron nearly shouted. Heavy breathing came over the line. Parkman jammed his room key in his pocket and slipped the toothpicks into the other one as he jogged back to the elevator he had just exited. It was still there.

"What happened?" he asked.

"Sarah's gone, Parkman. When I came back up, the room was empty."

"How is that possible? You said she collapsed on the bed."

"She did," he rasped. "A ruse, though. Looks like you were right. She's working something."

"What are you doing now?" Parkman jumped on the elevator and headed back to the lobby. "Where do you suspect she went?"

"No idea. I'm going to the lobby. I'll ask around. I'll find her."

"I'm on my way. Will be there in less than five minutes."

"Hurry."

The line clicked off.

Chapter 9

Eddie Coleman wiped the sweat from his face and blinked rapidly. The employee door at the back of the casino hadn't opened. Wallace Stern was late.

Ten cars over, Mark waited, engine idling. Wallace would die within seconds of exiting the building. Then Mark would die. It was perfect. Eddie would be rich and off on vacation— supposedly to the UK. He loved how he could change the plan on the fly and see that this was the better idea.

Brilliant.

But where was Wallace?

A good-looking, long-haired girl rounded the corner from the front and approached the employee door. She looked over her shoulder once, then again as she got closer to the door.

What was she doing? Why stop there at the employee door?

Blair Turner stepped out into the parking lot lights from

the other side of the building.

Of course. A drug deal in the parking lot. The timing couldn't be worse. Unless Blair was pushing his trade, this parking lot area was only used during shift change. If Wallace came out within the next minute, there would be witnesses. Druggies make unreliable witnesses but witnesses just the same.

When Eddie looked at Wallace's car with Mark behind the wheel, a white face stared back at him.

"Shit," Eddie said to himself. "This is the last thing we need."

Another man had rounded the corner behind the girl and waited in the shadows, leaning against the brick wall, his face hidden.

"Who the fuck are you, now?" Eddie shouted inside the empty car.

Eddie prayed it wasn't an undercover cop waiting to see Blair do a transaction. That meant a simple drug bust could thwart his entire plan. It would cost him if he couldn't get rid of Wallace and Mark. He would lose sixty-six percent of the money in one fell swoop. All because of Blair, the girl, and the man watching from the shadows.

He tightened his grip on the steering wheel. At that moment, he hated all drug dealers, far and wide.

Maybe there would need to be a few more people killed tonight.

Nothing would stop Eddie from getting what was his.

Nothing.

Chapter 10

A WEAKNESS HAD STARTED in her stomach, moved to her limbs, and everything shook. She definitely needed sleep. She needed to beat the drugs. This was no way to live.

And now she was seeing dead people. There was no way he was alive.

Sarah glanced over her shoulder. The man from the lobby had stopped at the corner and was obscured by shadows. He would wait. They would talk. She might even get a chance to introduce him to Aaron. The last time she saw him, they were having dinner at the Old Spaghetti Factory in Toronto after dealing with a serial killer who had kidnapped them. It was several years ago, but Sarah remembered it clearly. He was her first love, her first desire.

But then he was killed and dumped in Lake Ontario by Toronto. She had forgotten the exact details because that was the year Dolan Ryan and Esmerelda were murdered. It was a terrible year. A time when Sarah felt like she was the victim.

But here he was, in the flesh, waiting by the corner of the building for her.

She looked over her shoulder one more time.

He was still there.

She spun around at a noise behind her. Blair stepped out of the shadows and pointed at a black Camaro parked under an overhanging tree.

As she trudged to the Camaro, something caught her eye to the right. A man, white as a ghost, sat behind the wheel of a late model Buick. A small plume of exhaust billowed out from behind the car.

She glanced away. He was waiting for someone to get off shift. No big deal. Nothing to do with her. She was about to get a fix. She was about to do a deal she never thought she'd do unless she were going to bust someone. But what the hell? Vivian called, and Sarah answered.

Blair waited to open the car door for her. She walked around him, checked the back seat, and then eased into the low passenger seat. Blair closed the door and walked around the hood to get in on his side while Sarah checked out the guy behind the wheel of the Buick five cars over. She scanned the rest of the cars, hoping this wasn't a sting operation of some kind. Getting busted for buying drugs in Mexico would piss Aaron off and probably disappoint a few people who had risked their necks to get her clear of Enzo and his people, not to mention Casper. After all they'd been through in Amsterdam and Athens, this would really disappoint Casper.

Thinking of him saddened her. She hadn't given him a proper goodbye when she left the RV.

"What is your fancy?" Blair asked.

"My fancy? Is that what you call it?"

Her eyes stopped on another car about a dozen down from the white face in the Buick. Another man sat behind the wheel of that car, his face hidden in shadows. What tipped her off were his hands on the wheel at ten and two.

"Blair, when's shift change at the casino?"

Blair was fiddling with a black case behind his seat. He stopped and faced her. "Why? You nervous?"

"There are two men sitting in cars. One's idling. Like they're waiting to pick someone up. Or are they with you?"

Blair straightened in his seat and looked back and forth, studying the cars in the lot.

"Where?"

"The Buick, five cars down. Then another dozen to the right. I can't tell what kind of car that one is from here."

In his hand, resting on his lap, was a small bag of white powder. Sarah's eyes homed in on it and forgot about men in cars and men waiting to talk to her. For a moment, everything Vivian had said dissipated, and she was back in Enzo's place, feeling the rush in her blood as the heroin coursed through her.

"There's nobody there." Blair tapped the top of his steering wheel. "You had me there for a second. I hate getting arrested. Angers my mother, and when she's angry—" He stopped talking when he looked her way. She hadn't taken her eyes off the bag.

"How much?" she asked. Vivian had told her to buy something from the *dealer.*

"Depends on how much you want."

"All of it."

"You'll need a bank machine then, by the looks of you. No offense. Just saying."

The employee door at the back of the casino opened. Sarah glimpsed the movement and looked up. A man holding a black briefcase stepped into the parking lot.

The Buick to her left started out from its spot too quickly.

And the rest of Vivian's message played through her mind.

A man will die. Stop it ... another man needed to die ...

"There's Wallace," Blair said. "Saw him in the cage tonight. He looked sick or something. Preoccupied. I need to talk to him."

"Shit." Sarah grabbed the door handle and jumped from the Camaro as Blair did the same.

Chapter 11

BLAIR AND THE GIRL had disappeared in his Camaro. As long as Eddie stayed in the shadows, there was a good chance neither one would be able to recognize him as he drove into the driver's side door, killing Mark on impact.

He would aim his back their way as he jumped out and retrieved the briefcase. If only Wallace would hurry up.

It occurred to Eddie that Wallace might have gotten cold feet. If so, this was all over, and he was in jeopardy as two other people, Wallace and Mark, could finger him in an attempted robbery of the casino.

But the employee door opened, and Wallace stepped out.

"Finally," Eddie whispered.

Mark's car started forward. Everything was a go. In under a minute, two men would be dead, and Eddie would be free and clear. A cool wave of relief passed over him. It was his time. He deserved this.

"Fuck the casino."

He grabbed the keys in the ignition and was about to turn the car on when the employee door opened again, and Hank Olsen stepped outside behind Wallace.

"What the fuck?"

Eddie waited. Mark advanced.

Would he run Wallace down in front of Hank?

Hank looked right at Eddie. He had scanned the parking lot and found Eddie's car. Hank pointed and started across toward him.

"Shit! He thinks I'm waiting for him. Fuck off, Hank."

The nightmare went from bad to worse as Blair, and that girl exited Blair's Camaro and started toward Wallace, who stood by the door, the million-dollar briefcase in his hand.

Eddie caught sight of Mark's worried face through the driver's side window. Eddie turned his car on, then flashed the lights as a message for Mark to continue with the plan. The plan was still a go. Kill Wallace and kill Hank while he was at it. Who cared? It was a briefcase full of money they were dealing with. The body count mattered little once you added them up. This was Mexico. El Chapo never worried about body counts, and neither did Eddie Coleman.

He dropped the car in gear and put his foot on the gas as Mark accelerated the Buick toward Wallace, who stood dumb as fuck right in its path while Eddie started toward Hank Olsen.

"This ought to be good," Eddie said to himself.

At that moment, the stupid girl with Blair shouted something and started running.

"What the fuck is going on here?" Eddie shouted in a shriek of frustration.

Chapter 12

THEY WERE TOO FAR away. Shouting would only make them turn toward her. The guy had to get out of the car's path. He had to jump back inside the building or run because the driver of the Buick wasn't there to pick him up. He was there to run him down. Everything Vivian told her came together in an instant.

"Blair!" Sarah shouted. "What was that guy's name?"

The Buick's engine revved and shot forward.

"Wallace," Blair hollered behind her.

The man looked their way. Another guy had exited the building behind Wallace.

As Sarah's energy waned, she yelled, "Wallace, get out of the way, or you'll die." Her voice cracked, and she almost bent over at the waist but somehow managed to stay upright and continue running at half her normal speed.

At first, Wallace frowned, then turned to the Buick. He

took a tentative step back and held the briefcase up in the air.

The second man who had exited the building walked out into the middle of the parking lot.

The Buick veered toward Wallace at the last second. Simultaneously, Blair issued a warning too late, saying the name *Wallace* several times.

Like a perverted game of Grand Theft Auto come to life, the engine revved, metal en route toward flesh.

Seconds before impact with Wallace, someone leaped out of the shadows and bodily knocked Wallace aside. The car veered hard but not fast enough, clipping nothing but the brick wall immediately to the left of the employee entrance door.

Wallace got to his feet and scrambled away from the man who dove on him. Sarah slowed her step so as not to fall. Her physical state couldn't be trusted.

The other car's engine revved behind them. The car where she'd seen hands on the steering wheel. It raced toward the man—the name Hank popped into her mind—in the middle of the parking lot. He wasn't so lucky. The grill struck him mid-thigh, and he cartwheeled at least twenty feet to the left before the driver of the car veered toward the Buick that rested against the brick wall.

"Really, Vivian? What the shit is this?"

Chapter 13

Eddie Coleman was in shock. He couldn't believe what he was seeing. That stupid girl had shouted Wallace's name. She had warned him of Mark's intent, and somehow someone came out of nowhere and dove on Wallace, getting him out of the Buick's way in time.

Mark had missed.

All he succeeded in doing was ram the casino's brick wall and jeopardize the entire plan. He should have never involved Mark Struben. Mark's involvement had worried Eddie from the start.

He needed to have those two men dead. There was just no way around it. And if a car accident didn't accomplish that task, then he would have to use another method.

That's what the gun in the passenger seat was for. He wouldn't stop until he had the briefcase full of money and both men were dead.

If anyone got in his way, that would be unfortunate for them. Once he murdered Mark and Wallace and the police were looking for him, it wouldn't matter how many were dead. The police would still be looking for him.

He pressed the accelerator to the floor and aimed at Hank Olsen first. It was time to get that meddling ass fucker out of the way, then kill his partners in crime.

Hank Olsen hit the grill, bounced off the hood, and flew to the left. A quick pull on the steering wheel aimed his heavy weapon toward the driver's side door of the Buick.

Mark rammed his shoulder several times into the crumpled door, unable to exit the damaged car.

"Fuck you guys," Eddie shouted as he raced across the parking lot toward Mark.

Chapter 14

"AND NOW A MAN dies," Sarah whispered.

Blair said *Hank* over and over before he turned a pained glance her way. Something had clouded his eyes. Like shock settled over his system. "How do you know? You think Hank is dead?"

"There's nothing we can do to stop that car." She clung to Blair's shoulder, trying to catch her breath. Holding him helped her stay upright. "Look away. You won't want to see what comes next."

They were still twenty feet from the Buick. The driver had been unsuccessful in his attempts to exit the car. Wallace had gotten to his feet and retreated from the cars about to collide. The man who had knocked him out of the way stayed close to the brick wall of the casino.

... Another man needed to die ...

Maybe he already did. That unfortunate soul—Hank—

who got run down and tossed aside could be dead.

The grill of the approaching vehicle was lost in the crunch of metal as it made contact with the Buick. Airbags shot out from the dash, and the trunk of the car lifted at least four feet in the air before settling back down hard. Steam and a hissing sound emanated from the two broken cars.

Sarah moved toward the cars to see if they could pull anyone out safely. She picked up her step when she saw movement in the Buick. The driver of that car had slid across the front seat to get as far away from the vehicle about to hit him as he could, which probably saved his life.

Then who was supposed to die, Vivian? That man Hank?

Blair got to the Buick's passenger door, grabbed the handle, and yanked hard. It didn't budge. Five feet from the car, Sarah picked up a rock and continued forward. At the window, she cupped the rock in her hand and shattered the glass with the first blow. As she stepped back, Blair tended to the man inside the car. She had no strength to pull him out.

The other vehicle's driver crawled out and limped around the back of his car. His face was a mask of blood where, as far as Sarah could tell, he had broken his nose in the crash.

Light from the parking lot overhead lamps reflected off something in his hand.

A gun.

An arm wrapped around Sarah's waist, and she was lifted to the side as the weapon discharged. Then it fired again, and someone squealed.

Sarah couldn't breathe with that arm around her abdomen, her diaphragm sealed. She was still above the ground, moving rapidly away from the scene. Whoever had her was very strong.

Wallace dropped the briefcase and put his hands up. Blair crawled under the Buick. Sarah's feet touched the ground again. The arm released its grip, and she dropped to one knee, teetered, and caught herself before falling, panting like she'd swum five laps underwater.

At least a dozen white lights lit up the parking lot behind the damaged cars. The man with the gun fired again, taking a chunk of stone out of the brick beside Wallace's face. As far as she could tell, the man with the gun hadn't seen the bright lights, and neither had Wallace.

"The briefcase," the man shouted.

Wallace shoved the case away from him.

"Don't shoot," Wallace pleaded. "Take it. All yours. I won't say a thing—"

The gun fired.

The man holding the weapon on Wallace teetered to one side. As if the gun was too heavy, his wrist went limp, and he dropped it. A moment later, he fell beside his weapon, the last of the blood pumped by his heart oozing out of the new hole in his skull.

The gun that had fired was from the dozen lights. Some kind of Mexican SWAT team approached from the other side of the broken cars. Armed men ran up to Sarah and the man behind her.

Protesting, exclaiming they had nothing to do with it, Sarah and her friend from a long time ago were manhandled and shoved into the back of a police van. Blair, Wallace, and the driver of the Buick were put into another vehicle. Paramedics tended to the man who had been hit by the car— Hank—while the authorities surrounded the body of the shooter.

"This sucks," she said as she turned back to her old friend.

"Yeah. But I know you. This is part of being in your life."

"Gee, thanks. Cheers a girl up when she feels like shit."

"I'm just happy we have this opportunity to talk."

"With these guys, it's probably better if you keep the talking to a minimum. Or let me do the talking."

"In the state you're in? Not sure if they'll take your word as the truth that it is."

"Just watch." She snickered.

Is that it, Vivian? Am I done now? Vacation time?

She waited for an answer. As the van got underway, one came.

You're just getting started, Sarah.

Chapter 15

Parkman ran into the Beach and Casino Hotel lobby to meet Aaron. The area swarmed with every imaginable police, ambulance, and Mexican authority available. The casino entrance was blocked off, letting no one in or out. Something bad had happened in the short span it took him to get there from his hotel. Something very bad. It was like trouble followed Sarah wherever she went. Or haunted her.

He had asked one of the Mexican cops near the front of the hotel what had happened but got only grunts in response. They were either being tight-lipped, or they didn't know.

"Parkman," Aaron shouted from somewhere deep inside the lobby.

He bobbed left, then right, trying to see over the heads of everyone milling about until he caught sight of Aaron. They wended through the throng until they met by the couches on the west side of the cavernous lobby.

"Did you find Sarah?" Parkman asked.

Aaron shook his head in the negative. "This scares me." He waved an arm in a semi-circle at the crowd of people. "What happened here? We're supposed to be on vacation."

"You don't know what this is?" Parkman asked.

"No idea."

Parkman pulled out his cell phone.

"Who are you calling?"

"Buck. We have no authority here, and if Sarah's in police custody, we need to know about it. Casper's the kind of guy who can make that happen."

He studied the crowd as Casper's phone rang. On the third ring, it was picked up.

"Trouble?" Casper asked.

"Looks that way. But we need your help to find out."

"What do you need?"

Parkman filled him in on what he knew and described the scene at the hotel at the moment.

"Absolute pandemonium. No one knows what's going on. No one's talking to us. We've lost Sarah and have no way of contacting her. She could be on her way to her room or in police custody, for all we know."

"Leave it with me. I'll make some calls. Go to Aaron's room. Wait there in case she returns on her own. Keep your cell charged. I'll call when I know something."

Casper clicked off.

"Let's go," Parkman said. "Back to your room."

They started for the back of the lobby. The elevators were sealed off, so Parkman led Aaron to the left stairwell.

"What'd he say?" Aaron asked.

"That he'd look into what happened here tonight and get

back to us."

They hit the stairwell door.

"Hope he calls back soon. I feel like I'm losing Sarah. I can't lose her, Parkman."

"I know. Neither can I."

On the third floor, Parkman stopped to catch his breath. "What floor are you on?"

"Sixth."

"Great."

He continued up the stairs. Aaron followed close behind.

Chapter 16

THE HOLDING CELL HAD two overhead bulbs dangling from the ceiling. Only one worked. Dirt and grime had collected in the corners and on the baseboards over the years without the attention of a mop or cleaning supplies. Wafting through the air, a foreign smell came to her. Something like the smell of a dump site after rain. Wet, soggy rot.

Because Sarah was the only girl brought in from the parking lot, they had separated her from the rest of them and tossed her in a room with a brown-stained mattress on a wire frame. She chose the floor to lie on—instead of the bed—where she curled into a ball and waited for the shakes to pass.

This sucked. She could've stayed in her hotel room, under the warm bedsheets, curled up while Aaron took care of her. If she needed the bathroom, she had one. If the desire to take a bath came over her, she could. But no, she had to listen to her sister and try to buy drugs which would disappoint anyone who knew her.

She had changed. How much, she wasn't sure yet. The run-in with the Enzo Cartel had altered something in her. Something that dealt with survival and mortality. She didn't want to die. She didn't want to suffer. As someone who was always in control and confident, this weakness in her body weighed on her. The urge for a fix was still there, making her sick with desire.

The door clicked and then opened. She didn't move. Not that she didn't want out of this hellhole. She was just too damn weak to make the effort.

"Get up," a man ordered.

Sarah moaned in response. If they wanted her up, they could get her up themselves. She had done nothing wrong. Was warning people of an oncoming car a crime? She didn't even get to complete her drug purchase, so technically they had nothing on her. Zippo. Nada.

"Ramirez, Guzman, need a hand in here. Bitch don't want to listen."

Footsteps walked around her. Others bounded down the hall. Sarah took a deep breath, shivered with the cold, clammy feeling on her skin, and wondered if she'd vomit again.

Here we go ...

One of the men wrapped meaty hands around each ankle. The other two grabbed a wrist each and lifted. She moaned with the strain and cried out with the pain.

"Easy," she whispered.

They spoke in Spanish as they carted her down a cold corridor. A door opened. The men turned a corner and dropped her onto a concrete floor harder than they needed to.

She curled into a ball, hating her weak body, hating her weakened position, and hating Vivian a little more for her part in this.

Make it all go away, sis.

The door slammed shut. Sarah eased into a more comfortable position, then just lay there breathing, feeling the rhythm of her heartbeat, listening to the sounds of the police station outside the room.

This was just one day. There would be a tomorrow. Then another. She would beat this. She would heal. Then she would regain her strength and be as valuable as she'd been in the past. She'd fight, run, and maim whoever needed it when she was well again.

A better smell came from this room. Cleaner, newer. The lighting had improved as well. Through the thin skin of her eyelids, she detected a bright light to her right. She angled left and opened her eyes to slits.

A cleaner room by far. She moved slowly to sit up and lean against the wall. The interrogation room. Or, as some American departments now call them, interview rooms.

She knew the routine. They would come in, ask their questions, accuse her of something outrageous, claim they would charge her with umpteen criminal offenses, and she would spend a couple of decades in a Mexican prison if she didn't cooperate. This police business was like any other. It involved negotiations, deals, and master closers. The only way to beat the brilliant ones at this game was to be innocent. If they didn't have proof of any crime, they had nothing. Whether she was guilty of something or not, always better to play the innocent card. It kept their sails windless.

The door opened. At least they didn't make her wait as

long as other police departments would. They didn't want to sweat her. They wanted answers, and they wanted them fast. Being eager showed their cards early. Next time, they might not want to be so eager.

Two men filed into the room. They closed the door and locked it. Both men removed their suit jackets revealing shoulder holsters, and then, as if this was a performance worthy of a theater stage, they moved around the table and stopped on either side of her in perfect harmony.

"Impressive," she managed to say. "You guys look like you could be in a stage show called the Nutcracker because I'm sure all that was set up to make me think you're here to break my balls." She looked from one to the other. "Am I right?"

The man on her left reared back and kicked her in the side of the ribs as the man on the right sucker punched her in the cheek.

She missed the rest of the show as she passed out on the first punch.

Chapter 17

Aaron had left the hotel room twice for coffee while Parkman kept his phone by his side. They had been watching the news on the TV the entire time, but nothing came on about the incident at the casino downstairs. Sarah hadn't returned, and she hadn't tried to contact Aaron.

Sarah was gone in one scene, one accident, one slip-up, and there were no leads. Nothing.

In an hour, the sun would rise over Mexico, and they were no closer to learning Sarah's whereabouts than they had been the previous evening.

Parkman got up from his chair by the desk in the corner and paced the floor, glancing at Aaron on the bed a couple of times.

"I know we've gone over this repeatedly," Parkman said. "But is there anything else you can add? Any detail? Anything she said?" Aaron sat with pillows propped up behind his back on the bed. "Do you know if Vivian was in her head?"

"She never mentioned anything about Vivian. She usually does."

"When you got to the room and discovered her missing, you called me. Then what?"

"I ran back to the elevator, took it to the lobby, and scoured the front looking for her. I knew you'd be at least five to ten minutes, so I checked the casino. I walked the aisles, back and forth, but nothing. She had disappeared in the short time it took me to get downstairs and back up to the room."

"You mentioned she thought a car was following you. Did you check that out?"

"When we first got out of the taxi. I headed toward the car, but it did a U-turn and took off before I could get close enough to identify the driver."

"Okay, but did you go outside and see if that car had returned?"

Aaron shook his head. "No."

"So far, that may be the key, the only connection." Parkman shrugged. "It's all we have to go on. We need to learn if that car is connected in any way."

Parkman's cell rang.

He jumped and lunged for it. The phone bounced when he hit the bed, and he missed catching it on the first try. As he fell sideways, he attempted to snatch it out of the air but only succeeded in sending it flying to the carpeted floor. The ringing cut off in mid-ring.

"Shit and a fuck," he shouted as he rolled sideways, dropped to the floor, and retrieved his phone.

Everything worked fine. The power button must've been knocked when it hit the floor. He got to his feet and tried to search the recent calls menu when the phone rang in his hand.

Casper.

"Yeah, Buck. What do you have?"

"Everything okay there?" Buck asked. "I called a second ago, but it got cut off."

"Dropped the phone. You have anything?"

"Nothing, really. After what just happened a half hour's drive north of you in Tijuana, the Enzo Cartel compound still smoldering, no one wants to cooperate with the American authorities right now. At least not me, and on something they're deeming a local car accident."

"Car accident?" Parkman glanced at Aaron, who had jumped off the bed and was pacing now.

"Yeah. Someone smashed two cars up in the parking lot in the rear of the casino at Aaron's hotel."

"You got this from the Mexican cops? Even though they're not being cooperative?"

"No. They're tight-lipped. I got this from the guy at the front desk of your hotel."

Parkman shook his head. "Shit. We should have thought of that."

"Got through to the night manager. Explained who I was and that I had an interest in several Americans staying at his hotel. He relayed to me what he knew, which wasn't much, but said he would open their cameras to you if you wanted to take a look. Maybe you'd see Sarah on one of them."

"Yes. Great idea. We'll head down right now." At least they'd be doing something. Being proactive.

"Just one thing. He can't authorize you to see the control room for the casino. Nor can he let you see any of the casino cameras. Just the lobby and some of the outside ones."

"Understood. Better than nothing."

"Parkman, you find something. You locate Sarah. Get back to me. I want to know."

"Of course." He clicked off. "We're going to the front desk. They've agreed to let us see the hotel's camera footage, just nothing from the casino."

"Fine. Let's go. She's bound to be on one of them."

"She had better be."

They bumped into each other in their haste, trying to get through the hotel room door.

Chapter 18

Sarah didn't want to wake. The pain, the struggle, and the urge for heroin all remained. Just the act of waking up cast a shadow on the day. The old waves of depression rolled in like distant clouds.

What had that psychologist said to her before she got Cole Lincoln? He'd said something about a cube in the desert, a ladder, flowers, and a storm. She would never forget the horse representing how she felt about Aaron. But it was the clouds and the storm in the distance that came to mind right now. They represented her problems in life, and they always seemed to be right above her, a perpetual storm. How much could the cube take, the cube being her ego, her self-identity?

Sarah rolled to her side and drew her knees up to her chest. The wounds from the Enzo Cartel struggle mixed in with the new ones. Did it really matter? She could heal. She always did. The pain was never much of a problem initially. Adrenaline and endorphins were the body's natural Advil. It was always hours later, or even the next day, when the pain was made real, laid out on the table for all to see. Healing was the real pain. In healing, you felt every movement, every detail, and each breath.

Healing sucked, but it was also necessary and welcomed. To heal is to fight another day.

She willed her body to heal. She willed her body to stop yearning for the drug. Wasn't the heroin just another wound? One that could heal? It would take a few weeks, a month. But so did a broken bone.

But while the bone healed, she didn't yearn for another broken bone.

Fuck heroin.

She opened her eyes. Same dank holding cell. Same shit. Different country. Different rules.

Fuck it all.

She'd beat this. She'd beat them. She'd beat them as soon as the throbbing, shaking, and headache subsided.

Yeah, right.

Something was bound to happen. Vivian had to have foreseen all this. As always, everything was part of the bigger picture. Being human meant she was left out of the bigger picture—for now. When whatever was supposed to happen happened, she'd see it for what it was and be grateful she made it, she lived it. Happy for the people she saved.

But it always sucked in the moment.

The door to the cell crashed open. She flinched and moaned at the jolt of pain that shot through her.

"Get up," a man barked.

"You know what's funny?" Sarah asked.

"What?"

"A lot of things. Lighten the fuck up."

The man called out to his colleagues, and two minutes later, they were dragging her down the corridor.

"Is this round two?" she asked.

No one answered her.

This time the interview room had several chairs set up around a rectangular table. Whatever was going on, they wanted to talk this time. She looked forward to a talk. Maybe a cup of coffee.

They dropped her in a chair without restraints. Her first thought was how dangerous that was, but then she reminded herself how she looked and realized no one was worried about her.

Soon, three men stood on the other side of the table. No one took a chair. Only one man's badge was visible on his belt. All three were armed.

It was their court, their ball game. She was content to sit and wait them out. Eventually, one of them would speak. Or they would punch and kick her again. The withdrawal symptoms hadn't worsened, but they weren't showing signs of abating either. Her ability to rebuff an attack remained severely limited.

"Why were you at the casino?" the scruffy-haired man to her right asked.

"Try my luck. One never knows what corner Lady Luck might be hiding behind."

The man to her left adjusted his feet and rolled his shoulders as if preparing to take a shot to the head. Or maybe he was preparing to give one.

"I won't ask again," Scruffy said.

"You kind of just did."

They waited. She waited.

The man in the middle stepped forward. "Are you going to talk to us, tell us what we want to know? Or be evasive and answer nothing?"

"You know how many times I've been in an interview room? This has become so routine it's ridiculous. Been there, tried that." Her right leg bounced up and down. She stopped it. "So let's go around that block again." She shook her head and mumbled to herself, "Getting bored with these *interviews*, Vivian."

"You ever been in a Mexican prison, Señorita? I assure you, it's different than what you're used to north of the border."

She studied their eyes, one by one. "Okay, how about we make a deal?"

"What kind of deal?" Scruffy asked.

"A trade."

The men exchanged glances. Scruffy glared back at her with bloodshot eyes. "You have nothing to offer us."

"Ahh, but I do. I have something quite valuable."

"What's that?" the roll-the-shoulder man said to her left.

"Information." She slapped her leg. "Holy shit. You guys are thick. Isn't that what you've been asking me for? You want answers from me, so I want answers from you."

"Forget it," the man in the middle said. "This isn't a conversation in a coffee shop. This is an interrogation." He slapped his hands on the table, the sound reverberating throughout the small room. "Just answer our *fucking* questions."

"Wow, some people just know how to suck the nice out of you, don't they?" Sarah glared at him. "Nice Sarah just exited the building, so fuck you. I'm an American citizen. I've done nothing wrong. I want a phone call. I want a lawyer. Call the embassy and suck yourselves off. I'm done with you lot. Now, charge me or release me, asshole."

A vein bulged on the man's forehead as his eyes seemed to extend from their sockets from the internal pressure of his anger. She waited for the blow to the face, but it didn't come. Instead, the man on her left placed a hand on his colleague and pulled him up and away from Sarah. Quietly, he guided him out of the room. When she was alone with Scruffy, he sat down opposite her.

"Here's what we know," Scruffy said. "The Enzo Cartel compound is in ruins. Your name is linked to that. The cartel attacked a hotel outside Tijuana. Many of our friends and, in some cases, family died in that attack. Are you aware that Mexican police officers were killed while protecting you?"

"Yes. I am aware of that, and I am truly sorry. You have my condolences. As you are probably aware, I wasn't in the hotel the night it got hit."

"I know. You were saving a nun from being raped by two cartel men."

Sarah frowned. Usually, people didn't surprise her so easily. "How would you know about that? And me? How could you know that was me?"

"That nun is my sister. That is why you're not dead or on life support in the local hospital. My name is Manuel Hernandez, and I'm here to help you. But you have to tell me what you're here for. Why Rosarito? Why that casino? And how are Wallace Stern, Mark Struben, and Eddie Coleman involved with you? Did you know they were going to rob the casino?"

Sarah cleared her throat, sat up straighter, and turned toward Hernandez. She adjusted her chair and leaned in to rest her arms on the table's surface. Was he really the nun's brother? A cop? They could've easily gotten an identification from the nun and matched it to her. With all those dead men in the Baja Café just down the road from the church, they might want Sarah for murder. After all, she did enter that café with bloody intent.

Trust no one and hate most cops has kept her alive. Maybe it was prudent to stay true to oneself and not try to change things. If it wasn't broken and all that.

She cleared her throat. "Would you believe me if I told you I'm on vacation with my boyfriend? He's probably worried sick right now with all that's happening at the hotel, and I'm nowhere to be found. Any chance I could get that phone call?"

Hernandez studied her face. She met his eyes and didn't waver. After a moment, he pushed his chair back, a metal shriek sounding off the floor, got up, and walked from the room, leaving her to her thoughts.

Hey, Vivian, are we cool here?

No answer came.

Chapter 19

Parkman identified himself at the hotel's front desk and asked to speak to the manager. Aaron stood off to the side while the weary desk clerk, probably overworked and stressed about last night, paged the manager.

Five minutes later, a rotund American-looking man shuffled in from the casino. He was unshaven and looked close to having a coronary.

"How can I help you?" the manager asked without shaking Parkman's hand. The man's voice was high, whiny, and completely unexpected coming out of that body.

"My name's Parkman. I understand my colleague, Mr. Schaffer, called ahead."

"Ah, yes. Follow me."

The manager turned and strode toward the elevators. Parkman followed and motioned for Aaron, who hustled in behind him. The manager walked past the elevators, down a hall, and stopped at a door marked, Security: Private.

"Your names again?" he asked.

"I'm Parkman, and this is Aaron."

They shook hands. The manager's hand was clammy, cold, and wet. Parkman fought the urge to wipe his hand off on his jeans.

"Now, normally, this wouldn't happen. And if it did, the proper channels and procedures would be followed. But after what Sarah did to that cartel, not only do I want to help her friends, but I don't want anything on record that I did. Understood?"

Parkman and Aaron nodded.

"I wasn't here," the manager went on. "Neither were you. I will disavow any knowledge of this if word were to spread."

"We understand."

After a moment's pause, the manager slipped a key into the doorknob and turned it. He opened the door and stepped back.

"Bob?" he shouted into the room.

"Yeah?" a man said.

"Give these boys anything they want. Just no casino."

"Yes, sir."

A slight wind ruffled Parkman's sleeve as the manager slipped past him, heading back the way they had come.

"He talked like this was a presidential coup or something," Aaron whispered over Parkman's shoulder.

"It's all about being careful in Mexico. Staying off the radar."

They moved inside the room and let the door ease shut behind them. The place reminded Parkman of images he'd seen of the inside of nuclear power plant's control rooms. A long table with several chairs faced a wall of TV screens depicting several areas of the hotel simultaneously. It was like the inside of a network TV station.

"Hey, Bob," Parkman said as he looked over the screens, taking it all in. "We need your help."

"That's what I'm here for."

Bob was just as heavy as the manager, each side of his lower abdomen hanging off the chair. Candy wrappers littered his workspace, and a half-eaten Mars bar sat to his right. Parkman glanced in the garbage and wasn't surprised to see a McDonald's bag scrunched up in a ball at the bottom.

"We're looking for a girl—"

"Aren't we all," Bob guffawed, trying to make a joke. Something about him screamed creepy to Parkman.

He stole a glance Aaron's way. The firm eyes, tightened jaw, and taut skin on his knuckles told Parkman a story—he wasn't willing to entertain humor at this time.

"The girl is missing from this hotel," Parkman said. To elevate the sense of urgency and to keep Bob from joking further, Parkman added, "She may have been kidnapped from the premises."

Bob pulled his eyes away from the screens in front of him and faced Parkman. "Nobody is kidnapped from this hotel. Too much security. You're mistaken." Bob swiveled back to his screens.

The balls on some people.

"Last night. Twenty minutes before the shit hit the roof, maybe try the lobby cameras—"

"The fan," Bob interjected.

Parkman frowned and exchanged glances with Aaron,

who seemed ready to choke the guy. That would be an unfair fight.

"Excuse me?" Parkman asked.

"You said shit hit the roof. I believe the expression is shit hit the fan."

Parkman clenched and unclenched his fists. "You're right. The fan." He breathed deeply, exhaled sharply, then let his hands open. "The girl is a dirty blonde. It'll possibly appear as light brown hair on these screens. She would've checked in with this man to your left. About ten minutes later, she would've entered the lobby on her own. We need to see everything we can regarding her. Where she went. Who she might have met. Everything we—"

"Time?" Bob interrupted again.

"Aaron, you have an approximate?"

"Nine-thirty. Thereabouts."

The center console in front of Bob stopped recording. He typed on a keyboard, and a moment later, the camera started up again with a timer in the bottom right corner, last night's date and time stamped on the frame. The screen was at least a twenty-inch diameter, big enough for all three men to watch it whether sitting or standing.

"I'll increase the speed to two times." Bob adjusted something on the console. "If you see her, shout out."

They watched in silence. After a minute, it was almost nine-forty in the evening, and Sarah hadn't shown up yet.

"This is reminding me of Joanne's apartment building," Aaron said. "Scares me."

"Who was Joanne?" Parkman adjusted his feet and bent closer to the screen. "Your sister, right?"

"After she went missing, and the police were doing fuck

all about it, I went to her apartment building in Mississauga, a part of Toronto, and asked around. The superintendent let me in to view the cameras in the lobby. I saw Joanne leave the building with the man who killed her. It was the last time I saw her alive. On a camera."

"I'm sorry." Parkman didn't take his eyes off the screen. "That won't happen here, though. We'll find her. Vivian's got this."

"Let's just hope so—"

"There," Parkman shouted and pointed at the screen.

Sarah and Aaron walked by the camera's lens on their way to the elevators.

"Yes, that's us. Now take it about five minutes later. If she used the elevator, it'll show up. Are there other cameras in the lobby?"

"Yes, two more. Once we capture what we want to see, it'll be easy to load the other two to the date and time. This is the main one, though. Everyone usually shows up on this one."

Bob let the two-times fast-forward feature continue by the camera's clock for three minutes, then slowed it to real-time. Parkman adjusted his shirt as sweat formed under his arms. The temperature in the room increased. A stench wafted up from the garbage canister beside Bob's chair. Or maybe it was Bob himself.

"There." Aaron pointed. "I came off the elevator and walked to that couch. That's when I called you, Parkman."

"Okay, watch closely," Parkman said. "If she used the elevator, she'll show up any second."

Less than half a minute later, Sarah moved into the camera from the bottom where the elevators were. She watched Aaron, his back to her.

"She was right behind me. How could I miss that?"

Sarah moved slowly, heading to the left.

"She's going into the casino." Bob shrugged. "Without a court order, nobody sees casino footage."

"We know. Just keep your eyes peeled for her to exit the casino."

A few moments later, the Aaron on the screen got off the couch and headed for the small convenience store in the lobby for the Advil. After that, he entered the camera again on his way to the elevator. They didn't have to wait long for Sarah to show. It couldn't have been another minute before she walked on camera again toward the hotel's front entrance.

"She's leaving," Aaron whispered.

"Not so fast." Parkman jerked his head toward the screen.

Sarah had stopped by a couch. A man had approached her. They appeared to be talking, then Sarah dropped to the couch to sit. Parkman leaned in to get a better look at the man's face but couldn't.

Sarah got to her feet, leaned in close to either whisper something to the man or kiss him, then started past him. The man followed her off-camera and out the front door of the hotel.

"Who the hell was that?" Aaron asked, the uncertainty of what had just transpired written all over his face.

There was no doubt Sarah knew the man on the camera. Knew him in an intimate way. She would never get that close to anyone.

"Can you use another camera to show us a better image

of that man's face?" Parkman asked.

"Hold your horses. Already on it." Bob adjusted one camera, then another, and typed in the date and time. "I might even be able to utilize the cameras outside the building to see the vehicle they left in. If so, I've got the ability to read a license plate."

"Good. Just show me the face as soon as you can."

"Less than a minute."

There was something familiar about that man. Something ominous as well, though. Whoever it was probably wasn't good for Sarah. Parkman retrieved his cell phone from his back pocket and brought Casper's number up on call display. As soon as he got a name or just a picture of the face, he would need Casper's help in getting more on the guy. If that man had kidnapped Sarah, Special Agent Buck "Casper" Schaffer would probably come back to Mexico and spearhead the investigation himself.

"Got it," Bob shouted.

A face materialized on a camera closer to Aaron. Blurry at first, it started to take shape. The camera had zoomed in and was now filling in the blanks with a computer program.

As the man's hair took shape, the pit in Parkman's stomach got heavier. He had jammed the toothpicks in his back pocket in his haste to come to Aaron's aid last night. He retrieved one now and popped it between his lips.

The man's brow formed at the same time the chin and mouth took shape. Then the eyes.

"No," Parkman whispered. "No way."

"What?" Aaron said. "What is it? I don't recognize him."

"You wouldn't. No one would."

The face finished on the screen, and Parkman knew

exactly who it was.

"What's no one would mean?"

"No one would recognize a dead man."

Aaron stepped around Bob's chair and grabbed Parkman on each arm. "You're not making sense. Who is that?"

Parkman shook his head, averted his eyes, then looked back at the screen.

"That man is dead. He died years ago. His body was dumped in Toronto in Lake Ontario."

"He doesn't look dead to me. What's his name?"

"That dead man walking on that camera, the man who Sarah appeared to know and was shocked to see, used to go by the name Drake Bellamy. But who knows who he is now."

Aaron let go of Parkman's arms.

Parkman hit dial on his phone with a shaking finger. The toothpick fell from his mouth. As he tried to unwrap another, the phone rang on the other end.

It was time to get Casper more involved.

Chapter 20

FBI Special Agent Mary Fitzgerald and her partner, Special Agent Stacy King, sat in their cruiser, waiting for the call to authorize them to take Blair Turner into custody.

The taco from yesterday's lunch was cold and soggy, but King ate it anyway. She was hungry, and it might be several hours before she got the chance to eat again. Once they had Blair in custody, the briefing and stripping down would last into the night without let-up.

Blair Turner, eighteen-year-old drug dealer, was the son of Jane Turner, a rich widower of a man of Indian descent. She had reverted to her maiden name when her husband, Vihaan Singh, died. His death was still clouded in suspicion, but King and Fitzgerald weren't interested in her for that. They were interested in her because of her two trips to Bulgaria within the last six months. Particularly the small town called Sliven, about three-hundred kilometers east of

Bulgaria's capital, Sofia.

Jane Singh, nee Turner, had no family in Sliven. It wasn't a tourist destination like Greece to the south and Istanbul to the southeast. Organizations within the American government monitored chatter, which zeroed in on Sliven, where an old Russian military arms dump was located. As recent as February, Moldovan authorities, working with the FBI, stopped the sale of nuclear material to Islamic extremists by arresting the smugglers. They had successfully arrested smugglers and gangs four times in the previous five years, ceasing the movement of illegal arms.

With that much heat, the FBI wanted to know why such a rich woman as Jane Turner would be interested in flying to Sliven. And why did she transfer several million American dollars to a bank in London? Was her plan to relocate to Britain? Or was that money there to be transferred for a purchase of some kind?

Jane Turner was no criminal. If she was attempting to purchase something on the black market, she wasn't going about it discreetly enough. When that much money was transferred in and out of the United States, it raised eyebrows. As much as it was Jane's money, and she could do with it whatever she thought fit, with the world climate in regards to funding terrorism and extremist cells, governments around the globe were keeping a tab on transfers of that nature.

She had no ties to religious sects, no affiliation through her dead husband to any hostile groups, and lived a relatively quiet life in Mexico. But two trips to Bulgaria and a large money transfer raised questions Jane needed to answer. Even if she had valid reasons for her actions, she would be on their radar for a few more years.

"How can you eat that soggy taco?" Fitzgerald asked. "Looks gross."

King examined her half-eaten taco. "Not so bad. Rot in the hand or rot in the stomach." She shrugged. "Makes no difference to me."

"Gross."

King laughed. "I'm joking. It's not rotting. It's fine." She lifted what was left of the taco to show her partner. "A little limp, but good."

"Ewww." Fitzgerald reared back from it.

The street in front of the Mexican police station where they held Blair Turner and the others from last night's debacle at the casino hadn't seen a street cleaner in years. Filth, rubbish, and stains had built up over the years, leaving behind an odd collage of dark colors across the cracked pavement.

"What do you think happened last night?" King said with a mouth full. "You think Turner's kid had anything to do with it?"

"Who knows? The Mexican authorities are staying mum about the whole thing. Probably because they have no idea themselves."

"Why are we here so early, anyway?"

"Because." Fitzgerald glanced her way, then looked back at the police station. "I got word that the okay to pick up Blair was coming through this morning. When it does, I want to be close. If they let him leave or he walks out and disappears for a few days, that sets us back. What if Ms. Turner heads to the airport again? If possible, we need to nail this down, see what he knows, and get him on our side."

"You know how hard that's going to be? Get the kid to spy on his own mother?"

"Not hard at all." Fitzgerald examined King's face. "Do you have any kids?"

King shook her head. "No."

"Ms. Turner has only one, and she treats him like shit. Blair hates his mother. We're going to offer him a way to hit back."

"Sounds good. In theory. But in the end, don't we all innately love our mothers, even if they are bitches?"

"We have something that'll help Blair make up his mind."

"Yeah, I know. Threats."

"It works. You can't tell me it won't."

"Blair has been practically living on the street since he was sixteen. He's been in and out of scraps, the local jail, and half the girls' pants around here. You think threats will make him crumble, make him talk when his mother fixes everything for him?"

"My brand of threats will."

King sat up straighter in her seat. "What brand?"

"I'm going to threaten his mother. That's the one thing she won't be able to fix, and it'll be his fault."

"Wait, I'm confused." King scrunched up the empty taco wrapper and tossed it in the back seat. She tied her hair into a neat bun as she talked. "I thought you just said he hated his mother. So threatening her harm should please him, wouldn't it?"

Fitzgerald gave her a one-eye-half-lidded look, eyebrows raised. "Not if you threaten her life. Without Blair's help, his mother will die. Ultimately, he would be responsible for her death. Let's see if he doesn't help us then."

"How do you pull that off?"

"Her trips to Europe were by herself. He knows that. The money transfers were something she would've kept from him. I've been authorized to concoct a story around that. As long as he wears a wire and gets her talking, I'm authorized to lay anything on him."

King slapped the dash above the glovebox. "How come this is the first I've heard of it?"

"Just got word this morning when I was told the paperwork was being filed for us to pick him up."

"Great." She looked out her window at a dilapidated house a block away. They had been in Sliven coordinating with the Bulgarian authorities for a month. Back in the States, they were ordered to Mexico to follow Jane Turner. After all the action in Bulgaria, this had been a boring, shit job. Just last night, the idea was raised to bring Blair Turner in. He was now detained by the Mexican authorities, so more paperwork was necessary.

There could be no mistake, no letting this go. If Ms. Turner learned of their existence, all their work would dissolve instantly. If, in fact, she was attempting to use her transferred money for something illegal, she would simply back off and let it go until she wasn't under surveillance anymore. Then, when no one was looking, she would quietly buy what she wanted, and a price would be paid for their error.

If Blair wouldn't help, then he was to be kept in custody until they brought Ms. Turner in. If it turned out she had a boyfriend in Sliven and simply decided to send money to the boyfriend's family in Britain, a lot of people were going to be embarrassed. But if it turned out she was in contact with smugglers and was trying to buy something on the black market, a lot of lives would be saved.

Whatever the reason for Jane Turner's recent activities, Special Agents Fitzgerald and King were on the job, parked out front of the Mexican police station, eating day-old tacos, and waiting for her eighteen-year-old son to come out so they could threaten and cajole him to death.

"Shit, sometimes this job sucks," King whispered.

"Tell me about it."

Fitzgerald's phone rang.

"This has to be it," she said to King as she answered the phone. "Fitzgerald here." A pause. "Yeah? Really?" Another pause. "Interesting. Okay, thanks." She hung up.

King raised her hands. "Well? What was that? We got the go-ahead?"

Fitzgerald shook her head. "Not yet."

"Then what was that all about?"

Fitzgerald glanced over at the police station's front doors as a Mexican cop stepped out and headed for his cruiser.

"An interesting development." She faced King. "You ever heard the name, Sarah Roberts?"

"Yeah. It's that psychic girl or something. See her name in the papers here and there. Hey," King snapped her fingers. "Wasn't she involved with the sting on the Enzo Cartel?"

"The one and the same." Fitzgerald pointed at the station. "She's in there with Blair."

"What?" King sucked in air. "You're kidding? Sarah Roberts is working on this case?"

"I didn't say that. She was taken in with Blair last night, and it seems they were chummy before that car accident at the casino."

"Chummy? How?"

"Not sure, but it was just relayed to me that last night's bust was a setup. A man named Wallace Stern was working with the authorities to stop two other guys from robbing the casino. Wallace gave his statement last night, and in it, he says Sarah Roberts was with Blair in Blair's car. Although Wallace didn't know Sarah's name when he wrote his statement."

"No way." King shook her head. "Something doesn't add up."

"What doesn't?"

"Sarah Roberts is clean. She doesn't do drugs." She bit her lower lip. "We know Blair deals out of his Camaro, and she wouldn't have been buying shit from Blair."

"I agree. So she's working on our case, then. That's the only conclusion we have. That's why our contact in there," she pointed, "just called it in."

"Shit. This is going to get fucked up. We can't let someone like Sarah near this. Too many cooks in the kitchen or some shit like that. We're the FBI. She's just a private citizen."

"We won't let Sarah near this. Our authorization to nab Blair will come in any minute now, and we'll take him, leaving Sarah in this Mexican hellhole."

"I love what Sarah's done. I mean, what I've read about." King slapped her hands together. "But I don't want her working an FBI case. That's fucked up. She's not one of us."

"My thoughts exactly." Fitzgerald stared out the windshield. "Hey, any more of those tacos left?"

Chapter 21

From Aaron's room on the sixth floor, Parkman got through to Casper on the second try. He stared out of the window, coffee in hand, quiet. He seemed to be in a reflective state after seeing Sarah on camera. The moment she leaned into Drake. How close they got. How she avoided him in the lobby when she saw him on the phone. Her deception regarding the Advil errand. Aaron had a lot to think about and a lot to consider.

"Schaffer here."

"Casper, it's Parkman. We located Sarah on the hotel cameras."

"What did you see?"

"It appears she left the hotel with a man."

"You have a name?"

"Drake Bellamy. A Canadian. But there's a catch."

It sounded like Casper was writing the name down.

"What catch?"

"He's dead."

"Explain."

He liked that about Casper. No surprised inhale. No misunderstanding. Just a one-word response. All business.

"Sarah saved Drake's life a couple of times a few years back in Toronto. Later, when she was dealing with these religious zealots called the Rapturites, we heard Drake was found dead in Lake Ontario. His death had to have been faked to get whoever was after him off his back."

"It'll make finding anything on this guy extra hard, even if I do. He's probably got a new name. Everything."

"I know. Look, contact a cop in Toronto named Spencer. He was intimately involved in the Bellamy case. You may have to push, but Spencer would know something. He would've been in on the faked death of Bellamy."

"Done. What are you guys going to do now?"

"Not much we can do. Wait here for Sarah to come back or get in touch with us. Or wait until you call me back with something."

"I've called the local hospitals and the three closest police stations," Casper said. "Got nothing. I'll double-time this. Leave your phone on."

Parkman disconnected, grabbed his coffee, and stood beside Aaron. He waited a heartbeat, took a drink, then said, "Nice view."

"Yeah."

"She'll be fine, Aaron."

"I know." He dropped a hand on Parkman's shoulder. "She always makes it out, whatever's happening."

After another moment, Parkman asked, "What's on your

mind?"

Aaron turned to face him. "You saw her on that camera. Sarah lied to me. I've never seen this side of her."

"It's the drugs, then. Chalk it up to her not being herself because of what Enzo did to her. She'll make it out of that, too."

Aaron turned back to the window.

"I'm just afraid *we* won't make it out of this."

Chapter 22

Manuel Hernandez returned with another cop in a brown suit and white shirt. Would the new guy have a message for her, a new threat of imprisonment?

Whatever they wanted to discuss would go over better with food in her stomach. And water. She would need to use a toilet soon, too.

"Sarah Roberts," Hernandez said with a gesture toward the other man. "This is my superior."

Sarah nodded at him. "No name?"

The man in the brown suit shook his head in such a small spurt that she almost missed it.

"Let's get down to business," No Name said, his accent American, south.

"No." Sarah tapped the table with her fingers, one after the other. The men exchanged a glance, then turned back to her. "Not before I'm offered something to drink or eat. I'm ravenous."

"That can be arranged. In time." No Name sat down and leaned in close to the table. "How long have you known Eddie Coleman?"

"Food first. Water first."

No Name didn't bat an eye, didn't move. "Eddie Coleman?"

"Fuck you." Sarah crossed her arms. "Lips are sealed until something like water or food unseals them. We all know this is bullshit."

No Name leaned back in his chair. "You don't seem to understand the gravity of your situation here. You're in a lot of trouble, Miss. Half this police station wants you dead because they think you're to blame for several of their colleagues' death in a Tijuana hotel. Eddie Coleman was shot and killed last night by the Mexican version of our SWAT team, and a man named Hank Olsen is in critical care at the hospital after Eddie ran him over with his car. We have witnesses that place you at the scene uttering words like, 'Wallace, get out of the way, or you'll die.' Then you said, 'And now a man dies,' like you knew what would happen."

He adjusted his tie and placed his hands, open-palmed, on the tabletop. "Did you and Eddie plan this? Because, according to our inside guy, this was supposed to be a simple robbery, not murder. It's starting to look like you and Eddie will kill Mark Struben and Wallace Stern and make off with the money. At least, that's what it looks like to an outsider. That's attempted murder charges, Sarah." He waved at a wisp of hair that had fallen over his forehead. "Say something in your defense, for fuck's sake?"

She shook her head back and forth, pointed at her mouth,

then her stomach.

"Fuck a whale cock." No Name got up from the table, so fast his thighs banged it. "Get her something to fucking eat already. You're such a stubborn bitch. Must be a Taurus."

Sarah nodded at him.

Chapter 23

"PARKMAN, I GOT SOMEWHERE." Casper sounded out of breath on the phone. "But you're not going to like it."

Parkman had been lying down, dozing. He hadn't slept since before they were in the RV heading to the border. Without some sleep, he'd be useless to Sarah when she needed him.

Aaron had gone for a walk, unable to sleep.

"What?" Parkman sat up in bed and rubbed each eye with his free hand as he held the phone to his ear. "Tell me."

"The Mexican authorities have Sarah."

He was awake now. This was bad. Real bad. "How? Where?" He paused. "I'd need to know why, too."

"The information I got was spotty. Not many agencies are offering up free information. I had to call in a favor."

"I don't understand." He got off the bed and walked to the large window overlooking the ocean six floors down.

"Why would it be so hard to find an American citizen?"

"The FBI is there under the radar. Some international investigation. The local authorities were also at your hotel last night."

"I know. The car accident thing."

"There was an attempted robbery of the casino, and Sarah was involved. One guy is dead, and one is in critical condition."

"Oh shit." Parkman put a hand on his forehead and started rubbing. "Are they saying Sarah killed the guy?"

"No."

"Then what? She's a witness?"

"No. The report I'm getting is they think she was in on it somehow. There were witnesses."

Parkman exhaled sharply. "But that's what Sarah does. Of course, she knew what was going to happen. Casper, we have to get her out of there." Then a thought occurred to him. "Wait a second. When you called around earlier, you said you contacted the local police departments and got nowhere."

"I know. They lied."

His stomach did a flip. That could mean only one thing in this country. She would never see the light of day. "Why? I'm afraid to ask. What could that mean?"

"It could mean all sorts of things. Maybe I got a desk clerk who didn't care to look it up. Who knows how things work down there? But there is a catch."

"What?" Parkman didn't know how much more he could handle.

"The FBI is interested in the witness that was with Sarah. That's why they were there last night."

"So. They can have him. All we want is Sarah."

"I know, but that's the problem. The witness deals heroin, and Sarah was seen in his car in the parking lot of the hotel she was staying in. He's a known dealer in the area, and apparently, this is how he does his deals. In his car." Casper stopped talking, coughed, then added, "I'm sorry, Parkman."

Parkman waited for his emotions to release their grip on his vocal cords.

"Look, I've got a guy at the embassy down there working on sorting this out. He said he could get her out by sunset. Just be there when she's released."

Parkman needed a toothpick. He wiped his face with his free hand.

"Parkman?" Casper shouted into the phone.

"Yeah. I'm here. Shit, Buck, what am I going to tell Aaron?"

"Nothing right now. Just contact the local authorities and wait while we negotiate her release. I'll do what I can from Los Angeles."

"You're in LA?"

"Yeah."

"Sure wish we had crossed that border with you now."

"It would've been safer for Sarah to not remain in Mexico."

"One last thing."

"Shoot."

"Why would the FBI be interested in a drug dealer in Rosarito, Mexico?"

"I asked myself that same question. Came up empty."

"Anything on Drake Bellamy?"

"That's two."

Parkman frowned. He paced the floor in front of the TV.

"Two what?"

"You said one last thing. Then asked two questions."

Parkman stopped pacing.

"Nothing," Casper said. "Just playing. Lightening up the mood. Sometimes my humor doesn't work. Sarah always finds a way out of this kind of shit. She's been in worse situations."

"What about Drake?"

"Got nothing. He's a ghost. The official record shows he drowned in Lake Ontario, as you said. As far as anyone is concerned, that's it. I talked to that cop Spencer in Toronto. Repeated what I found out on Drake."

"I saw Drake Bellamy on that camera. He's alive." A pulse beat in his throat and temple. "People are lying to you."

"I know. I hear you. I'll get to the bottom of this. Just go get Sarah. She's eight blocks away." Casper gave him the address. "They'll lie. Say she's not there. Persevere. You'll get through. After what happened at that hotel in Tijuana, I don't like the thought of Sarah alone in a Mexican police station. My embassy guy is working on it. Just hang there until you get her. Then find an airport and leave Mexico."

As Parkman clicked off, the hotel room door opened. Aaron stepped inside and closed the door behind him. He had aged at least five years in the hour they'd been apart.

"Anything?" Aaron asked.

"You need to sit down for this, but you can't. I'll tell you on the way. We haven't got much time."

Chapter 24

Two pre-packaged sandwiches later and two water bottles, Sarah was full but sick now. She controlled her breathing, sat still, and waited for the food to settle to quell the urge to throw up after finally eating. Every second, every minute it remained inside her was good.

No Name was back, alone this time.

"You ready to talk?" he asked.

"Sure. I'll talk." She leaned back on her chair, balancing on two legs. Thought better of it as the movement upset her stomach, and slowly set the chair back to the floor.

"Earlier, you heard the predicament you're in. Why were you at the casino last night?"

"My boyfriend and I are on vacation. Just happened to be out enjoying the night air."

"Bullshit. You're doing one of your psychic dances here, and the Mexican authorities don't like it."

"Psychic dance? Sounds new ageish."

"Sarah, wherever you are, death follows, just not yours."

"That's good, then. Right?"

No Name got up from his chair and walked to the wall where he rested a shoulder against it. "You're a smart-ass little bitch. They have enough shit to charge you with that you won't leave Mexico until you're in your fifties, and you crack jokes like a wise ass. The only reason I'm here is to see if you'll talk to me, shed some light on how you know Blair Turner, and why you were there last night."

Something clicked in her mind. Through her symptoms —which seemed to have subsided some—she was able to perceive that No Name's real objective was Blair Turner. The man hadn't offered his name because he technically wasn't here and would deny he talked to her. They were working a case on Blair and wanted what she knew about him. On that count, they would be sorely disappointed.

And what happened to Drake? Where had they taken him? All she'd seen were the Mexican cops and this No Name guy.

"What'll it be?" No Name asked. "You gonna talk to me?"

"I am talking."

He pushed off the wall. "Fuck's sake. You know what I mean."

"I don't know these people. Never did. And anyone can see a car racing across a parking lot and predict someone will die when that car is aimed at them. Now, can I go?"

He stood beside her, looking down, his eyes bulging with something like rage. Or hatred.

"Can you go? Can you go? No, you cannot go. This isn't

the principal's office in high school. You're in a Mexican police station waiting for charges to be filed, so you cannot *go*." He walked behind her. She planted her feet in case she needed to jam the chair back into his abdomen. "What you need to do is help yourself." Then he was on the other side of her. "You need to talk, little lady. Think of talking as a currency; you're buying your way out of this place."

"I think I need a nap."

No Name spun around and brought his face up close to hers. "What did you just say?"

"I ate. Now I'm tired." She offered him a polite smile, then dropped it. "I want a nap. Send me back to my cell." She turned to the door. "Guards."

No Name slapped the table in front of her, the sound reverberating throughout the small interview room.

The door opened, and two armed men entered with another man in a suit carrying a briefcase.

"Leave the room," Briefcase man said. "Now."

"Who the fuck are you?" No Name asked.

"Her new lawyer. She's being released. This interview is illegal and will not be admissible in court. Now get out."

Lawyer? Wow, how did you pull this off, sis?

No Name looked like he was about to have a coronary on the spot. His head swiveled from Sarah to the lawyer, then back to Sarah. He kicked the table like a little boy who couldn't get his way and stormed from the room, nearly smashing into the lawyer.

"Sarah, I need you to sign a couple of documents saying you'll stay in Mexico until the investigation is complete, and we need to be able to get in touch with you. Sign these, and you are free to go." The lawyer turned to the guards behind him. "No one will try to stop you."

Sarah signed the papers and was escorted to the back of the police station, where Blair Turner waited.

"Oh, shit. Did they do that?" he asked, examining her bruised cheek.

Her ribs ached, but nothing was broken from the first beat down. They had sent a message. Letting some of their angst out. She had gotten used to cops over the years.

Blair didn't look so good. His posture appeared crumpled like he tried something but was defeated. His complexion had paled an unhealthy yellow-white. She wondered what had happened to him in there.

"That was you back there?" she asked, ignoring his question. "The lawyer?"

He looked down at the ground, where he kicked a rock. "My mother's lawyer. Everybody in here listens to that guy. Got me out, too. Did you read the paper the lawyer had?"

"Your mom's a powerful woman."

He glanced up, eyes bloodshot. Before he looked away, she saw that he'd been crying. "Did you read the paper you signed?"

"No."

"You've been remanded into my mother's custody until these fools say you're not."

"Wrong." Sarah stepped around him.

"What?" He ran to catch up. "Sarah, you signed them. You need to come home with us, or you void that document."

"Consider it voided." She stopped at the sight of Drake sitting behind the wheel of a red car a block away.

"My mother wants to meet you, have you for dinner. She's in the car waiting. Entertain me. Do this. You won't regret it." Blair pointed at a black Mercedes, the sun glinting off its roof. A thick man sat behind the wheel. It was the only way she could describe him. His neck was as thick as his skull. The rear windows were tinted so dark nothing inside was visible.

"You coming?" Blair pleaded. "After all, she did post your bail and gave you free legal counsel." He started toward the car, stopped, and looked back when she didn't follow. "Sarah?"

The back area was a small parking lot where the Mexican cops parked their personal vehicles. One road traversed the back. On the left, the way the Mercedes was aimed, the road was empty. On the right, Drake's red four-door sat at the end by the connecting road. His vehicle was like something you could rent at any car rental company. Upon closer inspection, she was absolutely sure it was Drake Bellamy behind the wheel. Instead of going with Blair, she should be going with Drake. They needed to talk and catch up. She had so many questions for him.

"I'm sorry, Blair." She stepped closer to him. "I don't know you or your mother. Thank her for helping me out."

"She's going to be very disappointed. She usually doesn't get this kind of response."

"I'm not your usual kind of girl."

She started toward Drake's car. The moment she did, his hand became visible over the steering wheel, palm up in a *stop* gesture. Her pace faltered. She stopped. What was he trying to say? Her internal radar pinged, even as her legs were still weak from withdrawal and her stomach roiled around like it was filled with balls of lead.

Over her shoulder, she saw Blair about to enter the

Mercedes. She pivoted back to Drake. He gestured for her to go to Blair. But why? What did Drake know? She felt so far out of the loop her head spun.

Sarah, go with Blair ...

That sealed the deal. Even Vivian wanted her in that Mercedes. Vivian was the reason she was here in the first place. Otherwise, she'd be in Santa Rosa with her parents or swimming in the hotel pool with Aaron.

"Shit cake," she whispered to herself. "With yellow fucking icing." Maybe she would get that one more fix of heroin after all. Maybe that's what Vivian wanted for her. A fix. She got her to meet up with Blair to buy drugs, and now she was heading to Blair's lair.

A door opened behind her. Blair spoke to someone inside the car. The tone was hushed, too low for her to make out the words.

"Blair," she shouted over her shoulder. "Wait. I'm coming with you."

She stared at Drake's car a moment longer, imperceptibly nodded at him, then headed for the Mercedes.

You better be right about this, Vivian.

With each step, she dreaded the thought of getting a fix at Blair's place. She had almost beaten this thing even though it had only been a day since she left the Enzo compound.

But if he did have a little heroin, it could smooth out the edges for a day or two. Get back to Aaron soon. Beat this thing after the vacation.

That could work.

She was lying to herself and would never let that happen. She was too strong. She could resist. Had to. For Aaron, she would resist. For Parkman. For herself.

She only hoped, when the time came, that was true.

Chapter 25

FBI SPECIAL AGENTS FITZGERALD and King had finished every morsel of food in the cruiser, and now King needed a toilet.

"Can't we walk in there, identify ourselves, and they let us use the toilet as a professional courtesy?"

Fitzgerald shook her head. "We're unofficially here until that call comes in and makes us official."

"Where do I piss then?"

"Hold it."

"Can't."

Fitzgerald cast a pained glance her way. "I have to go, too. Shit, sometimes I hate stakeouts."

"Is that what this is? A stakeout?"

The phone rang. Fitzgerald grabbed at it so fast she dropped it under her feet.

"Shit."

By the third ring, she answered.

"Fitzgerald."

King watched her partner as she nodded and listened to the speaker on the phone. After a moment, Fitzgerald brought the phone down, clicked it off, and slipped it inside her pocket.

"Paperwork's being faxed over to the station as we speak." She smacked King's hand. "Let's go get our boy. The okay came from high up the Mexican food chain. No way they can refuse us."

King hopped from the cruiser, squinting at the protest her bladder offered her.

"Before the prisoner's release, I must release my bladder."

"Me too."

At the front doors, King pulled on Fitzgerald's sleeve.

"We talking to this kid here?"

"Never. Too many ears." Fitzgerald opened the doors and slipped inside the police station.

King followed. "Where then?" she mumbled as she pulled out her FBI ID.

Fitzgerald was already at the counter. She had identified herself and asked to see Blair Turner.

The Mexican officer behind the counter was overweight, his shirt undone at the top. A mustard or taco sauce stain covered at least an inch of the fabric on his collar. King wondered why that wasn't addressed. Don't they have superiors that fixed these things if the staff's standards weren't high enough?

The cop responded in Spanish, which wasn't King's strong suit. Knowing a few nouns and names wasn't enough to string sentences together. Without Fitzgerald, if they didn't speak English, King was done.

She stepped in beside Fitzgerald.

A few more words were exchanged in Spanish before Fitzgerald turned to King, her ire evident.

"They're saying Turner's gone. He was released fifteen minutes ago. You believe him?"

"Fuck no. We were outside the whole time. We didn't take a piss break on purpose." She faced the Mexican, thinking he didn't speak English. "Don't tell me I held my piss for nothing." Even as the words came out, she remembered that he was a cop and there was a high chance he spoke English.

"FBI came looking for Turner," he said. "Must be important."

"None of your concern." Fitzgerald's anger showed through. "Where is he?"

"Not here." The Mexican cop raised his hands and then set them back down. After a moment, he grabbed a pen and started writing something on a form in front of him.

King snatched the pen from his grasp.

Startled, he looked up at her.

"The paperwork was faxed to this station. Blair Turner is to be handed over to our custody. Stop writing on that paper and go get him. Or better yet, bring him to us."

The Mexican cop lowered down to rest on his elbows. "The man you seek has left the building with his fancy lawyer and that girl. Call his lawyer. Go to his house. He is not here, so there is no one to hand over."

"What girl?" Fitzgerald asked.

King's mind reeled at the possibility that the cop would

say the name Sarah Roberts. There was no way. There just had to be no way she was involved, or their investigation would fall apart.

"That American girl, Sarah Roberts. The bitch of Tijuana." He grunted like he laughed on the inside. "Lucky she left. She might not have made it another day in here."

Chapter 26

Parkman jogged most of the way to the police station, with Aaron following close behind. He detailed his phone call with Casper to Aaron, even the part about Drake Bellamy and how Casper couldn't get anything on the guy. At this point, Drake was a mystery, and until that mystery was solved, he had to be considered a threat.

Aaron had no problem with that.

Parkman slowed down as the police station came into view. Between breaths, he said, "Casper's working on getting her released today. We'll take her back to my hotel. It'll make it harder for anyone looking for her. She can rest. You guys can talk."

"We need to talk." Aaron was right beside him.

Up ahead, two well-dressed women stepped from what looked like an unmarked American police cruiser. To Parkman's trained eye, if he wasn't mistaken, those two women were Feds.

"Aaron, after what happened in Tijuana, there's a lot of interest in Sarah."

"I know. That's what I'm worried about."

"Bad interest."

The grim look on Aaron's face said it all. He was quite aware of the gravity of the situation. Sarah's safety was in question. If a cop wanted to take a shot at her, who would stop him? Vivian? Parkman knew Vivian was pretty powerful, but could she stop a bullet?

They made it to the front doors a minute later and entered the building.

The two women who had entered ahead of them were arguing with a large Mexican cop at the front counter.

One of the women said something Parkman couldn't make out. As he drew closer, the Mexican said, "The man you seek has left the building with his fancy lawyer and that girl. Call his lawyer. Go to his house. He is not here, so there is no one to hand over."

"What girl?" the woman on the right asked.

Parkman stopped five feet behind them, Aaron at his side.

"That American girl, Sarah Roberts. The bitch of Tijuana." The cop grunted, a deep rumble in his distended belly. "Lucky she left. She might not have made it another day in here."

Aaron leaped at the counter. "What the fuck did you just say?"

The woman on Parkman's right reacted fast, grabbing Aaron's arm and yanking him back, but Aaron was faster. His arm swung in a circle, spun back down, and had the woman in his grasp, twisting her arm away from him.

"Don't touch me," Aaron barked.

The woman on the left stepped closer, opening her blazer to expose the weapon strapped to her waist. "FBI. Release her."

Aaron let go.

"Sorry about that." Parkman moved in. "Sarah's boyfriend can get fired up."

"Aaron Stevens?" the Mexican cop said, standing up straighter. "The guy kidnapped by the Enzo Cartel? Here? In my police station?"

"Hey, Aaron," Parkman said. "Maybe it's time we leave."

"Not until they tell me where Sarah is."

"Aaron Stevens," the Mexican cop yelled loud enough for everyone in the building to hear. "Right here. Right now."

Tables moved. Chairs shifted. Cops came out of cubicles, from behind desks, and out of rooms where doors were closed. Within seconds, a wall of cops moved toward Aaron, Parkman, and the two women.

The woman on the right massaged her wrist where Aaron had twisted it. "I think it's time we leave."

"Aaron, you heard the lady," Parkman said. "Let's go. Nothing we can do here."

Parkman was proud of Aaron in that moment. He listened without protest. He simply started walking backward, fell behind Parkman, who stayed behind the Feds, and walked outside close-knit as if an imaginary rope surrounded them.

Once outside, the agent let go of her wrist, pulled cuffs from her belt, and held them up in Aaron's face.

"If you ever touch me again like that, I'll use these."

Aaron nodded his understanding. Again, Parkman was

proud of him. If he'd opened his mouth, regret would follow.

The agent put her cuffs away and introduced herself and her partner.

"What are you two doing here?" Fitzgerald asked.

Parkman moved in front of her. "Came to pick Sarah up. It was all a misunderstanding. She shouldn't have been in there. How about you two? Here for Sarah as well?"

"We can't discuss why we're here. But I will tell you we have no interest in Sarah. Actually, we'd prefer it if she'd just go home. Leave this alone. Get out of Mexico before something happens to her."

"What's going to happen to her?" Aaron said too sharply.

"You got a leash for him?" King asked Parkman. "One more bite out of him, and he won't wish the trouble he'll be in on anybody."

"Look, he took your comment as a threat. Before something happens to her, sounds ominous, like you know something."

"After what just happened in Tijuana?" Fitzgerald moved closer to Parkman. "All those cops killed in a hotel? You're kidding, right? Sarah was there. She survived. They were organized together, waiting to extract him." She pointed at Aaron. "And she just shows up in this police station the day after the Enzo Cartel is destroyed. Then he walks in," she pointed at Aaron again, "the bandage on his missing finger. You two have some balls being upset with us. It's you two and your little psychic girl that are fucking everything up."

She walked away, her hands balled into fists.

"Where's Sarah?" Parkman called after her.

"I have no idea. The sooner we find her, the sooner we can leave Mexico."

Fitzgerald stopped at the open door of her car. King opened hers and looked back. It was as if Fitzgerald was watching the clouds as they lazily roamed the sky, but Parkman knew she was debating what to offer and what to leave out. After a few moments, with Aaron breathing heavily behind him, Fitzgerald lowered her eyes and met Parkman's.

"I'll tell you where Sarah is."

"Where?" Aaron shouted.

"Sarah is in trouble. That's where she is."

Fitzgerald dropped into her car and slammed the door.

"Fuck you," Aaron yelled.

The FBI cruiser turned on, dropped in gear, and squealed away, leaving a black rubber mark behind it. Parkman watched the vehicle until they turned a corner.

"What now?" Aaron asked. "What the fuck now?"

"Back to the hotel. Call Casper."

"Then what?" He advanced on Parkman. "Huh, tell me, Parkman, what next? Sit around the hotel room, drinking coffee, calling people, waiting for Casper to call us back? All the while, Sarah's out there somewhere."

"It is what it is." Parkman didn't want to say the next part but felt Aaron needed to be reminded. "This is part and parcel of knowing Sarah. Part of being in her life."

"Fuck that," Aaron shouted. The front door to the police station opened. Cops filed out the door. "Is being lied to part of knowing Sarah? Is being deceived part of knowing Sarah? You know what's the hardest part, Parkman?"

"What?" He avoided looking over at the throng of officers easing out of the building to his right.

"The hardest part about being lied to," Aaron said, his

tone calming, quieter, "is knowing you weren't worth the truth."

He looked the other way, his eyes clouding over, and headed down the road the way they had come.

A red car eased by him as he stood in the middle of the street. It slowed, stopped five feet away, then moved again. Parkman noted the color and bent down to look inside. It sped away, the back of the driver's head all he could see.

"Does everyone have a problem here?" Parkman said to the back of the car. He turned to face the line of cops. "Damn. I need a toothpick. For shit's sake." Parkman started after Aaron, hoping none of the officers would follow them. "Wait up."

Chapter 27

THE INSIDE OF THE car was so immaculate Sarah wondered if she would be allowed in at first. She had spent the previous night lying on the floor of a dirty holding cell. She needed a shower and new clothes. She was bruised, sore all over, and fatigued in a way that only a ten-hour sleep would satisfy.

"Sarah Roberts," Blair's mother said. "I'm Jane Turner. Please, call me Jane."

They shook hands—more of a touch with Jane's hand limp—before Jane appeared to wipe her hand on the seat beside her leg.

Jane Turner was in her fifties but didn't look it. Late thirties, early forties was an easy sell. The wrinkles around her eyes gave away her true age. No amount of makeup could disguise that from this range. The aura she emitted was the stereotypical rich woman, the regal bitch feel, the I-can-have-anything-I-want expression on her face.

Sarah pondered the reason this woman would help her out of that holding cell and couldn't come up with anything solid.

Unless she wanted a girlfriend for her wayward drug dealer of a son. If that was the case, Sarah wasn't interested.

Jane Turner didn't strike Sarah as a criminal. Anything but. So why did Vivian want her to go with Jane? Was Jane's life in danger? Was she being blackmailed, stalked by a creeper, or something worse? Was meeting Blair a bid to get her close to the mother?

Is that all this is, sis?

"Blair tells me you helped him out last night."

She glanced at Blair, paused when she saw the anguish on his face, then turned back to Jane. "I wouldn't go so far as to say I helped him. He wasn't involved in what happened last night at the casino." A thought struck her. Maybe that's what had Blair in turmoil. She turned his way. "Or were you?"

He shook his head back and forth in a jerking motion to dispel that idea quickly. "You could've told the police why you were in the parking lot. You could've told them about me and what we were going to do in my car—"

"But you didn't," Jane finished for him. "Please, as a thank you, you're invited to my house for dinner. We'll get you new clothes, fix you up. After that, my driver will take you wherever you want to go."

Something about that sounded so good. Decent food, a shower, and new clothes. She needed to get back to Aaron. He was going to be pissed she was gone all night and now all day without even a phone call. He probably called Parkman already. Soon, all her friends would be back in Mexico looking for her, and it would be all her fault.

"I appreciate your offer," Sarah said. "But I didn't do anything special." Her mouth seemed perpetually dry. She wasn't feeling well at all. The seat was comfortable, but the driver appeared to be going too fast. "I just need to return to my hotel and continue my vacation. Could your driver head that way?"

Jane watched traffic pass by the window. She placed one hand over the other as if it was a signal for something.

It was.

Blair reached under the car's seat and came up with a bag of heroin. "All yours. The bag you wanted to buy last night. It's free. A thank you from my family to you."

Even as her body rebelled against rational thought and the desire to snatch that bag out of Blair's hand reared up in her consciousness, she heard herself say, "I couldn't."

"Don't be ridiculous." Blair leaned closer. "Take it. You need it. The ache is written all over your face."

"I can't." The timbre of her voice scared her. She hadn't been this weak since her teenage days. Wasn't she a strong woman? Didn't she fight, take shots, stand up for what was right, and do the right thing? "I can't." Tears welled up in her eyes as Blair set the baggie beside her. "I can't." Her voice broke this time. She crossed her legs, then uncrossed them as she drew back into the car seat, making herself as small as she felt.

"Then just take one hit. After that, you'll be stronger, able to beat it for good."

"Really?" She met Blair's eyes, hoping there was truth in them, but all she saw was pain and anguish. A hopeless young man who had let his dreams fade. Selling drugs on the street didn't have a retirement savings plan. The only people who retired from the streets, died on the streets. Blair was smart. He could read people. She saw that in him right away. But somewhere along the way, he let that go. Why? With the riches his mother possessed, why wasn't he in school studying to be a chemist, a lawyer, or a doctor?

She touched the baggie before she knew her hand was reaching and before she understood the depth of her longing. That simple touch had the same effect on her body as if she was touching Aaron. Stimulation coursed through her at the thought of one shot of the stuff in her grip. The excitement made her realize she couldn't walk away from it now. To come this close to a hit and walk away was maddening. Staying away was one thing. Out of sight, out of mind. But holding it in her hand was something completely different.

"Idon'tknowhowtodoit," she managed to say, the words jumbled together as one-off her arid tongue.

"What?" Jane asked, turning from the window. "Then how are you dependent?"

She swallowed and grimaced at her dry throat before raising her eyes to look at Jane. "This was done to me. While I was at the Enzo Cartel compound."

"I read about that." Jane stared out the window again. "Blair. Help her."

Blair slid across the seat and leaned toward Sarah. He pulled tools from a small case in a compartment under his seat and began setting up. Inside her, a tiny voice screamed to stop him. Her hand twitched. She almost did. But one shot of heroin wouldn't hurt anybody. Just one. Then she would beat it. She would win. She always did. This was it. One shot.

Jane stared at her.

"While he's getting ready, tell me about your sister."

Overwhelmed, even intoxicated at what Blair was doing with the heroin beside her, she didn't completely understand what Jane was saying.

"Yes," Jane said. "Your sister. Tell me about her."

"She's dead."

"I know that. But she talks to you? Keeps you safe? Correct?"

Blair tied something around her right bicep. He then tapped her inner arm.

"You could say that." Why the questions about Vivian?

Something sharp pricked her arm. She laid her head back and closed her eyes as Blair pulled the strap off.

Almost instantly, the pain all over her body receded, and she began to feel better. Fantastic, really. She even felt her mouth form a smile as her mind raced on. What now? Where to go? What to do? Nothing made sense, and everything was all right again.

"Your sister," Jane persisted. "Is she around now?"

"Always. Around."

"Did she tell you to come with me?"

"Yes."

"Can you hear her at all times?"

"No."

"When *can't* you hear her?"

"Brain addled."

"Addled?"

"Booze. Whiskey. No Vivian."

This thinking thing wasn't fun. She didn't want to talk. She wanted to rest. Sleep for a week. Then she'd beat the drug. But for right now, just relax. Enjoy the ride wherever they were going.

"How about drugs?" Jane asked.

"Same as alcohol. Unless Vivian's angry. Nothing stops my angry sister."

"Enjoy this trip, then. It'll be your last."

Sarah was falling. Fading away. Moving fast along a tunnel of some sort. An eighties song by Def Leppard popped into her mind. Something about fading away and burning out.

"What was that song?" she heard herself ask.

"Blair. Lock her in her room when we get home. She doesn't leave that room until she's clean. Get Dr. Wesson over to help her deal with it."

"Yes," Sarah said as if in a long tunnel. "No more drugs. I'm good now. No more."

The tunnel cracked in the middle, and she dropped down somewhere. Her mouth opened, and nothing came out as she fell under the spell of her new best friend.

Chapter 28

At the hotel, Aaron collected their things and checked out. He followed Parkman to his hotel, where Aaron had agreed to stay until they found Sarah, and everything was over.

"What if Sarah comes back to our hotel?" Aaron asked. "And I'm not in that room?"

"There's a high chance you won't be in that room when she returns if you didn't make this change."

"Really?" Aaron set the bag with their meager belongings in the corner. "How so? You really think the Mexican authorities are going to come after me?"

Parkman was about to dial Casper.

"It's just too dangerous. They won't come as cops. They'll come in their regular clothes, but they'll come. Too many for one man to handle. What we saw at the police station when they all exited the building like that was a warning. 'Leave Mexico' was written all over it."

"You think I should leave?" He sounded angry now. "Tail between my legs with Sarah out there somewhere?"

"No, Aaron. I don't think you should leave. But you need to calm down. Have a drink. Mellow out. I'm not the enemy here."

Aaron glanced around the room and found an inviting chair. When he dropped into the seat, he deflated like a spent balloon.

"You're right. I'm sorry."

"I'm calling Casper now." Parkman dialed out. When Casper answered, Parkman relayed everything they had learned.

"Okay, maybe it was me who was in the wrong here," Casper said. "I shouldn't have left Mexico." He cleared his throat. "I'll get someone to come to your hotel. Watch your room."

"That won't matter if a dozen cops come looking for blood."

Parkman waited on his side of the line as Casper thought to himself. Aaron held his face in his hands. Parkman opened the sliding door and stepped onto the balcony.

"Parkman, I'll send three of my best men. They can watch front and back entrances. Give you a heads up if trouble's coming. There's something to be said about a warning. You'll be able to get out of wherever you are in time."

"What about Sarah? They let her go. She could be anywhere. Don't you have some kind of jurisdiction over certain FBI cases?"

"I do. But not this one. For some reason, no one is talking about what the FBI is doing in Rosarito. To tell you the truth, it scares me, and I don't scare easily."

"Why?"

"Because whatever it is, it's huge. International ramifications. And Sarah's smack dab in the middle of it with no external support. They're tracking inquiries on the case as well."

"They are? How? Why?"

"After making my initial calls, I got a call back from Washington—"

"FBI?"

"No. Homeland Security. Something had come to them from the National Security Agency in Fort Meade. It all centers on Rosarito."

"How did you know about the NSA connection?"

"A friend of a friend."

Parkman let out the air he'd been holding. "Who do you *not* know?"

"Evidently, the right person to fill in the blanks here."

"Okay, we will sit tight until we hear more. How will I know your guys have shown up?"

"I'll call you back with names. My guys will have ID. Just don't get killed in the meantime. And don't go anywhere. I'll need a few hours."

"Call me when you can. I've got a plan in the meantime."

"What is it—wait. I don't want to know."

"I wouldn't say over the phone."

"Stay safe, Parkman. We'll get Sarah back. It's just a matter of time."

"I know."

Parkman clicked off and stepped inside to tell Aaron about his plan, but the room was empty.

Aaron was gone.

Chapter 29

WAKING UP WAS A chore. The weight of her body pressing into the mattress seemed heavier somehow. She couldn't have possibly gained that much weight in the time she'd slept. But how long had she slept? She tried to open her eyes, but the headache kept them closed.

Nothing felt good. Her bones, her muscles, or the aches and pains. Pins and needles pricked at her skin, roaming her body as if every limb and every joint had fallen asleep and was now just waking up.

She tried to move her arms back and under her to sit up, but something held her down. Something offered a dull ache in her right arm.

What the hell is that?

She considered her situation. A Mercedes. The Turners and their offer of dinner. Did she eat dinner with them? Get drunk? Do drugs?

The reality came sweeping in. Heroin. Blair had shot her up. That was the last thing she remembered. The high. The rush. But now what? Was this the coming down part? The sobering up or whatever withdrawal was called?

She tried to open her eyes again but failed the second time.

"Be still," a man said.

She hadn't detected him earlier. "Who are you?"

"Dr. Wesson."

"Was there an accident?"

"No accident."

She swallowed, her throat drier than the last time she was awake.

"You're helpful," she whispered.

He moved away from her. After a moment, he moved closer again, this time on the other side.

"You're experiencing withdrawal symptoms, Miss Roberts—"

"Sarah's fine."

"Your pupils are dilated. Your mouth is probably dry. Over the next few days, until you're off heroin, you will likely experience some of these symptoms: restlessness, sweats, chills, possible muscle and bone pain, insomnia, diarrhea, vomiting, and cold flashes, to name a few. I will help you through it as much as I can without getting you hooked on anything else, Miss Roberts. You'll be past the worst inside a week."

"Sarah," she muttered, her voice feeble, weak.

She focused on the sounds as he moved throughout the room to determine his whereabouts. He was moving away. Far away. A door clicked. The hinges squeaked.

"Why did you just say your name?" he asked.

"Call me Sarah. Not Miss Roberts."

"You will always be Miss Roberts. You're a patient, a number. We're not friends. I won't use your first name."

She cleared her throat, opened her mouth to lick her lips, then said, "I'm a number? Gee, thanks. Make sure you look both ways before you go fuck yourself."

After several seconds, the door eased closed. The light behind her eyelids faded. She tried to open her eyes again but gave up after a minute, drifting back to sleep under the influence of whatever Dr. Strangelove gave her.

Chapter 30

PARKMAN DARTED ACROSS THE room and bounded into the hotel corridor without slowing down. He lost control and shoulder-smacked the opposite wall.

It was empty. Aaron wasn't there.

He ran for the elevator, wondering why Aaron would just leave without saying anything. What purpose would that serve? They needed to work together. Most importantly, they needed to stay together. Either something big happened because of the Enzo Cartel ordeal, or something was already underway, and somehow Sarah had gotten herself tied into it.

With Homeland Security calling Casper to question his interest—or to quell it—the threat level to Sarah and those involved with her raised to THREATCON One. This had the potential to swallow them whole.

The elevator door opened maddeningly slowly. Before there was room, Parkman squeezed through the opening and attacked the close-door button. A young couple clutching small carry-on suitcases leaned back to give him room. He nodded at the male before facing the door as the elevator descended toward the lobby. Soft music chimed from tiny speakers above his head. For an excruciating moment, he imagined the elevator getting stuck. The three of them calling out for help. Sarah lost somewhere in Mexico, and Aaron running nowhere in particular.

A short, sharp shake of his head dispelled negative thoughts. They'd never dealt with Homeland Security, the NSA, or any other CIA-type agency other than the FBI in the past. It scared him to think what they could do to Sarah or Aaron. If they got tied up with a spy or an organized crime network, or worse, a terrorist, any one of them could end up on a no-fly list or be incarcerated for years under some kind of Patriot Act or something. Akin to gambling, you had to bet on the house winning every time in a case like this. As Franz Kafka once said, "In man's struggle against the world, bet on the world." As far as Sarah Roberts was concerned, Parkman would bet on her. All in.

The elevator doors finally opened in the lobby. Parkman squeezed through, stumbled into a luggage-laden cart, pivoted around it, and regained his balance. People were checking out, checking in. Others were storing their luggage, and still, others were heading into the smaller casino his hotel offered. But Aaron was nowhere in sight.

He tried Aaron's cell number. After five rings, he disconnected. His eyes darted left, then right. He rocked on his feet, back and forth. What would Aaron be thinking? Where would he go? Would he leave the premises entirely?

Parkman pushed through a family of five and trudged

down the hotel's front steps so fast he almost lost his footing. At the bottom, he looked up the street toward the hotel where Sarah and Aaron had rented their room.

Did Aaron go back in hopes of meeting Sarah there? If so, would a rogue police officer be waiting for him?

Parkman wrung his hands together for a moment, contemplating his next move. Casper's men were on their way. Protection was coming while Casper worked his magic. All Aaron had to do was sit tight. Instead, he'd gone off alone without a word to anyone. Parkman shook his head in denial. Sarah was the only person who could get through to Aaron. He was just too headstrong.

Parkman had to find out if Aaron was at his old hotel. He had no choice. Worst case, if he were wrong, he'd be back within fifteen minutes, way before any of Casper's men showed up.

He walked up the street, cell phone in hand. Halfway there, it occurred to him to execute the plan he'd mentioned to Casper. He wanted to call the Toronto police himself and see what he could find out. Maybe he could get through to the police station, get Spencer on the phone, and have more answers before he found Aaron.

Parkman made the call. He was directed to homicide, where a young female voice answered.

"Detective Martin. How can I help you?"

"I'm looking for a detective by the name of Spencer."

"Got anything else?" Martin asked.

"Anything else?"

"More than one name."

"Just Spencer. That's all I remember."

"May I have your name?"

Parkman didn't have time for this. He was almost at Aaron's hotel now. Slowing his pace, he found a bench and sat down to focus on the call.

"My name is Parkman. I worked with Detective Waller before he retired. My colleague and I worked with Spencer regarding the Drake Bellamy incident at the Roger's Centre about four years ago. Right now, I really need to speak with Spencer."

The woman on the line cleared her throat. The line crackled. He feared she'd set the phone down. The sound of keys being pressed on a keyboard resonated to him.

"Excuse me, Detective Martin. I need your full name."

"My name is Detective Tracy Martin. Detective Waller doesn't work here anymore. Hasn't for some years. Just looked him up. Nothing."

"I don't need to speak to him. I need Spencer."

"Right, well, can't help you there."

"Is he retired? Change departments? What? How can I find him?"

"There's no record of Detective Spencer on my computer."

Had he got the name wrong? He didn't think so. He usually remembered names well. It was his job.

"Is there something else I can help you with, Mr. Parkman?"

"Just Parkman," he muttered.

"I'm sorry. I missed that."

Parkman stared across the street, his vacant eyes picking nothing up as he thought of his next move. "Can you see all the detectives, or is there no Spencer in homicide?"

"No Spencer, period."

"Then someone has erased him."

"Excuse me?"

"There was a Spencer. He saved Drake's life—" He probably shouldn't have said that name. "I need to go."

"Sir? Parkman, what did you just say about saving someone's life?"

"Nothing. Gotta go."

"Sir. Stay on the line—"

Parkman disconnected. In a daze, having no idea what was going on, he got to his feet and entered Aaron's hotel from last night. With only a few people in the lobby, it was easy to see Aaron wasn't there.

He entered the casino that had reopened after last night's attempted robbery and car accident out back. After a five-minute walk-through, Aaron was nowhere to be found.

Aaron wouldn't go back to the police station alone, would he? That would be suicide. If he had, he was on his own. Parkman couldn't risk going back there. Sarah needed someone on the outside available for her.

Shoulders slumped, head down, he started back for his hotel. As he ascended the stairs to the lobby, his cell phone rang. He stayed outside for better reception. Caller ID came up *private*.

"Parkman here."

"Toronto police calling you back." A man this time. "I understand you have a question about a dead man."

"Who's this?"

"Doesn't matter who I am. Who were you looking for?"

"Detective Spencer." Parkman looked skyward, waiting for an answer.

"And if you were to locate Detective Spencer, what

would you need from him?"

Weird question. "We'll find that out when I locate him."

"Good luck, then. There's no such man."

It sounded final like the caller was going to hang up.

"Wait." Breathing on the other end indicated the man hadn't hung up. Parkman weighed his options and decided to go forward. "I would tell him I just saw Drake Bellamy in Mexico even though Drake Bellamy died several years ago in Lake Ontario. I would ask Detective Spencer how this was possible, and I'm sure I would understand his answer. Finally, if Spencer were to take my call, I would express my deepest concern for Sarah Roberts."

"Why would that be?" The voice had changed, the tone firmer, clipped.

"Sarah Roberts was last seen leaving a hotel lobby in Rosarito, Mexico, after a brief visit with Drake Bellamy, who followed her out. As I'm searching for Sarah now, I want to know how Drake is alive and what he's doing here at Sarah's hotel."

The silence that stretched worried Parkman. He looked over his shoulder, then into the hotel. A chill ran through him like he was being watched.

"Drake's alive, Parkman."

He frowned. That voice. "Spencer?" Parkman whispered.

"New name. New game."

"What's that supposed to mean?"

"Too much said over the phone already. Where are you? Rosarito?"

"Yeah," Parkman said. *New name, new game?* What the hell did that mean?

"I'll be there in the morning. Don't leave the city."

"How will you find me?"

The line clicked dead.

Parkman lowered the phone from his ear, his hand descending like the slow hand on a large clock.

"What the fuck is going on?" he said to himself, barely above a whisper.

A hand dropped on his shoulder at the exact moment someone shouted from behind him.

"Hey!"

Parkman lifted a foot in the air and twisted at an odd angle, his nervous system in a quandary of sorts. He landed awkwardly, twisting around fully.

Aaron stood there, smiling. "Where did you get to?" Aaron asked. "I left a note on the dresser. When I came back to the room, you were gone."

"Fucking shit!" Parkman burst out. "I feel like a cat dangling from a shit chandelier. You scared the cank out of me."

"What the hell is cank?"

"Everything you scared." He tried to catch his breath. "And then some. And I can see you're enjoying it, too. That smile of yours." He held a hand over his chest. "If you weren't a black belt, I'd drop you right here."

Aaron's smile widened as he turned sideways. He offered his right arm. "Here, one shot for payback—"

Parkman drove a fist into Aaron's arm before he could finish his sentence or reconsider his offer. Parkman added what power he could to the jab, but Aaron barely moved an inch.

"I have to admit, that felt good." Parkman gestured at Aaron's arm. "You good?"

"Yeah, but I've had houseflies bump into me harder."

Parkman jabbed at him again. "You little fuck." Aaron deflected everything Parkman tossed his way until a small crowd had stopped to watch. It was over as fast as it started. They headed for the elevators, Parkman feeling the tension and confusion leaving him after the friendly tussle.

"Where did you go, Aaron?"

"The gym. Needed a workout. Let some of the steam off."

"Guess I should look for a note next time."

They got on the elevator. Parkman pushed the button for his floor, then filled Aaron in on his call with Casper. On their floor, they started down the hall while he told Aaron about the strange call to Toronto and how he thought Spencer—with a new name—was coming to Mexico tomorrow.

"It's very strange. Nothing is making sense." He pulled the keycard from his pocket. "Why would Spencer change his name? What's Drake doing here in Mexico? Or has Drake's name changed, and Spencer is his handler? Maybe that's it. I got nowhere when I dropped Drake's name to Detective Martin and then asked for Spencer. That would explain, *new name, new game.*" He unlocked the hotel door and opened it. "And what has Sarah gotten herself into?"

Parkman entered the room, Aaron close behind. The door shut. The air thickened. His senses pinged. Something smelled funny.

They had company.

He ducked down, lowering his center of gravity in preparation for taking a hit. To warn Aaron, he shot a hand back, but Aaron wasn't there anymore.

"Good afternoon, Mr. Parkman. Mr. Stevens."

The smell was urine. One of the police officers from the station they had visited stepped into view from the balcony area. His uniform was stained with sweat. He carried the smell of a men's locker room around, permeating everything. Behind Parkman, two beefy cops held Aaron's arms. A third man had a gun placed under Aaron's chin to guarantee his struggles were minimal.

"We need to have a word with you two," the overweight cop by the balcony door said.

Another cop—five in total now—materialized from the left side of the hotel room, where the desk and chair sat against the wall.

"Don't try to run. You will be shot. Don't try to fight. You will be shot. Resisting arrest in Mexico is a serious offense."

The speaker crossed the space between him and Parkman slowly, bringing his fetid smell with him. The man stopped when he stood nose-to-nose with Parkman. Sweat ran down Parkman's ramrod-straight spine. His hands flexed at his sides while he raced through escape options.

That stench!

"Please, don't try anything," the overweight cop said again. "We would hate to have to report that we were simply asking questions of an American citizen when they went for my gun and were killed in the ensuing gunfight. Please don't make me or my men kill you here." He looked at the carpet as if he'd dropped something. Or was he simply studying the pattern? When he met Parkman's eyes, he grinned, revealing yellowed teeth. "It would be sad to ruin such a nice Berber floor covering, now wouldn't it? Killing you outside the city makes for a quieter death."

A struggle started behind him. When he looked back, Aaron was on the floor, the three men holding him down, knees in his back, forcing his hands together to handcuff them.

"Hey—" Parkman started, but something smacked the back of his head mid-word.

A bright light and white-hot pain shot through his shoulder blades before he fell unconscious.

Chapter 31

WAKING UP GOT LESS painful for Sarah. Dr. Wesson said she was doing better. Her body was dealing well with the withdrawal symptoms, which caused her minimum unpleasantness. She had ample water and kept the little food he gave her down.

The sun had dropped out of sight, the lone window in the room dark behind the white curtains. The room itself was pleasant enough. Better than a hospital. Light blue walls, white furniture. Pictures on the wall were spaced evenly. All the pictures were landscape scenes of oceans, waves rolling in, and sunsets. The one on the farthest wall showed a thin girl holding the handlebars of a bike as she watched the sun set behind a rainbow. To Sarah, the pictures were depictions of lost hope. In each shot, the sun was setting. There was loneliness, loss, and a feeling that something was ending.

The vast room wasn't filled with furniture. Instead, the

interior decorator—probably Jane Turner—simply placed a bed, a dresser, and a chair by the window in this room, added pics on the walls, and left it at that. A perfect guest bedroom. If they wanted to depress their guests.

She closed her eyes and rested, drifting in and out of sleep. According to the doctor, being secured to the bed wasn't so she couldn't escape. It was so she didn't hurt herself during the withdrawal process.

"Hurt myself?" she had said to him. "Yeah, right, and I've got a bridge to buy in London."

A soft knock on the door brought her out of her semi-dream state. She opened her eyes and waited. Did she dream the knock, or was there someone at the door?

The knock came again. The doorknob turned.

"Come on in," she whispered. "Door's open." *Like I could do anything about it.*

Blair eased inside the room and quietly shut the door behind him. Barely above the soft whisper of rubbing linen, Blair tiptoed across the bedroom floor and stopped by the chair beside the window.

"May I?" A hand gesture toward the chair.

"It's your house."

He placed the chair by the bed and sat down, resting his arm on the edge of the bed, his head hung low as if the world's weight was on his shoulders.

"How are you feeling?" he asked without looking up, his tone subdued, demure.

"Couldn't be better." She kept her tone low, calm. The drug still pulled at her, but whatever Dr. Wesson gave her eased the draw considerably.

Blair looked different somehow. It wasn't the dressed-down look in track pants and the loose sweater he wore. It was his demeanor. His smile was gone. He seemed spent like he'd tried something important and lost. Maybe they ought to move her to another room and give this room to him. He'd fit right in with those pics on the walls.

"Are you angry with me?" he asked, finally looking up.

At this distance, his eyes—windows to the soul that they were—offered insight into his mental state. Something was tearing him apart on the inside. A pained, grief-ridden expression looked back at her.

"Why would I be angry with you? Have you done something that I should be angry about?"

"Well, no." He avoided her eyes. "It's just, you're here and not on your vacation."

"Why *am* I here?"

The chair groaned as Blair leaned back on it. "My mother's crazy."

"Why am I here?" Sarah repeated.

"Because of my mother."

"You're avoiding the question. Those aren't answers."

He made a fist and pressed it to his lips, then glanced at the window, letting his hand fall away. Whatever bothered him went deep.

"My mother wants you to help her with something, but she won't tell me what it is."

"Is that why she's offering me a forced rehab here?"

"I guess so."

"And asking about Vivian?" Sarah rolled her head sideways to follow his gaze and look at the window. Blair stared at his fingers as he fiddled with them.

"You tried to save Wallace." He bit his lower lip.

Released it. "You tried to warn Hank."

"They were in danger."

"You whispered things. About a man dying. Then Eddie was shot and killed."

"And? So?" She closed her eyes. *Oh shit. Here we go.*

"You were right. Then I looked you up online."

"What did you find?"

"A lot of stuff. Did you know there's even a website dedicated to tracking the amount of people you've saved from accidents, kidnappers, and murderers?"

"Can't say I knew that. Although, I'd be curious to hear where they get their numbers."

Her backside had numbed. The doctor unstrapped her routinely and rolled her onto her side when he was here, but until he returned, she would remain on her back.

"Anyway, you're Sarah Roberts. You can see the future."

"Not exactly."

"Yeah, I know. What your sister tells you."

"Are you doing okay?" she asked him. "The accident shake you up?"

"You could say that."

"How so? What part shook you up?"

After an extended pause, she opened her eyes and looked at the empty chair. He'd gotten quietly to his feet and walked to the window. He stood with his back to her and wiped at his eyes.

She wasn't in the best of places, the best of times, to be able to read between the lines. Something was going on with Blair, and she couldn't figure it out. She stared at the back of his head, his neat hair gelled in place. The silver earrings in each ear. A tattoo on his left arm. He was in good shape and maintained his appearance, but so did a lot of men. This wasn't something new or odd.

He had been confident at the casino. But he was deflated now.

"There was another man there that night," Sarah said. "A man named Drake. I think he was the one who tackled Wallace out of the way."

Blair nodded.

"What happened to him?" she asked. "Did he get bailed out by your mother, too?"

"Can't say I recall another man. Never heard that name before, either."

Drake had been in the red car at the back when she got in the Mercedes. Was he waiting for her? Or watching Jane Turner? If he was watching Jane, then he knew where Sarah was. Based on that, Drake was probably outside watching the Turner house at that moment.

"I'm gay," he said, barely audible enough to hear. He said it so low that she almost missed it.

"Okay," she replied, not sure how else to respond.

He twisted away from the window.

"That man who got hit by Eddie's car, Hank Olsen, he and I were going to run away together. He was the pit boss that allowed me to work the casino. We're in love."

"Good. Nothing wrong with that. Love is love." A sudden weariness came over her. If the conversation didn't end soon, she'd drift out of it on a wave of melatonin.

"Now, he might not make it. Still critical at the hospital. Even if he does leave the hospital one day, Hank's paralyzed from the waist down."

"I'm sorry," she said, barely above a whisper.

"That's why my mother hates me."

"What?" She forced herself to mentally climb up out of sleep. "No. She loves you."

He was close to her again. She could feel him close.

"At fourteen, I told her I was gay." Blair stood beside the bed. "Her response was to beat me."

"I'm sorry."

"As long as I'm gay, there's no money, no schooling, no nothing. I'm cut off."

"That can't be."

"It is. That's why I fend for myself. Sometimes I think she wishes I were dead."

Sarah nodded her understanding, her head sinking into the pillow.

Blair continued, "If Hank leaves that hospital, I'll take care of him. I'll be there. Gay or not gay, we love each other, and that's what's important, isn't it?"

"Of course."

"My mother would never understand that. She doesn't know what love is."

"She has you, doesn't she?"

"My mother doesn't love me."

"I mean, she has you to show her what love is. Even when she shuns you, love her back. Over time, she'll crumble."

"No, not my mother. She hated my father."

Silence again. She listened to see if he was walking away or staying close. A slit was all she could muster when she tried to open her eyes. He stood over her, crying, wiping his tears aside.

"I'm sorry," he mumbled. "This isn't your problem. Just

happy to have someone I can vent to."

"Of course."

Blair let it out. He dropped into the chair and wept, leaning his forearms on the bed. Sarah would've held his shoulder, but her hands were bound. She thought about asking him to untie her and roll her over but thought better of it. This was his moment.

"I'm resigned to the fact that my mother will hate me as long as she lives because I'll never change."

"That's a hard thing to deal with. A mother *hating* their child is harsh. Are you sure it's hatred?"

"She used a leather strap on me when I told her. Fifty lashes, meted out over five days, ten lashes per day. Said if I were back in India, where she met my father, the punishment would be worse. She thought she could beat the disease out of me."

"That's frustrating. Lower educated thinking."

"I've had to lie, keep it from her in order to live here. She suspects I'm still gay, though. Until she's sure I'm hetero, I'm off the books. Can you believe that?"

Sarah rolled her head back and forth with great effort as the fatigue fought to make her sleep.

"Well, fuck her. As soon as Hank is well enough, I will tell her, and let's see what happens if she tries to give me a single lash. She's the one who will get a beat down."

Sarah drifted deeper. She couldn't keep this conversation going. Sleep was winning.

"Even if I have to kill her," Blair added.

Kill her? Who is he talking about again?

"I'll murder her in her sleep, and you could help me."

Murder her? In her sleep?

"If we don't, she'll kill you, too. Whatever she has planned for you, Sarah, you won't like it. I think she aims to have you killed."

Then she dropped further and left the conversation where it was.

Chapter 32

PARKMAN WOKE IN THE back seat of a car as it bounced along a pothole-filled road. Both shoulders ached with his hands cuffed tightly behind his back. He groaned as the car bounced over rough terrain. Pain sliced up his spine. For some reason, his right cheek was inflamed, too.

What had they done to him?

He thought of Aaron and hoped he was still alive.

He tried to sit up but found it too difficult with his hands bound at the small of his back.

From his twisted position in the back seat, he watched the star-filled night sky out the back window. Two heads moved slightly with the car's motion in the front seat.

After several minutes, the car's tires hit the smooth ground and glided briefly, making it easier on him. Sweat rolled down his swollen face, and he blinked the drops out of his eyes.

The Mexican authorities had him. They had Aaron if he was still alive. Spencer was coming from Toronto, and Casper had sent three men to watch over them.

But it was all too little, too late.

They would be dead long before anyone could intervene. Unless either one of them figured out a way to fight back. This couldn't be the end. Vivian would have seen this coming and gotten Sarah involved somehow. At least, he hoped that was the case.

His hands had lost most of their feeling. He fiddled with them in an attempt to examine what bound his wrists so tight. Cold steel. The cuffs were placed low on the wrist, limiting his hand movement. He got as comfortable as he could and waited.

Would they drive him out of town just to release him? No, they hadn't covered their faces. This was a one-way ticket.

He stopped trying to convince himself of some other motive. The police were going to execute Aaron and Parkman for their role in losing so many of their colleagues in that hotel attack in Tijuana. It wasn't their fault directly, but because the authorities were gathered there to deal with Aaron's abduction, it was indirectly their fault. At least to the men in the front of the car, they were responsible. And it seemed these men wanted someone to pay for the loss they had to endure.

Quite a few of the authorities worked for local cartels. It wouldn't be a stretch to think the cops in the front seat weren't acting alone. It could be any number of cartels happy to avenge the Enzo destruction with their heads on the end of a stake or their bodies dangling from a bridge over a busy highway.

What shouldn't concern Parkman as much was what *they* were going to do. What should be of utmost concern to him was what *he* was going to do.

It had been stupid to allow Sarah and Aaron to remain in Mexico within days of the Enzo Cartel's destruction. No matter how much Sarah protested, they should've forced the issue and taken her across the border. Better to have her pissed off than dead.

It was reckless and careless to have thought this was a sane move. The car accident at the casino, Casper making calls and getting return calls from people concerned with what he was up to, and now Sarah missing. Nothing good at all had come from staying in Mexico.

The vehicle slowed, then stopped. The men in the front seat exited the car, leaving their doors open. Parkman waited, listening. A crazy thought struck him. What if these were Casper's men, and the only way to get Aaron and him to safety was to abduct them? If that were the case, they didn't have to be so rough during the abduction.

No, these were hitmen. Their day jobs were officers of the law, but hitmen just the same. They had one objective, and Parkman wasn't disillusioned as to what it was. That left him with a fight *and* flight option. Or die bound and gagged, and something told him this wasn't his time to go.

The passenger door opened behind his head. He looked up as someone grabbed him under the shoulders and pulled. His butt dropped to the ground hard, then his feet, which weren't tied together. A grunt escaped his lips upon impact.

The man rolled him over and stepped away.

"Get up."

Parkman had put hundreds of men in handcuffs in his time on the police force but never really considered how uncomfortable it was or how hard it was to maneuver with his hands bound. With a leg under him, balance corrected, he pushed upward and got to his feet.

"Got any toothpicks?" he asked.

He didn't get an answer.

There was enough moonlight to see the wide-open countryside in all directions. Not a single street light or sign of civilization offered him hope. A small, rundown, sun-weathered shack stood to the right of the beat-up car. It had seen better days. The roof sloped in where it appeared to be about to collapse, and the walls had graffiti and holes where the windows once were.

Inside the shack, several candles flickered, sending a chill through him. He hadn't thought it would come to this for a long time and could come up with no reasonable way to get out of this situation. These kinds of men didn't listen to pleading or begging. No amount of money would dissuade them. Whatever their plan, they'd done it before and would do it again.

"Where's Aaron?" Parkman asked, his voice stronger than he expected in this situation.

"Inside," the man closest to him answered. He was one of the men that had held onto Aaron back in the hotel room.

Parkman didn't know what the man meant by *inside*. Is Aaron inside the shack? Or was he ordering Parkman to go inside?

"I don't see another car," Parkman persisted. "Is Aaron here?"

The man nodded. "He's inside." He grabbed Parkman's

arm and shoved him toward the shack. "Go. Now."

Parkman stumbled, caught himself, and walked to the half-open door of the wooden structure. Was this what a life's work amounted to? Was this where he would die? In a broken-down building in a barren part of Mexico?

He ducked his head and entered. Aaron sat in a chair facing the door, untied. A gun rested sideways on his thigh, gripped in his right hand. The tip of the weapon aimed at the empty chair across from him.

A thick candle burned on a small, square table in front of Aaron. Under the table sat a black case with a red digital readout that looked strangely like a bomb setting. The digits sat unmoving at five seconds.

The other empty chair in front of Aaron was presumably placed there for Parkman.

In the yellow light, Aaron's eyes were red and glazed. He'd been crying and probably stressing about what to do.

Someone shoved Parkman forward. He managed to stay on his feet as he neared the empty chair.

"Sit," the man behind him said. "We're going to play a little game. I understand you Americans like games, no? Am I right?"

Parkman looked at Aaron and felt sorry for him at that moment. He didn't ask for this. Sarah's life, and the violence that came with it, had been thrust upon him. He wasn't prepared. Even being the fighter he was, he couldn't handle it. It wasn't fair. Life wasn't fair. If it were, they'd be dining with the royals at Buckingham Palace and spending money like the Warren Buffetts of the world.

He took a seat opposite Aaron. After a moment, Aaron's eyes met his. The torment in them caused Parkman to shiver.

What had they done to him while Parkman was unconscious?

"Where are we?" Parkman asked.

Only one man entered the shack behind Parkman. He held up a key for Parkman to see. Then he leaned behind Parkman and worked on the cuffs.

"There is a sensor on the chair," the man said. "Now that you have sat down, you cannot get up. When these cuffs come off," the man stopped what he was doing, leaned forward to look Parkman in the eye, then said, "you will be free. I will give you a gun."

Audibly, the cuffs unlocked, and Parkman's hands fell away from each other. Relief coursed through his arms as blood flowed to places lacking it. He leaned forward and groaned. He knew he should be attacking the man beside him, but he needed a moment as his arms regained feeling. Aaron had a gun. Now was the time to fight back.

But why send one man inside the cabin with them? It was too risky with Aaron armed.

The man moved until he stood next to the small table.

"Under each chair is an explosive device, like a landmine. Stand up, and you will be blown apart."

Parkman shivered under a cool sheen of sweat. Beneath Aaron's chair, something was clamped under it, behind the top of his calf muscles.

"If, for some reason, you both decide to leap from your chairs simultaneously and miraculously survive, the unit under this little table here, the one with the five-second counter, will begin its countdown. I assure you, this bomb is big enough to flatten this shack. Our insurance."

Parkman took in the scene for what it was. He had a chance to escape before he sat down, and now he didn't. But how could he have known that? Why didn't Aaron warn him?

It was over for them, and Aaron knew it. Sometimes a man's luck runs out, and there's nothing a man can do about it. It's just the way it was.

The man produced a weapon, checked its safety was off and leaned close to Parkman.

"See here," he said. "One bullet in the chamber. Just one." He handed the gun, butt first, to Parkman. "That bullet is for Aaron. Your friend here has his gun with one bullet. For you."

Parkman took the gun and thought about shooting the man on the spot. He took a huge risk by handing him a loaded weapon.

"You probably think you're in a dismal situation and want to shoot me. I know I would. But there is a chance to walk out of this alive." He looked at both men. "Shoot me, and you both die."

Tears ran down Aaron's cheeks. He was resigned to his fate. But Parkman wouldn't buy it. There had to be a way for both of them. There always was.

Or he'd give his life for Aaron to live. Sarah would understand.

"The game is this. When we hear a gunshot, that means one of you will be dead. You cannot win by suicide. One of you has to kill the other." Parkman couldn't believe what he was hearing. "Once either one of you is dead, we will release the other."

"Bullshit," Parkman muttered.

"It isn't bullshit. You have our word. There is a time limit, though. The candle on the table will burn out. The wick is attached to the five-second bomb under the table. We estimate you have an hour or so to decide who dies. Otherwise, you both die in the explosion." He stepped back toward the door. "Armed men will cover the two windows on each side and this door. For some reason, if you are able to avoid death by chair and hop out a window, you will be shot. There is no escape here. Only the death of one of you releases the other."

"What happens to the man who lives?" Parkman shouted. "You just drive him back to the hotel?"

The man moved outside before he answered. "I won't lie to you." The sound of his voice diminished as he walked away from the cabin. "The man who lives will be brought to the police station and charged in the murder of the man who died. He will live. You have our word. But he will live with the torment of what he did and spend the rest of his years doing hard time for his crime." The man's voice was almost too far to hear unless he shouted. "There really is no escape here."

Was this a joke? A nightmare?

Parkman sat across from Aaron, who hadn't uttered a word the whole time, while he cried and stared back. Aaron's hand jittered, the gun moving slightly with the movement.

"Aaron? You okay?"

He nodded once, his eyes locked on Parkman.

"We can't do this," Parkman said. "I can't kill you. I won't. I'd rather die than spend the rest of my life in a Mexican prison."

Aaron lifted the gun in his hand and aimed it at Parkman.

"Hey, wait, that wasn't an invitation. Look, man, the candle. We have time. A half hour at least." The gun steadied. "Hey," Parkman yelled. "What has gotten into you? Put that thing down."

"It's the—" Aaron choked, sobbed, swallowed something, and said, "It's the only way. Just don't fall off the chair. I'd hate both of us to die because you're careless."

To Parkman's surprise, he detected the movement of Aaron's finger. The gun discharged its only bullet, loud and shocking in the small shack.

Parkman jolted as the bullet hit his body.

Chapter 33

DRAKE BELLAMY, NO LONGER known by that name, had waited outside Parkman's hotel after he heard from Spencer. He had wondered how long it would take for Spencer to learn of his whereabouts. Spencer couldn't raise too many alarms to look for a missing colleague named John Whitman when that name was fake.

Sure, they'd given Drake—John Whitman—a new ID and passport, but John had never tested the passport by traveling out of Canada. With the money he'd saved and the will to help Sarah, he'd raced to Mexico, rented a car, and prepared to aid in any way he could.

Sarah had startlingly finished the Enzo Cartel, killing most of Enzo's men, including Enzo himself, and destroying the compound in one spectacular helicopter crash before Whitman arrived.

John had located the RV Sarah was traveling in on the

property's perimeter as they were about to leave. It had been quite a few years since he'd seen Sarah. He felt nothing when he saw Aaron with her. They were a couple now. He had no place. He wanted to return the favor she had offered him by being there for her if she needed a hand.

Without Sarah, Drake would have died during a baseball game in Toronto. Angry Hungarians were hunting Drake after he had successfully repelled their initial attack on him. He didn't ask for it, nor was he involved in the original slight. Nonetheless, the Hungarians didn't stop their onslaught.

After several more attempts on his life, he begged Spencer, the Toronto cop who had worked hard to save Drake's life, to put him in witness protection housing. But Spencer had a different plan, so a new ID was created. Drake's "body" was located in the lake. For all intents and purposes, it was ID'd, bagged, and buried with an authentic death certificate, thereby dissolving the Hungarians still hunting him.

Drake Bellamy became John Whitman, a police informant. After a few years of schooling, he was hired full-time to work with Spencer behind the scenes, cracking whatever case they had trouble with. Whitman kept a low profile, preferring to work alone and at odd hours of the night. Oftentimes, Spencer would wake to text messages with the information he was looking for or the detail they needed to arrest a perp. John Whitman hid in plain sight and became an asset for the Toronto Police Department as a detective of a different kind. One that thought outside the box. One that had no history on paper. He was a man even the bad guys couldn't find or figure out, even if they got his name. An asset to Spencer.

It was highly unlikely Sarah had any idea—unless Vivian told her—what Drake's new name was or what he was doing with Spencer in Toronto. In fact, when she saw him, he was pretty sure she had thought him dead all this time.

When Whitman heard of Sarah's plight, he got to Mexico when it was all over. Thinking he'd have dinner with the couple and get to meet Aaron, he'd followed them in the taxi they hired to take them to Rosarito. He watched them hesitate on the hotel's front steps, with Sarah's keen eye picking him out as a tail.

Then Aaron started toward the car. That wasn't how he wanted them to meet for the first time, so Whitman made a U-turn and got out of there, only to return minutes later. After parking the car, he entered the lobby and was astounded to see Sarah heading for the exit at the front.

Their first meeting in years was heartwarming but too short. He followed her outside, saw what was happening, and jumped on that man before the car could hit him. When the local authorities began to arrive, Whitman suspected Spencer wouldn't be overjoyed to hear he had been detained in a Mexican police station, but what could he do? They placed him in the van with Sarah and released him within minutes of arrival at the station. His police ID got him out of the building without being written up or offering a statement.

Waiting had always been his strong suit. He hunkered down and decided to wait for Sarah to be alone so they could talk. One hour, maybe two. With or without Aaron. He just wanted to talk. Then he'd be on his way back to Toronto, back to the new life he'd built for himself as John Whitman. Back to work for Spencer. He'd waited all these years to contact Sarah; he could wait a few more days.

But could Spencer wait for his return? No one knew a thing until Parkman called asking about Drake. That had fucked things up for him. And how did Parkman get involved? Whitman had kept himself hidden. Only Sarah had seen him. He made sure to wait to speak to Sarah first, get her to understand the importance of his new identity, then let Aaron or Parkman know if necessary.

Whitman had to stay as Whitman. If the Hungarians learned that Drake Bellamy didn't die in Lake Ontario, the old nightmare would start up again.

When the police station released Sarah into that woman's care, he thought it best she went with her. Whitman figured his only play was to watch Aaron. Eventually, Aaron would meet Sarah, and then Whitman could talk to them together. If that didn't work, he would approach Parkman and let him know what had happened. With Spencer on his way to Mexico now, Whitman would be collected and returned to Toronto like a piece of misplaced luggage.

He had come here to see if Sarah needed any help with the Enzo Cartel and was stuck trying to locate her by staking out her boyfriend. Not exactly a successful trip. Sarah didn't need him or his help. Evidently, she was quite capable of taking care of herself. All this did was expose his new identity to people who knew him as Drake. Something Spencer told him to avoid at all costs.

How angry Spencer was going to be remained to be seen. What struck Whitman as curious, though, were the two cars filled with five men that looked strangely like the same officers at the police station where they'd taken Sarah. The same ones who told him Sarah had been released.

These two cars were driven around the back of the hotel.

When Whitman sauntered back there, the vehicles were empty. Not a good sign considering Aaron and Parkman were inside the hotel. They, too, had been to the police station earlier and made it known they were looking for Sarah. This was the same Aaron Stevens that just escaped cartel custody. The boyfriend of the girl who caused so much havoc in Mexico over the previous few days. It was quite plausible to Whitman that those two vehicles were filled with five men bent on revenge. Five men who, at that moment, could be killing Aaron and Parkman.

John Whitman had run for the hotel's back door but stopped short and dove behind a large garbage bin when three men came out pushing a bound Aaron toward the first car. Once he was inside, the car drove away.

Whitman ran around to the front, deducing that the other car was for Parkman and the other two men. Both vehicles would be gone forever, and Sarah's colleagues with them, if he didn't get to his car and drive around to the back in time.

Which didn't happen.

But lucky for him—or lucky for Parkman and Aaron—the second vehicle drove by his parked rental just as he turned the key in the ignition. In his mirror, he watched them turn a corner. Then he did a U-turn and raced after them, following as close as he could all the way out of the city, heading south into open country.

When they turned off the highway, Whitman passed the dirt patch of a road and continued on so as not to be detected. His cell phone had rung several times with Spencer's name on call display, but he ignored it. He was in strategy mode. He had to think. What were these members of the law community going to do with Aaron and Parkman? Why bring them out here?

Of course, this had all the earmarks of an execution, but at what gain? The Enzo Cartel was dead. Who were they working for? Was this part of Mexico so lawless that they would risk taking them out of the hotel without masks on? Unless the cover story was Parkman and Aaron were arrested. Then escaped and were found here, shot execution style.

Whatever the reason, Whitman had enough certainty to believe this was the end of the road for Sarah's men, and he was the only one who could do anything about it.

He parked the rental a dozen feet off the highway, obscured by bushes, got out, and doubled back. He walked down the dirt patch of a road, mindful of where his shoes touched the ground. After a hundred yards, he found a thick piece of wood on the ground that resembled a baseball bat, just a little shorter.

Sarah had saved his life at a baseball game in Toronto. And now he would take part in saving Aaron's life with a club that could pass as a bat.

He kept moving in the moonlit darkness until the vague shapes of the two vehicles came into view up ahead. A dim light flickered in the darkness to the right of the vehicles. After another ten steps, he made out a small building, like a tiny barn. The light flickered on its windowsill.

Voices to his left stopped him in his tracks. He got to his knees and closed his eyes to listen. Two men whispered a few feet behind the vehicles. After a moment, he opened his eyes and glanced toward the sound of their voices. A cigarette flared.

Something moved to his right. He now counted three

men of the five.

After another moment on his knees, the fourth man exited the small barn. He walked to the men with the cigarette. Aaron and Parkman were probably inside the barn. He hoped they were still alive. He prayed he wasn't too late. Sarah would never forgive him, having come this far.

He tightened his grip on the piece of wood. They had guns. That didn't stop him before.

He got up off his numbed knees and started toward the trio of men standing behind their cars, using the few trees behind them for cover.

Twenty feet from them. He inched forward. Their volume increased as he neared them. His stomach tied itself into a knot. Who would he hit first? Could he get to the second man before a gun came out? These were trained police officers. What would happen if luck wasn't on his side? He had the element of surprise, but that would only last for the bashing of one head. And if he got shot?

But what would happen to Aaron and Parkman if he did nothing? And could he live with that, knowing he would be rotting in a grave if it weren't for Sarah.

This was for Sarah. He owed her his life.

Ten feet. Each step tentative, each step careful. Six feet. He was close enough to jump and swing. He would connect with the first man quite easily.

One more step. A branch broke underfoot. One of the men turned toward him.

A gun went off inside the little barn. The men turned that way.

One ran toward the barn while the other two produced guns from their waistband.

Was that it? Who was dead? Aaron or Parkman? Did the man who had just run inside go in to finish the other one off?

He got here too late. He had failed Sarah.

The least he could do was kill a few dirty cops in her honor. When they cleaned up this crime scene, she'd hear the whole story and know someone had been watching over her men.

Another weapon was fired inside the barn.

There goes the other one, he thought with dismay. *I'm so sorry, Sarah.*

John Whitman jumped from cover and swung his wooden club.

Chapter 34

PARKMAN TRIED TO IGNORE the pain. Fought back the screams and chills and listened to Aaron rattle off his plan in a hushed tone. They exchanged guns. Parkman now held the weapon Aaron had used. The empty one.

Aaron gripped the loaded weapon down at his side and sat up straight.

One of the cops entered through the open door, a stunned look on his face. He grinned at the sight of blood running through Parkman's fingers, a gun in his right hand, concealed behind his leg.

Aaron had set his presumably empty weapon on his thigh. He gestured at Parkman with his empty hand.

"I did what you asked." He looked frantic, haggard. "One bullet. I shot Parkman. Just like you asked." Aaron's eyes were glazed over in tears.

Parkman lifted his hand away from the smeared blood

and showed the Mexican the wound. It wasn't nearly big enough or in the right spot to kill him. Nothing more than a graze on his arm.

The Mexican laughed. Shoulders hitching, gut clenching with the effort. He laughed and shook his head back and forth like he couldn't believe it.

He held his hand out, open-palmed at Parkman. The cop wanted Parkman's loaded gun. Parkman tossed it aside. It clanged down behind the cop's feet and slid into the wall under the window with the burning candle. He didn't want him to see that that weapon had been fired.

The man jerked around to face Aaron, his laughter cut off. The cop's gun came up, aimed at Aaron's face. Parkman's breath caught in his throat.

Aaron's reflexes kicked in. He jerked to the side as fast as the cop moved, his weapon up high, in kill-shot range. Then he was falling to the side, off the chair. Aaron's aim stayed true, over his shoulder. He fired the one bullet in the gun at the exact moment the cop's weapon spit at Aaron.

Parkman's heart skipped a beat, then lurched into the base of his throat as he waited for the explosion from under Aaron's chair. A blanket of understanding covered Parkman by the time Aaron smashed onto the dirty floor. There was no bomb attached to the chairs. Nothing exploded. The Mexican had laughed because the joke was on them.

But he wasn't laughing anymore because Aaron's aim had been true. The cop dropped to his knees, paused for a maddening second, then fell sideways, his face twisted toward Parkman. A hole had opened in his mouth, his mouth grotesquely larger than it was supposed to be. Blood pooled outward from the head wound slowed, then stopped after the man's heart ceased to pump.

Parkman clutched at his chest. A gasp restarted his breathing. Aaron rolled, spun over, and jumped to his feet, staying down.

"Those fuckers," he whispered between clenched teeth. "They lied to us about the bombs."

"Now one of theirs is down," Parkman said under his breath.

Aaron dropped to the dead cop and coaxed the gun from his thick fingers. "We can handle this." He held the gun up. "And we've got hope."

Gunfire erupted outside. The sound of hammers smacking dead wood resounded throughout the shack as bullet after bullet connected with the shack's frail wooden walls. They dove for the floor as bullets whizzed by their heads. Aaron's arm wrapped over Parkman's back. It seemed like ten minutes or more, but it was probably only ten seconds until the gunfire stopped.

"There's no escaping here," a man shouted on a bullhorn. "This is the end of the road."

"You hit?" Parkman asked.

"No." Then, "What next? We can't shoot blindly out a window into the darkness. Don't have much ammo."

"We wait."

"Wait? For what?"

"No idea. But I'm sure I'll come up with something soon."

"Great."

"Or they'll come in blazing, and you can pick them off one by one with that." Parkman gestured at the gun in Aaron's hand.

Aaron rolled away from him and disappeared into the darkness behind the candle that still burned on the center table.

Someone shouted a maniacal wail in the distance somewhere. The sound of a dull thud was accompanied by grunts and shouts of pain. Maybe help had arrived. Maybe, just maybe, if someone did come and wounded the men outside the shack, they could walk out of here.

Maybe.

Parkman had lost so much blood his energy waned. He sunk lower, closer to the floor. He had managed to stem most of the bleeding but was weakening. Aaron needed to fashion a tourniquet soon.

"Someone's out there," Aaron said in a hushed tone. "I think that someone is on our side."

Parkman made out Aaron's silhouette by the window in the corner and thought about how crazy human nature was. To imagine hope in such ways. They were driven to a remote spot in Mexico to be executed. These were the kind of cops who had done it before. They knew what they were doing. These kinds of people would've known if they were followed. The only person who could be out there was Sarah. If Vivian had told her where to be and when to be there, she could've lain in wait for them to arrive and be, right now, attacking the cops one by one. But he knew Sarah's body wasn't in that place physically. She was still wounded by the heroin Enzo had pumped her body with. It wasn't Sarah outside. And if not, then who? Who was attacking the Mexican police officers?

Another fusillade of gunfire roared out of the darkness covering the shack with new holes from the back.

Parkman kicked the table from between the two chairs and huddled behind it, praying the bullets would stop before they punctured him somewhere he wouldn't walk away from.

Chapter 35

WHITMAN LANDED THE CLUB on the back of the closest man's upper neck before his feet touched the ground. The man barely emitted a sound as his knees collapsed, and he fell to the baked earth like his pockets were filled with lead. The other man was so surprised that he reared back, took in the scene, and began to bring his gun around.

Before the man's gun was in place to fire, the club knocked it from his grasp. Continuing in a circle, the club came around in a vicious backswing that broke teeth out of the man's mouth. He stumbled, hands up to ward off another attack. Whitman swung, fueled with anger, the end of the wooden club glistening crimson in the moonlight. The audible crack of the man's nose sounded in the quiet night as someone else began shooting from behind the barn.

The man fell beside his colleague, and Whitman dove to the ground, thinking the shooter was firing at him. The wood of the barn crackled and splintered as it took bullet after bullet. Evidently, someone on the other side of the barn thought either Aaron, Parkman, or both of them were still alive.

The cop rolled to the side, blood covering his face, and tried to reach his dropped gun. Whitman got up on his knees, raised the wooden club two-handed, saw the fear in the cop's eyes, then swung like he was trying to drive a golf ball three hundred yards. The man's jaw snapped off its hinges, knocking the man unconscious.

He foraged in the pockets of the wounded men and came up with a wallet from each man. ID confirmed they were police officers.

"Shit," he whispered to himself.

Upon further examination, he discovered a brand new iPhone in the guy's pocket to his right. Luckily, it wasn't locked. Whitman was able to open the camera feature and press record. It was dark, so the camera wouldn't pick up much, but it would gather audio. When they were clear of this situation, he'd take the ID and the iPhone as proof of self-defense.

Balancing the camera on a nearby rock, he aimed it at the barn-like building. When Whitman turned back to the carnage, he broke the scene down mentally, cataloging events as he was trained to do, which was something that had grown on him naturally.

Five cops. Two down. One in the barn, probably wounded or dead, after two gunshots came from inside the barn. Had to deal with the other two cops before he considered the one inside.

He snatched the gun from the unconscious man's leg and

crouched. Staying low, he ran for a nearby tree to study the area. The noise of weapons ceased. He waited. If they fired again, he might see a flash from the gun.

A rustling came from inside the cabin. He got lower to the ground and tightened his grip on the gun, his hand slippery now with sweat. The night air was warm. The breeze carried the smell of discharged firearms, similar to a gun range. He counted his breaths, slowing his heart, focusing. When dealing with armed men, calculated attacks and well-thought-out ideas won over rash decisions and stupid ideas. The only enemy he had out here was time. As soon as the two men at the back of the barn realized their friends were down, they would run for it. That could be any moment, any second.

They would run to their cars.

Whitman turned back to the vehicles five feet from him. One last look to the rear of the cabin, then he rolled to the first car. Pressing the tip of the gun to the rubber of the back wheel, he pulled the trigger. With an audible hiss, the wheel discharged the air. He did the same to the front right tire, then moved on to the next car.

When he was done, and both vehicles were handicapped, he hunkered down behind the front hood of the vehicle farthest from the barn and waited. Without checking, there was no way to tell how many bullets were left in the gun.

He set the wooden club down and wiped the sweat from his brow. They would come, and he was ready. There was no walking out of this desolate area. These men needed their cars, but they wouldn't get very far in either of these vehicles.

Gunfire erupted from behind the barn again. Something clanged inside the barn, like a chunk of wood smashing down. Whitman didn't think Aaron and Parkman, if still alive, would remain so if the onslaught of bullets didn't stop soon. He couldn't wait here until they ran out of ammo.

"Hey!" he shouted. The guns ceased. He decided on another tactic. "Hey. What are you guys doing on my property? Why are you assholes shooting up my barn?"

Chapter 36

PARKMAN CURLED INTO A ball and prayed none of the bullets would find their mark on him or Aaron. Thunk after thunk hit the shack wall above him, shattering it into broken strips of wood. The candles had been destroyed in explosions of wax and flame. The inside of the building was darker than the outside now.

As suddenly as the gunfire started, it stopped.

"Hey," Parkman heard a man shout. "What are you guys doing on my property? Why are you assholes shooting up my barn?"

Had the owner of the property just shown up? Somehow that didn't fit. Why would dirty cops bring them here without knowing if the place was safe? Unless they intended on blaming the property owner for their murders.

"Nobody owns this land," someone shouted in reply.

"Fuck you. Who built that barn? I did."

A shuffling noise beside Parkman. Aaron was moving closer. He waited until Aaron was right beside him before he spoke.

"You hit?" he asked in a whisper.

"No. You?"

"No."

"You think that's the owner?"

"Not sure. Whoever he is, he's stopped the guns for now. You think we could crawl out of here?"

"If we go through a window. The door is too exposed, and the angle those bullets came in makes me think they can see the door."

"Then out a window we go—"

"We're Rosarito Police," someone shouted from the back, cutting off Parkman. "We have armed fugitives inside the barn."

"If someone was alive inside that barn, they're dead now," the owner's voice volleyed back.

Parkman could barely make out Aaron's face in the dark. Enough light from the moon filtered in a window two feet from him to catch the silhouette of his profile.

"We need to get out of here," Parkman said.

"How's your arm?"

Parkman eased his hand away from the wound and felt a small trickle of blood run down the back of his triceps.

"Doing okay. It's clotting."

"Can you walk on your own?"

"Yeah. Sure. To get out of here, I'll run a fucking marathon bleeding from both arms."

"How about jumping through a window head first?"

"To save my life. Yeah."

"Then let's go." Aaron grabbed Parkman's good arm and helped him to his feet. Before they got halfway across the shack's floor, something crashed just outside the outer wall. A gun fired. Then another gun from another direction.

They dropped to the ruined floor of the shack again.

What the hell?

Parkman curled into a ball as pain in his arm flared up, and the guns outside spat repeatedly.

"Could use a break here," he shouted.

Chapter 37

Whitman got ready. As soon as they said they were police, he had zeroed in on the location of the voice good enough to get into position. He waited an extra moment, confident his idea would work but not entirely sure. The idea was schoolyard worthy. Something kids would play on their friends as a trick. He needed this to work. If it didn't, Parkman's and Aaron's chances would slim to almost nothing if they were still alive.

He knelt by a tree, placed his arm on the stump, and aimed the weapon in the general direction of the voice. The wood in his other hand, he swung it by his side once, brought it back, then swung it again and let it go. The wood sailed quietly through the air until it came down beside the barn's wall.

As a kid in Toronto, he remembered growing up in the Greek community near Danforth and Pape on Hunter Street when he would go to the park with his friends at night and play Hide 'n' Seek. His goal was always to make them think he was somewhere else as they neared his location. He would hide with a large stone or stick. When the seeker got close, Whitman would toss the stone as a diversion. After a while, the other kids caught on to his tactics but couldn't do anything about it as they still had to find him, and the stone could've been thrown from anywhere.

Tonight, under the waxing gibbous moon, there was enough light for Whitman to play one more version of Hide 'n' Seek, but this one had deadly consequences for the opponent.

Upon the thunk of the wood, the cop fired blindly in its general direction, allowing Whitman to see the muzzle flash. He was already in position, arm resting on the tree stump, hand steady.

He squeezed the trigger. The gun fired. Something fell hard from the direction of the muzzle flash.

To the left of his aim, another muzzle flashed. The whiz of the bullet traveled close to his head, sounding like an angry carpenter bee. He adjusted his aim and let loose, firing the weapon in his hand until it clicked empty.

He dropped the empty gun and lowered himself to the ground. The night was quiet around the ringing in his ears. He waited. No gun now. No wood. Now, only armed with the hope that all five assailants were down, he raised himself to his feet.

The cops had chosen their execution spot well, so Whitman wasn't concerned anyone had heard the gunplay. But remaining at the scene of five dead Mexican police officers would end with his untimely demise.

"Parkman?" he yelled. "Aaron? Either one of you still breathing?"

"Yeah," one of them shouted, to Whitman's relief. "Who are you?"

"Are you both alive?"

"Yeah. Parkman's hit. Arm wound. Still bleeding."

"Okay, we can fix that. You guys ready to leave?"

"Yeah, but who are you?"

"John Whitman—" he stopped. "You might know me as Drake Bellamy, but I'm no longer him. I'm Whitman now."

There was a pause. While Aaron considered what Whitman had just said, he listened for movement, for anything that would reveal the Mexicans were still alive.

"If you guys want to get out of here," Whitman shouted. "Don't use the door, just in case. Come out the window on my side. Listen to my voice for direction."

"We're at the window now."

Whitman stared at the window and was barely able to see a man crawl out. Then another man. No one fired a weapon. Getting them to exit without confirming all the assailants were dead had been a gamble, but he was reasonably sure they were safe.

With Aaron leading the way and Parkman's arm around Aaron's shoulder, they started toward Whitman. He wiped his prints off the weapon by his feet, then tossed the empty gun aside.

The closer they got, the easier it was to see them. He stepped out from behind the tree stump.

"Sorry that took so long," Whitman said. "I wasn't carrying as I wasn't prepared for this."

"Fuck that," Parkman said. "We're just happy to see you.

How did you find us?"

Whitman slipped in beside Parkman as they walked away from the carnage. "Was watching the hotel for signs of Sarah. Saw you two get in the cars with the police. Didn't think that looked good. Decided to follow you, and here we are." They stepped onto the access road and started toward the main highway. "My car's up ahead. Once we clear this area, I'll do a field dressing on that arm."

"Why were you watching for Sarah?" Aaron asked.

Whitman expected that question. "She saved my life several times a few years back. When I heard a cartel kidnapped you and Sarah was in Mexico, I flew down to see if I could help. Caught up with you guys just as the RV left the Enzo compound."

"Was that you who followed Sarah and me to Rosarito?"

"Guilty."

"Should I be concerned about your intentions?" Aaron asked.

"Aaron," Parkman said, a tone of caution in his voice. "Really? You want to do that right now? After Whiteman just saved our asses? Isn't that a display of his intentions?"

"Whitman."

"Whatever."

"Just checking," Aaron said.

"There's nothing to be concerned about, Aaron," Whitman added.

"See," Parkman snapped. "Can we just get out of here?"

Halfway to the car, something metallic smashed behind them. Whitman spun around and saw that Aaron was already turned around, his hands up in a defensive gesture.

Shit, he's fast.

The bang came again.

"Sounds like one of the cops is alive," Whitman whispered. "We need to move. He could radio for help."

"Roadblocks?" Parkman added.

"That too. Let's go."

They started to jog.

A car started behind them. The engine revved. Neither car would be going very far with flat tires.

"Shit," Aaron said. "How far to your car?"

"Two minutes."

"We won't make it."

"Their vehicles aren't going anywhere. I saw to that."

Aaron glanced his way. Whitman met Aaron's gaze with the confidence of a man trained by retired Joint Task Force Two members in Toronto. After the required amount of male bravado eye stare, Parkman stepped between them.

"Seriously, guys, I'm going to bitch slap the both of you if we die out here." He turned to Aaron. "I'm still bleeding because you shot me. Now move. We must get in Whiteman's car and get out of here."

Parkman held his wound as he jogged. After a minute, with Whitman's car in sight, he corrected Parkman again by saying, "The name's Whitman. Not *White*man."

"You're Bellamy to me. Always will be."

"Use that name publicly, and the wrong person might hear it." Whitman opened the door for Parkman to get in the back seat. "Is that the thanks I get for saving your ass?"

"You're right. I'll try to remember the new name."

Once they were in, Whitman turned the car on, left the headlights off, and pulled away from the shoulder. He was a mile away when he realized his mistake. The pit of his stomach dropped, and he felt like shit.

When Aaron had asked who he was back when they were in the shack, he had answered to reassure them and get them to come out. Whitman had identified himself and even used the Drake Bellamy name.

One of the cops was left alive, and now he knew the name of the Toronto man who had killed his colleagues. It wouldn't be long before every cop in Mexico would be hunting John Whitman for the murder of four of their own.

And he'd left the cell phone behind. Recording. There was no way he could go back to retrieve it.

Maybe it was time for him to leave Mexico.

Not before finding Sarah. He came down here to do that, and he wouldn't leave until he did.

Dead or alive.

Chapter 38

Special agents Stacy King and Mary Fitzgerald grew weary of stakeouts. Stake out this, stake out that. All to talk to Blair Turner and get him to spy on his mother. All this to discover what Jane Turner was up to in foreign countries. The stakeouts were murder on the bladder and butt, and King was done with it. She could only play Scrabble on her iPad so often without losing her mind.

"We need to find a new way of doing this," King said. "Sitting a block from the Turner residence waiting for days on end for Blair to come out and play isn't what I signed up for."

Fitzgerald rolled her window down, spit gum from her mouth, then rolled the window back up. They had at least two more hours until sunrise, and King did not want more coffee.

"That's the job. You know why, too. There's nothing we can do but wait. Jane Turner hasn't broken any laws. We can't bring her in."

King clicked her iPad off and tossed it in the back seat. "Then why are we here? Really? If we can't approach the mother, what good will the son be to us? He's been locked inside that house with Sarah for a day and a half now." She checked her watch. "Scratch that. Two days. We're getting nowhere here."

"These are our orders." Fitzgerald's tone warned caution. She spoke slowly, sounding out each word. "It's what we do. Unless you have a better idea."

"It's not what Jack Bauer would do. Or Ray Donovan. They'd go in, get the answers needed, and move on to the next crazy."

"Right, but this isn't fictional TV, and if we did something like that, we'd be up on charges." Fitzgerald turned the air conditioning off. "What's really bothering you? I've been on stakeouts with you before. What's different about this one?"

King stared out her window while biting on a fingernail. "I think it's Sarah. It bothers me that she's in there. I don't want her anywhere near our case." King dropped her hand and faced Fitzgerald. "I mean, why is this her business? This is FBI business. She needs to go home and let the professionals do their jobs."

"I knew it." Fitzgerald slapped the steering wheel. "You're anti-religion, anti-new age, anti—"

"Anti-everything," King cut in. "I believe in the here and now. Flesh and blood. Dust to dust and all that shit. From what I know of her, Sarah plays a different game and dances to a different drummer. One that does not recognize the *Band of the Hand*."

"*Band of the Hand*? What the hell is that?"

"A movie." King tilted her head sideways and eyed Fitzgerald suspiciously. "Don't tell me you haven't seen it."

"Never heard of it."

"Michael Mann did it. The same guy who produced over a hundred *Miami Vice* TV shows."

"What's it about? Or should I ask?"

King stared out the windshield, a blank look on her face. "This is why we don't connect all the time. Why we don't get one another."

"Oh, shut the fuck up," Fitzgerald said, playfully slapping King on the shoulder. "Just tell me what the movie's about."

"I'll tell you this. I watched it on my VCR back when VHS was still around. It's the only movie I watched, rewound, and watched again in one sitting. It's that good. A masterpiece. To this day, not a single movie has knocked it out of my personal number one spot."

Fitzgerald pulled her cell phone out and began typing.

"What are you doing?" King asked.

"Looking it up."

King rested her head on the back of the seat and closed her eyes. They had another four hours before relief came. Her bladder was cooperating today. Less coffee would do that for a girl. But less coffee meant more drowsiness.

"Found it. The synopsis sounds pretty good, but it got a low rating. The box office wasn't that high." Fitzgerald turned toward her. "Are you sure we're talking about the same movie?"

Fitzgerald's cell phone rang in her hand.

"Shit."

She answered on the third ring.

"Fitzgerald here." A pause. "Okay." She smacked the steering wheel. Seemed to be a pastime of hers. "Fine." She keyed the engine and pulled away from the curb. "On our way."

Before she could end the call, King sat up straighter and asked, "What's going on?"

Fitzgerald dropped the phone beside her and signaled to turn left.

"We're being pulled off surveillance."

"What? Why?"

"Don't be in too much of a rush to question it. You got what you wanted. No stakeout."

"What I want is to learn what Jane Turner is up to. Not drive home with our tails between our legs."

"We're to leave Mexico immediately. Plane tickets are waiting for us."

"Where are we going?"

"Las Vegas office. We're to report to the Special Agent in Charge there."

"Got a name?"

"Samantha Puig."

"Did they say why?"

"No. I was told to drop the surveillance and go to the airport."

King sat back and ran a hand through her hair. "That sucks. Wonder if they made us."

They rode in silence for a while.

"You think Sarah Roberts has something to do with this?" King asked.

"Would you fuck off with the Sarah shit?" Fitzgerald

snapped. "She's got nothing to do with what the FBI decides either way."

"Geez, sorry," King said in a mock hurt voice. "Didn't know Sarah was a sore spot for you."

"She isn't."

"Right. I can tell."

Five minutes later, King said, "*Band of the Hand*. Good movie. You should watch it."

Fitzgerald didn't even glance her way.

Chapter 39

WHITMAN FOUND A MOTEL on the outskirts of Rosarito and checked them in using American dollars. Once they were settled in the room and Aaron had given Parkman a towel to stem the bleeding in his arm, Whitman announced he was leaving to get supplies.

Within five miles, he found an all-night drug store where he got disinfectant, a small sewing needle, a roll of thread, and cotton swabs. Bandages were by the counter, where he got orange juice and pre-packaged muffins. Parkman had lost some blood and would need his energy levels raised. At this hour, unless he wanted potato chips or chocolate bars, the muffins and juice would have to do.

Whitman returned to the motel, knowing this was only a pit stop. The cop they left behind would have every cop in the country hunting them in short order. They had an hour, maybe less, to get on the road.

And go where, exactly? Border patrol would be watching for three guys. There would be descriptions of Parkman and Aaron. Sure, he saved their lives tonight, but he might have signed their death certificates for tomorrow.

He entered the room to find Parkman asleep on the bed farthest from the door. Aaron sat beside the bed holding the white towel—now stained deep red with blood—against the arm wound.

"Clotted?" Whitman asked.

Aaron nodded. "Mostly."

Whitman unpacked his purchases and set everything up on the table beside the bed. The room came equipped with a coffee maker and sealed packets of filtered coffee. He poured water into the basin and turned the machine on without the coffee. In moments he would have hot water. Hopefully, it was hot enough to cleanse the needle and thread.

Once he was set up, he turned to Aaron. Sarah's boyfriend had heavy eyes, but they watched Whitman with an intensity that made Whitman think of a cougar watching him from atop a large boulder, waiting for the right moment to pounce.

"Wake him," Whitman said.

"Why?"

"I need to stitch his arm closed, and then we leave."

"Leave? Where?"

"We can't stay here."

"Because of the cop you left alive back there?"

Whitman dropped the needle and thread into the hot water. He'd been around enough hostility to last a lifetime. It didn't bother him any more or less than usual. He only felt concerned because he didn't want his reunion with Sarah to be marred by anything as trivial as a jealous boyfriend. He paused momentarily, watching the needle at the bottom of the coffee pot.

"Aaron, if you have an issue with my intentions, then speak. State your claim." He faced Aaron. "Say your piece. Or don't. But what you won't do is accuse me of a hidden agenda. Sarah saved my life. I would be rotting in the ground if it wasn't for that woman." He moved across the carpeted floor and stopped in front of Aaron's chair. "Sarah is everything to me. As a friend. As a role model. As a woman. She is not someone I think of intimately. I don't seek a relationship with her. She's yours. You have nothing to concern yourself with. If you can prove otherwise, I will walk away from this. Now, if you'll excuse me, I want to clean and disinfect Parkman's wound and stitch it up. Then we can carry on with the saving our lives part. Are we cool?"

After a moment, with Aaron neither speaking nor nodding, Whitman walked back to the coffee pot, withdrew the needle, threaded it, and started back to Parkman.

"Sarah is my world," Aaron said. "We've been through a lot together." He nudged Parkman to wake him. "Understand something for me."

Whitman nodded.

"What you're feeling isn't jealousy. It's caution. You show up after several years, back from the dead. Makes me wonder why. What do you want? Why now? You say your intentions are clean. All I'll say is that remains to be seen."

"Saving your life back there isn't worth something?"

"It is." He pushed Parkman again. "The true test will be when you're with Sarah."

"Then let's go get her, and you and I will learn together

what I'm here for."

"I warn you, if for any reason—"

"There's no need to warn me. Sarah can take care of herself. As I've heard, you can, too. Now, can we get Parkman fixed up?"

Aaron waited a heartbeat, nodded slightly, then shook Parkman awake.

"Parkman, I need to disinfect the wound," Whitman said. Parkman's eyes opened slightly. "I need to clean and disinfect it completely to leave nothing inside. If anything is left inside the sub-dermal layer, it can become septic almost immediately."

"Go ahead," Parkman mumbled.

"It might hurt, but once I'm done in a few minutes, you'll be on the road to healing. Also, I have muffins and juice. You need to eat and drink to get your energy up." Whitman touched Parkman's flesh around the wound. It was cool and damp.

Whitman decided to talk to him to keep Parkman's mind off the process. There was no local anesthetic to administer, so Parkman would be sewn up raw.

"The body expels foreign material using abscesses and pustules." He dabbed the disinfectant-soaked cotton into the inner part of the cut. Parkman winced and drew back. Aaron held him, forcing him in place. "If I sew it into the skin, that would be bad."

Once the wound looked clean, Whitman brought the needle to it. A minor amount of blood seeped out, running down Parkman's arm. He pressed the skin where he wanted to place the needle, rotated it in his fingers to aid in the numbing, and pushed the needle in.

"I'm starting with the closest edge of the wound and sewing away from me. This area should be mostly numb from the injury, so you shouldn't feel much."

"It's good," Parkman said. "Just do it. No problem."

Aaron opened an orange juice and handed it to Parkman, who drank it back.

Whitman sewed in a zigzag pattern up the wound until he reached the end, where he tied it off in a firm knot.

"There, all done." He dabbed at the little blood with the stained towel. "I'll apply a large bandage, and we're good to go."

Aaron unwrapped a muffin and handed it to Parkman. He unwrapped another and bit into it.

"If you need to use the bathroom, do it now. We'll be on the road for a while and shouldn't stop that often."

"Where are we headed?" Aaron asked. "Sarah's in Rosarito somewhere. We need to go back there. Find her. Then leave."

"Not possible," Parkman said.

Whitman was relieved he wasn't the one who had to say that.

"Not with one cop still alive from the shack. We are wanted men in Mexico now. We need out."

Aaron got up and walked to the other side of the bed. "What about Sarah? Just leave her here? When she's at her weakest?"

"We have no choice. We'll be dead before the sun sets if we don't."

"And if she dies?"

"Aaron, she won't. It's Sarah. She has Vivian."

Aaron moved to the motel room window and peeked out

the curtains, clearly battling with the decision to leave the country.

"Drake, have you got a cell phone?" Parkman put his hand out.

"Whitman. And yes."

"I need to make a call."

Whitman handed him his cell. A moment later, Parkman was talking to a man he called Casper. Then he clicked off the call.

"Casper's sending a helicopter."

Aaron turned from the window. "Where? You didn't tell him where we are."

"Leave this cell phone on. He's tracking it. The helicopter will be here inside an hour. I'm going to sleep. Wake me when it gets here." Parkman leaned back and rested his head on the pillow.

"Wow, this man named Casper is powerful," Whitman said. "Who is he?"

"Works for the U.S. government," Parkman said. "Helped us out of a few jams."

"Good to have someone like that around." Whitman stepped into the bathroom to wash up. Several minutes later, when he returned to the room, Parkman was asleep, breathing loudly.

Aaron was nowhere to be seen.

He had left the room.

Chapter 40

SARAH WOKE WITH A splitting headache that felt like a toothache had flared up in the middle of her skull. Rubbing her temples didn't ease the pain. Slow on the uptake; it occurred to her that her arms weren't restrained as she rubbed the side of her head.

Other than the headache, she didn't feel sick anymore. Her stomach had settled. If anything, her body felt rested, like she'd slept for twenty hours.

She kept her head on the pillow and her eyes closed as she thought of heroin. The urge seemed to be gone. In fact, the idea of shoving that stuff in her arm disgusted her. She sighed in relief. It was time to get back to herself, to live her life again. The addiction was over. From here on in, even if the idea appealed to her in the slightest, she'd be able to beat it. In the worst moments of withdrawal, she had almost won. From here on, there would only be the best moments.

She forced her eyes open. It was the same room as before, with the same dismal artwork and sparse furniture. Although now, she wasn't tied to the bed, therefore not a prisoner.

The headache's pounding eased off. She rolled to her side, dropped her legs over the edge, and pushed off the bed into a sitting position. A moment of dizziness halted her movement. When it passed, she took in her surroundings from an upright position. They had left her alone. The doctor and all his equipment were gone. For all intents and purposes, no one would see anything other than a girl waking in a room after what might appear to be a wicked hangover.

"Yeah, some hangover."

Her voice was deep, gravelly. She cleared her throat, squinted at the small flare of pain behind her eyes, and tried to speak again.

"What am I doing here, Vivian?"

Her sister's presence flowed into her consciousness.

"Good to know you're still around," Sarah whispered. "Haven't chatted much lately."

Vivian's knowledge was imparted upon Sarah in seconds and transferred to her consciousness. It was suddenly there like she'd only recovered a thought from before. Vivian's words entered her mind like it was something she just knew. Instead of speaking, Vivian could plant an entire idea, a plan, or a way of thinking into Sarah's consciousness through mental osmosis. Almost at once, the planted thoughts took on a cognitive awareness for Sarah that became her new understanding. In essence, what Vivian planted became Sarah's new knowledge and, ultimately, her thoughts, even though Sarah knew they were foreign.

In the time she sat waiting for her headache to subside enough to get off the bed and walk around the room, she understood why she was here, why Vivian allowed her to be used as a heroin test subject, and what she needed to do. Vivian failed to reveal the end game, though. Why did it all matter so much? Why was she supposed to stay here and do what Jane Turner wanted her to do? Sarah was left wondering how that connected to the drugs but felt it had something to do with Jane's son, Blair.

Vivian explained her process had to be the way it was, or she wouldn't have met Blair if she wasn't addicted to heroin. She wouldn't have wanted to buy anything from him. Actually, knowing what he was up to in his Camaro, she probably would've wrecked his car and put him in the hospital. Instead, she became his customer. To witness the accident. To whisper the prophecy. So he could overhear her and tell his mother about it. So she would be interested in Sarah and research her. According to Vivian, all that had to happen started with allowing Enzo to cause her addiction in the first place so that Sarah could be in this room at this exact moment. It was all like a blueprint, prewritten in immaculate detail for each event to happen in real-time.

"And now I'm supposed to just play along?" Sarah asked the empty room.

Vivian whispered *yes*, then retreated from Sarah's consciousness.

"Great. Thanks." She thought of another question. "Hey, Sis, what about Aaron? Where's he right now? Probably worried sick about me. How many days have I been here? And what's he think about these glamorous plans of yours?"

"This is your third day," a metallic female voice said

from the corner.

Sarah jerked her head to the left too fast and winced at the pain. The voice emitted from speakers somewhere because the room was empty.

When she hopped off the bed and landed on her feet, her knees gave way, and she dropped to the floor, bracing her fall by thrusting her hands out in front of her.

"Shit," she muttered under her breath.

"It'll take a little time to walk," the voice said. It had to be Jane's voice. Cameras must be giving her visual access to Sarah's room. Why though? To see when she wakes up? To see what she does?

That made it creepy. Sarah understood this room was the guest room, which meant Jane spied on her guests.

"Not a very trusting person, are you?" Sarah said.

"What was that?" the voice asked.

"Toilet. I need to piss."

There was a moment's pause. Then, "You will find what you need through the door on the far left."

With the use of the side of the bed, Sarah got to her feet, wobbled for a moment, then started across the hardwood floor.

"You've been in bed for three days. You'll recover quickly, though."

Like I need to be told that.

It felt like a burst of acid filled her stomach, and she felt nauseous again.

I thought that shit was over.

"There are no cameras in the bathroom. But neither are there ways to escape. I'll wait for you out here."

Ways to escape? Wait for me?

So now I am a prisoner.

Two minutes later, she felt a lot better after flushing, washing her hands, and splashing water on her face. She emerged from the bathroom and looked around the room. The cameras had to be small or hidden because nothing stood out.

"You're looking for the cameras," the voice said. "You won't find them. Surgically implanted in the room. I have six cameras that cover everything but the toilet."

Sarah made her way over to the window and pulled the curtain aside. The sun was rising on what would probably be a gorgeous day. A quick glance revealed the ground below was at least thirty feet away. Too high to break the glass and jump. From her limited view, the wall below the window was smooth without the required footholds to climb down. The surrounding grounds looked immaculately tended, but no tree came close to the house. The only way out of this room was through the door.

"Banish thoughts of escape," the metallic voice droned on. "I have an offer for you. Once we agree to the terms, you'll be on your way. Free to go back to Aaron and Parkman."

Sarah started across the room on less wobbly legs. Jane Turner had done her research. This woman was dangerous. Rich and powerful. She could get what she wanted. Like pulling Sarah from a Mexican jail. For what, though? An offer? A deal? Hold her as a prisoner until the deal had been reached?

"What kind of an offer?" Sarah asked.

"One you might find quite appealing."

"Somehow, I don't think so." She made it to the door and

tried the handle. Locked. She knocked on the door. It looked like wood but sounded solid like it was made of steel.

"Reinforced vault door," Jane said. "The kind of material a bank would use on their vaults. I had it made for this room. Without the combination, which, mind you, is only accessible on the other side of the door, there's no opening it unless you rammed it with a tank. Somehow I doubt anyone's bringing a tank to the third floor of my house."

Sarah stepped back from the door. She examined the walls, looking for pinholes where cameras might be. Her anger—familiar, comfortable—came back. She felt herself again. Somehow, even being captive in this room brought her back to who she always was.

"Why do you hate your son?" Sarah asked.

There was no immediate response.

Hit a nerve?

"I don't hate my son."

"Sure you do." Sarah walked back to the window. There had to be a way out. "With all this money, why is he selling drugs in casinos?"

"His choice. He wants to be an entrepreneur. As any good parent would, I allow him to make his own choices." After a moment, she added, "But we're not here to discuss my son or my relationship with him. We're here to discuss you and my offer."

Sarah pulled the curtains aside and watched as the sun crested the Mexican terrain in the distance. As she thought of Aaron and what personal hell he was probably going through, having no idea where she was and who was probably involved in locating her, she realized her headache had vanished.

"Go on. What offer?"

"I have a very important deal coming up. I want you to travel with me and help me make this deal."

Sarah frowned. Sure, Jane couldn't see her face as long as she continued to stare out the bedroom window. "Why me? I have no experience making deals at the level you're used to. I don't come from a family of this kind of wealth."

"I want you as my personal security."

Vivian rushed into her consciousness with two words: *Do it.*

"Not interested," Sarah said.

Vivian whirled around inside her head and shouted something unintelligible. Sarah jerked slightly, then Vivian shot away, leaving Sarah's mind.

"You will be interested when I explain my terms."

"And what are they?" Sarah gripped the curtains on both sides and tightened her fists. "Come on, hit me with it. I'm ready."

"One million dollars in untraceable cash. Half up front, the other half when my deal has been completed."

One million dollars. That would finance her for years to come. Act as security for a woman making a prearranged deal? For one million dollars? There had to be a snag somewhere. It smelled bad, no matter how she looked at it.

"What's the catch?" Sarah asked.

"There is no catch. One million to act as security for approximately one hour."

"There's a catch. There always is. Why would you hire me, a drug addict, to protect you when you could hire dozens of professionals for that kind of money?"

"I want you."

"Why me? Answer that satisfactorily, and I'll give you my decision."

"Because I think the people I'm arranging this deal with want to kill me and everyone with me. Since you're Sarah Roberts and you have Vivian in your ear, she won't let you die so easily. If I bring you to the deal, my chances of making it out alive rise a few hundred percent." Jane paused. "I don't want to die on their terms, Sarah. I want to die on mine."

Chapter 41

The violent thunder of a helicopter startled Whitman awake. He jumped to his feet and looked around the room frantically to orientate himself. Parkman slept on the bed, but otherwise, the room was empty. Aaron hadn't come back yet.

He ran for the window and peeked out. A large helicopter with an American flag on the tail had landed in the clearing on the other side of the road. The sun had just risen above the horizon, behind the chopper. The rotors of the chopper sliced through the early morning rays.

Whitman turned from the window to see Parkman getting up off the bed.

"Help me," he said. "Little weak this morning."

They couldn't have gotten more than two hours of sleep. Whitman felt the grogginess like a weight throughout his body. Considering the blood loss and the wound, he imagined Parkman would feel a lot worse than him.

He grabbed Parkman's good arm and helped him to his feet. At the door, Parkman put a hand on the wall to stop them.

"Where's Aaron?"

Whitman shook his head. "No idea. He left the room after I'd stitched you up."

"Without saying a word on where he was going?"

"Not a word."

Someone knocked on the door. "Parkman? Aaron? You in there?"

"Yeah," Parkman shouted back.

When Whitman opened the door, they were greeted by three men in full uniform, as if they were on a raid, sporting machine guns.

The man closest to the door leaned into Parkman. "Agent Buck Schaffer is waiting in the chopper. We need to double-time it. We needed to be in the air five minutes ago. Mexican authorities are tracking us." The man started running toward the helicopter, shouting over his shoulder. "Go, go. Go."

For a wounded man, Parkman made running for the chopper look easy. Whitman was at least fifteen years younger and had to turn it up to stay on his tail. The side door was open as they approached. Two of the soldiers helped Parkman in, then Whitman.

A man in the corner—probably the Buck Schaffer the soldier had said was waiting in the chopper—leaned forward and shouted at Parkman, "Where's Aaron?"

Parkman sat beside Schaffer. "No idea. He left the room a few hours ago. Didn't come back."

A stern look crossed Schaffer's face as he leaned back on the bench seat he occupied. The soldiers piled in and slammed the door shut. The leader twirled his hand in the air, index finger aiming skyward, and the chopper lifted off almost immediately.

One of the men handed Whitman headphones. By the time he got them on, and the mouthpiece dropped in place, Parkman was also wearing a set. He could hear the men talking clearly through the extreme noise the rotors made only a few feet above their heads.

"Parkman, who is this?" Schaffer asked.

They all looked at him.

"My name is John Whitman. I'm a friend of Sarah's."

Parkman nodded at Schaffer. "He's clean. Saved our lives earlier tonight. Did a damn fine stitch job on my bullet wound, too." Parkman pulled his arm up to show Schaffer.

"Do you know who shot you?" Schaffer asked.

Parkman nodded. "Yeah. Aaron."

Schaffer frowned, lines on his face converging, then smoothed out as the frown melted away. "What?"

"Long story. I'll tell you about it later."

"We can't fly back to the States right now. Too much heat."

"Heat?" It was Parkman's turn to frown.

"Four Mexican cops have been found murdered. Bludgeoned to death and shot, to be exact. The authorities down here are looking for three men, two of which look exactly like you," he gestured at Parkman, "and Aaron. We're flying to our embassy, so at least for now, we'll be on American soil."

Whitman exchanged a glance with Parkman. "It was necessary, sir."

Schaffer turned his way. "Explain why it was necessary

to murder four Mexican police officers. As far as I can tell, all four work at the same police station where Sarah Roberts was held for several hours. The media will ride this wave to the moon and back. But a man I had just met told me it was necessary. Back that claim up."

Without missing a beat, Whitman said, "I witnessed five Mexican police officers enter Parkman's hotel. Ten minutes later, three of them escorted Aaron out to a car and drove off. The other two carried the unconscious Parkman to a car and left the hotel. I decided to follow at a safe distance. I tracked them to a remote area south of the city where they had placed Aaron and Parkman in a shack to execute them. I had to stop it. Killing them was my only option. Sorry for the noise this is causing, but I regret nothing when it comes to saving their lives. I did it once; I would do it again."

If Schaffer had the capacity to be surprised, that's what Whitman read on his face. After a moment, Schaffer turned to Parkman.

"I like this guy. We should keep him."

"My thoughts exactly."

The chopper took a sharp right and began to descend. Whitman looked out the window, watched the land get closer and the sun rise and wondered where Sarah was and what she was doing.

And where was Aaron? He would die on the streets in Mexico with every cop in the country looking for him. He needed to find sanctuary and find it fast.

Whitman had Aaron, and now he was gone. If something happened to Aaron, Sarah would never forgive him. Since the Mexican authorities had Parkman's and Aaron's descriptions but not his, he was the natural choice to start looking for

Aaron as soon as they landed.

He had come back to see Sarah and help Sarah if she needed it. Not make mistakes and lose her boyfriend.

Even if Aaron didn't want to be found, Whitman had no choice. It was either find Aaron or never be able to face Sarah.

The helicopter landed softly, as did Whitman's decision.

It was time to go hunting in Mexico, and he would need a big gun.

Chapter 42

F OOD WAS DELIVERED USING a slot behind a picture on the wall. Jane gave her instructions on the speaker system, and Sarah followed them. Eating and getting her strength up was a mutual goal of theirs.

After she'd eaten the chicken, potatoes, and broccoli, she lifted the picture aside and placed the dirty dinner plate back in the slot. Minutes later, the picture locked into place as the plate was retrieved from the other side.

Sated, she lay on the bed and thought she'd nap. There was nothing else to do in the rich woman's house unless she agreed to her terms, and Sarah wouldn't. The woman had a deal to conclude, an arrangement. If she wanted security for it, hire a security firm. Pay the right people who do that sort of thing for a living.

Even though Vivian told Sarah she was there for that purpose, Sarah refused to go along. This was a first of many firsts. It was time to set things right. She told Vivian that she needed to be brought in on the planning. It had to be that way. If there was a blueprint, let Sarah read it as it pertained to her life and well-being. Wouldn't it have been easier to explain that she needed to meet Blair and impress him so Sarah could win Jane's trust? Wouldn't that have been a better plan than getting her addicted to heroin and then making her withdraw from it? And to what extent did Sarah's body pay for the methods Vivian undertook?

What about Aaron? How did he fare in all this? He had no idea where Sarah was. Because of the drugs, she had deceived him. Sent him down for Advil when all she wanted to do was meet a drug dealer. Sarah was Vivian's pawn, and it had to stop.

If it was only Sarah, maybe she could come to an arrangement with Vivian. But this involved her family and her loved ones. Because of events Vivian set in motion, Aaron lost a finger.

To be fair, Vivian had forewarned Sarah about Aaron's abduction, but it didn't happen in time. Had she stopped what she was doing in Europe to save Aaron, a lot of young girls would still be trafficked. In the end, a finger was a lower price to pay.

Tell Aaron that.

Sarah wondered what Vivian would do next. They had never really gone to this place in the past with each other. Ever since Sarah was eighteen, she had been blindly listening to Vivian, doing as she asked.

Vivian whispered, *And staying alive because of it.*

That was the internal conflict. Sarah had grown to love her sister in ways she never thought possible. She trusted her, and over the last year or so, they had gotten even closer as Vivian could talk directly to her. Sarah would never deny that she loved having Vivian in her head. It was a comfort, and she preferred this over the original days when Sarah had to write down all of Vivian's messages.

If you're listening, Vivian, which I think you are, all I'm asking for is forethought. You already have the big picture. Offer that to me, and we'll move forward as a team. Right now, I feel like a little silver ball inside a large pinball machine as I get buzzed around, banging into one life moment after the next, never knowing where I'll end up, but at least knowing I'll get to the finish line. That's not enough anymore. That's just not enough. I get hurt. The people around me get hurt. And what if I want to marry Aaron and have a baby one day? She rolled onto her side and stared at the curtains by the window. *What if we have a baby one day?* she repeated for Vivian's sake. *What would happen to my baby if you suddenly needed me to take off and fight some terrorist fundamentalists? Vivian, I need assurances. I need more than you've been giving me. I'll be turning twenty-seven next April. We have evolved to this new place where you're in my head. Evolve a little more, and I would be honored to do your bidding. If trust is your problem, you have no reason not to trust me.*

Sarah waited for an answer, but none was forthcoming.

The door clicked. Sarah glanced over as the door swung open. Her one chance to bolt from this fancy prison cell, and she's lying on the bed.

Jane Turner entered the room, followed by two tall men. The men took positions on either side of the door as it was closed from the other side, the lock falling back into place.

The men had handguns on either side of their waists, along with what looked like an Uzi in their hands. The man on the right had to be almost seven feet tall and over three hundred pounds. Definitely someone she didn't want to tussle with. The man on the left was smaller and leaner. He reminded her of Aaron's physique. Strong, tight, like a black belt fighter should be. The Uzi in his hands didn't fit his image. He would be more menacing without it.

Turner walked to the window, an ugly smirk on her face. She was rich and got what she wanted from the people in her life, or she ostracized them. Just look at her son. This woman wasn't used to not getting her own way.

"I came here to tell you a story," Turner said. She pulled the curtains aside and leaned on the windowsill. "One that will shock and disgust you. When I'm done, I will ask for your help again. If you refuse, you will stay here as my guest until the deal is done. When I return, you will be free to go. I have lawyers and papers drawn up that show you asked to stay here to aid in your withdrawal symptoms." She turned from the window. "My doctor and my son will testify to that fact if you choose to take legal action against me for this," she waved a hand in the air, "forcible confinement."

Sarah sat up on the bed. "Coffee? Let's talk over coffee."

Jane appeared surprised. She probably didn't expect that response after her little speech. She gestured at the two men at the door. The lithe one on the left slipped a hand inside his pocket and pushed something. The door clicked and began sliding open. He moved sideways and disappeared into the hall as the door closed behind him.

"If you decide to work with me, I have papers drawn up to offer you the one million in cash, as I mentioned before."

"Fair enough." Sarah lay back on the bed. "Your story?"

Without pause, Jane stated, "I was very young when I got married. I was raised in India, even though I don't look Indian. My marriage was arranged when I was ten years old. It's different here and in America. But that sort of thing still goes on in India."

"I've heard of that. Isn't it a custom, a way of life over there?" Sarah could listen, have coffee, and wait for her sister to respond to her plea. Whatever happened, she would leave this room doing her sister's bidding or dropping the vigilante stuff for good. If Vivian couldn't see that Sarah was ready for the big picture, then she wasn't ready for any of it anymore.

"Is rape a way of life?" Jane asked.

Sarah met Jane's eyes. She was telling the truth. Standing water glistened in her wide, round orbs as she fought back the tears.

"Rape?"

"I was raped several times before I was five years old. I nearly died on the operating table in New Delhi."

A pang of anger sliced through Sarah's abdomen. How could anyone do that to a child?

Jane moved across the room and sat in the chair her son had occupied when he told Sarah how his mother hated him because he was gay. That talk seemed so long ago.

"The men who raped me over and over were never brought to justice. Even though they were known to my family."

Vivian whispered, *What she's saying is true. Listen to her, Sarah. Open your heart. Then you will know why you're here.*

Sarah closed her eyes and focused hard to dispel the

voice on the inside. Until Vivian offered her the whole picture, she was offline.

Instead, she turned her attention to Jane, now even more invested in the story. Vivian could piss her off, not tell her everything, and get her beat up and hooked on drugs, but one thing Vivian would never do was lie to her. That meant Jane's story was true. Getting to Jane's house had been a tough road. It wouldn't hurt to find out more about Jane.

"How is that possible?" Sarah asked. "How could they never get caught when your family knew them?"

Jane looked down at her feet, then slid them under the chair. Sarah had almost forgotten the man by the door.

"It was a different time in India."

The door clicked. Lanky was back. He held a tray with a French press and two coffee cups on it, cream and sugar. Jane waited until Lanky poured coffee into both cups, then retreated to the door.

"That will be all," Jane said without looking up.

The men by the door quietly exited the room.

"That puts you in a risky position," Sarah said. "Us, alone."

"No, it doesn't." Jane mixed cream and sugar into her cup, brought it to her mouth, and sipped. After a deep swallow, she said, "I read a lot about you while you were here sleeping. You're a kind soul. One is not taken to violence unless provoked. Now, cream? Sugar?"

"I drink it black. I never dilute my coffee or my whiskey." Without missing a beat, she said, "I'd consider holding me prisoner against my will in this large panic room as a provocation."

"In case you do, you would not escape this fortress. I

have fifteen men roaming the premises, watching and guarding, two right outside that door. Any attack on me would prove fruitless."

"Not entirely fruitless." Sarah couldn't resist the coffee any longer. They drank from the same French Press. The chances her coffee was drugged were slim.

"How so?"

"I'd garner a certain level of satisfaction from it." She sipped, burned her lip, then swallowed. "But we're getting off-topic. Please continue with your story."

Jane nodded slightly. "I was very young. Memories at that age, with the trauma, are hard to formulate. Things are clearer when I was seven years old. Then again, when I was ten. I remember one summer using the toilet." She drank from her cup. "I should stop and tell you that our village didn't have running water. We used the stream to clean our clothes and bathe in. The toilet was a rough hole in the ground with a wooden seat built over top of it. My father would move the wooden seat weekly, burying our waste as he went."

Sarah looked around the room. "You made good with your life coming from that."

"It wasn't all me. But I'll get to that."

Sarah set her cup down to let the coffee cool.

"When I was ten, after helping my mother with the clothes and chopping vegetables for dinner, I walked alone to the wooden box. I was taken away by four men who gang-raped me until the next day when they left me to die a mile from my house. My dad found me, cleaned me up in the river —I still remember the sting of my wounds when the water touched me—and brought me home. He told my mother that

I had tried to run away and had to teach me a lesson. That explained my injuries. She beat me for it, too."

To Sarah's surprise, Jane didn't shed a tear. It was like something had closed over this woman's heart and sank it to depths where she couldn't feel anymore, like the maelstrom that took down Captain Nemo's submarine.

"I'm sorry," is all Sarah could think of saying. She picked up her coffee cup and sipped from it to do something. The air in the room had changed. She was a good listener when she needed to be, but she wasn't good at hearing these kinds of revelations.

"I've stayed on top of the statistics in India," Jane said as she got up from the chair. She set her cup down, rubbed her hands together as if they were cold, and walked to the window where she parted the curtains and stared outside just as Sarah had earlier. "Rape is the fourth most common crime against women in India." She swiveled to face Sarah. "Nearly twenty-five thousand rapes are reported annually. Ninety-eight percent are known to the victim, but do you want to know the worst part?"

Sarah swallowed audibly. "Not really. But go ahead."

"Reported rapes, you know, the ones we hear about, stand at an alarming one percent of the total number of rapes in that country. That means that out of every one hundred rapes, only one is reported to the police. And do you want to know why?"

"No. But I feel sick now." Sarah held her stomach.

"When a victim comes forward, it is widely known that the police in India mistreat the victims and humiliate them. Sometimes it's as simple as a caste system."

"Can you explain how that relates?"

"Family status. For instance, here's a true story. Two girls from the Dalit caste, another word for Untouchables, were raped and hung from trees. Initial evidence pointed to the rape and murder of these two girls. But the perpetrators and the police belong to the Yadav community, supposedly a higher class. Guess what happened in that case?"

"I have no idea. The perps were arrested and charged with murder, among other things?"

"There were arrests all right, but without breaking the case down, no charges have ever seen the inside of a courtroom, and the case was eventually overturned and deemed a suicide. It's a complete cover-up by the CBI because of the caste system."

"What's the CBI?"

"Central Bureau of Investigation in India."

"How is it possible that they can get away with this?"

Jane turned back to the window and placed her hands open-palmed on the pane. "Things are changing, but slowly. Protests still happen. But it's not only an Indian problem. I read that the U.N. studied countries around the world. Only eleven percent of all rapes are ever reported globally. That's disgusting to me."

Sarah dropped her eyes. Half her coffee was gone already. She'd been held so rapt by Jane's story that she didn't notice how much she'd drank. She set the cup down and addressed Jane.

"What has this got to do with me? Why am I here?"

Jane stepped away from the window and stood in front of Sarah.

"I'm buying a device from a friend in Bulgaria; something called a dirty bomb. We are meeting in Las Vegas to do the deal in"—she looked at her watch—"fifteen hours. There's a conference in Las Vegas for international lawmakers soon after the deal that will have a large Indian presence. I want you to help me buy that device so I can plant it at the conference in the Sands Expo at The Venetian and send as many Indian men to hell as I can." She breathed in deep, then loudly blew the breath out. "How about it, Sarah the Vigilante? Will you help me buy a bomb and kill a bunch of Indian rapists? My personal helicopter is outside waiting to ferry us to my private jet at the airport."

Sarah got to her feet and moved close to Jane. Their noses almost touched.

"I will do it," Sarah said, her tone filled with conviction. She could still hear Vivian's words telling her to help Jane. "You have my word. I will help you buy the bomb." An idea occurred to her. "But on one condition."

"What's that?"

"You bring Blair with us to Vegas."

"Fine. Blair comes."

They shook hands.

Chapter 43

A MEDIC SAW TO Parkman's wound, cleaned and redressed it. Parkman met with Whitman, where they were supposed to take a two-hour nap after Casper built a profile on Aaron.

He watched Whitman and Casper in a small room, sitting across from each other at a metal table where Casper recorded everything Whitman told him about the attack. Whitman was a wealth of knowledge regarding Aaron's hotel, Parkman's hotel, and what happened in between. Parkman broke into the conversation to add as much as he could on his visit to the Mexican police station, what he knew of Aaron, and where he thought the man might be.

Casper told them he'd found out Sarah was released into the care of a rich woman named Jane Turner. He had men assigned to discover everything they could about Turner and why she would vouch for Sarah. He assured them he would do everything he could to get Aaron back safe and left the room to direct the operation on the ground further.

"Wait," Parkman said. "What about Sarah? Why can't we just drive to the Turner house and pick her up?"

"We're working on it. We can't do anything short of a military operation on foreign soil. The woman has a veritable army surrounding her house. If Sarah's inside, it's not due to her own free will, but we don't have the same legal channels down here that we enjoy north of the border." Casper held the door open, swinging it back and forth as he talked. "Even if we did, we're unwelcome here. No one's talking to us, and we need to maintain a low profile. Until something cracks with Sarah, I'm afraid there's not much I can do right now."

"There's your reason, then."

Casper stepped back into a room. "My reason?"

"Why Aaron went AWOL. He saw this coming and is hunting Sarah his way."

"You may be right. But his way will get him killed. There are a lot of police officers in Mexico, and each and every one is looking for him. His odds of success are extremely low."

"Aaron doesn't bank on odds. He banks on himself."

Casper pulled the door open and stepped into the corridor. "That catches up with you eventually," he said over his shoulder. Before the door closed, he added, "And it fucking hurts." The door closed.

Parkman glanced at Whitman. "What now?" he asked. "What are you going to do?"

"Sleep. We're no good to anyone burnt out."

"Agreed." Parkman moved for the door. "I want to be up in two hours. I want caffeine, chocolate, and cake. Something to juice me up. Then we find Aaron and Sarah and leave Mexico." He stepped into the corridor with Whitman following. "Agreed?"

"Absolutely. Find them and leave. Top on my agenda as well."

They moved away from each other and headed to their bunks, as detailed by embassy staff when they arrived.

Parkman rolled the green blanket aside, lay down on the bed's thin mattress, and winced at the sharp pain in his arm when he put weight on it.

Pain seemed to be more intense with age. He wondered how Sarah dealt with it. Toothpicks would help. What embassy didn't have toothpicks in the mess hall or the receiving area? He would've sent someone to a local grocery store, but they were in lockdown mode.

Just my luck.

He was asleep before his head was on the pillow for a full minute.

Chapter 44

Whitman entered his small room where a bed waited. He sat on it and tried to decide on a tactic. He wasn't American. He held a Canadian passport. Yet he was in an American embassy on lockdown. Normally that would please him. But he didn't want to be on lockdown. He wanted to be out there, looking for Sarah and Aaron.

He still had his cell phone on him. Since it was on vibrate, no one heard the phone when Spencer texted him that he was in Rosarito at a casino waiting for Whitman.

But how could he leave the embassy on lockdown? He thought back to other times in his life when he needed to leave a building without being stopped, like the apartment building in Toronto where he discovered a dead body. He had left his fingerprints all over the crime scene, then found the body. The police were already knocking at the door. Yet he escaped and managed to stay alive when every cop in

Toronto was looking for him. He did it once; he could do it again.

Although, that was Canadian police. Americans might be more apt to see through his ruse. Whether they were better trained or not, he felt the risk level needed to be elevated when dealing with the Americans.

"Fuck it," he whispered and got up off the bed.

Out in the corridor, he headed toward the rear of the building. When they landed in the helicopter, he saw where the embassy was in relation to where he wanted to go. Leaving through the back, where the vehicle came and went, was his answer.

He made it up to the street level without seeing anyone but was stopped by a guard standing at his post near the rear door.

"Where's the toilet?" Whitman asked the guard.

"Back downstairs," the guard said. "By the room Agent Schaffer has put you in."

Whitman nodded. Everyone knew him here. He was Schaffer's guest. He turned back and headed down one flight of stairs and stopped when he was unobserved.

Everyone knew him here, and soon enough, all of the Mexican police would also have his description. It wouldn't take long to travel along the road from the four dead cops to the motel where Whitman's car rental was still parked and where a loud helicopter dropped in at sunrise to pick up three men. The police would trace the car to the rental agency and ultimately get his name. That would lead them to Toronto, the special investigations unit, and ultimately, Spencer, who was just now wandering around the Rosarito Casino and Hotel looking for him. It was a stretch, but within an hour or so,

Whitman believed the Mexican police would pick up Spencer, and after questioning, he would never be heard from again.

A simple text to Spencer wouldn't work.

Whitman pressed his back against the wall of the corridor. And what about Sarah? The authorities knew where she was. They know the woman who has her. It's only a matter of time before they raid that woman's home to take Sarah out.

Without action on Whitman's part, the Mexican authorities would get their man or woman in this case.

He had to stop it.

Whitman grabbed the fire alarm, held it while saying a short prayer, and then pulled it.

Whitman ran for the back exit as the blaring sound resonated throughout the American embassy.

If there were a chance he could steal a car, he would. One with diplomatic plates would work well.

If not, he would venture out on foot. Either way, he'd get Spencer, and together they would find Aaron and Sarah and leave Mexico.

He just hoped he wouldn't fuck this up and leave Mexico in a body bag.

Chapter 45

FBI Special Agent Stacy King slept on the plane while her partner, Special Agent Mary Fitzgerald, didn't. The car that came to McCarran Airport in Las Vegas to pick them up wasn't exactly a car as much as it was a decked-out, black, bulletproof Suburban. Even the driver had the trademark FBI sunglasses.

King slapped her partner's arm. "Mary, wake up."

Fitzgerald stirred beside her. "Huh?"

"Wake up. We're almost here."

Fitzgerald blinked in the Nevada sun. "Where's here?"

"FBI office. Vegas. You want to tell me why we're here?"

"Don't know."

"We're here because we're being reassigned, is why. We fumbled the case. Sarah Roberts got involved. After all Sarah's done for the bureau over the years, they've handed our files over to her."

Fitzgerald wiped her eyes. "Your sarcasm won't win you any favors where we're going. Certain agents applaud Sarah's work."

"Yeah, sure. Applaud the woman. I actually like what she's done, too. But don't fuck with a case we're in the middle of and then get us pulled from it."

The SUV slowed for a traffic light, then turned into the FBI building's parking lot.

"I just hope our reassignment isn't brutal. I'd like to avoid being sent to Alaska or some shit."

Fitzgerald was waking up fast as the SUV came to a stop. "You really think they'd fly us to Vegas to reassign us? What about the Hoover building? Why Vegas?" Fitzgerald opened her door and hopped out. "Let's hear the Special Agent in Charge out. See where it goes."

King shrugged. "Whatever."

They were escorted through the main building, signed in, and taken upstairs to the agent in charge's office.

Samantha Puig, the SAC for Las Vegas, didn't make them wait long. She ushered them into her office, and after the required amount of handshaking and greetings, Puig offered them a beverage and sat behind her desk.

"I've ordered you here for a few reasons."

Here we go, King thought. *The punchline of my career.*

"We have reason to believe there's a device in Las Vegas. We haven't been able to find it. This device is for sale and can cause considerable damage in the wrong hands."

King raised a hand. "Agent Puig, with all due—"

"Sam's fine."

"With all due respect, we were very close to meeting

with people regarding a similar device on a different case. When you pulled us off—"

"Same case."

Agent Puig seemed to enjoy cutting people off in mid-sentence. King would have to be wary of a woman in her position.

"How is it the same case?" Fitzgerald asked.

"Jane Turner has been going to Bulgaria to buy a device. We have reason to believe that device is in Vegas right now."

King cut in. "How are you in possession of our case files that—"

"When the Bulgarians brought the device onto American soil, information was brought to my attention that a transaction would take place in Vegas. We have intel on the Bulgarians entering the U.S. in Los Angeles. Then we lost them." She put her hands together on the top of her desk, interlacing her fingers. "Jane Turner is coming here. We have not been able to locate the device yet. Furthermore, my team discovered your investigation using my clearance to access open cases regarding the Bulgarians. We coordinated efforts and thought it best if you came here to work the case from Vegas." She turned to type something on her computer. "It appears that the Turner family in Mexico has chartered a private jet for a flight from Rosarito to Las Vegas, landing here tomorrow morning at oh-eight-hundred hours." Puig turned back to them. "You are being reassigned geographically to work the case you started here in Vegas. You will see your case to completion from this office. I can think of no one better than the two agents that have been working on this case from the beginning."

King and Fitzgerald exchanged a look.

"I agree," Fitzgerald said. "We'll get started immediately."

"That is all for now. You have until tomorrow morning to be updated on all we have. A team is being assembled to meet Turner's plane in the morning. We will follow her people until the deal occurs, then do what we do best."

Fitzgerald stood. King followed suit.

Puig typed on her computer again.

"Go sleep a few hours," Puig said. "Get cleaned up. I'm sure it's been a long night."

They had been dismissed, but that was okay. Agent King didn't mind Agent Puig after all. She was a no-nonsense kind of woman. But one thing Puig didn't know was that Sarah Roberts was with Jane Turner, and because of that, things could change at the last moment.

With Sarah Roberts, King was worried everything could go to hell with that familiar handbasket before the device was seized and destroyed and all the bad guys swept up and charged accordingly.

Call it a hunch. Call it whatever they wanted. Because Sarah was involved, King was sure things wouldn't go as smoothly as a newly ironed shirt.

No fucking way. Nothing was simple with Sarah.

King was happy to be wrong about being summoned to Vegas. They weren't being reassigned after all. They were being tasked to finish what they had started.

With pleasure.

She couldn't wait to see the look on Sarah's face when this was all over, and the FBI had her in custody.

Chapter 46

Jane had asked for biscuits and tea from her security guards as they continued their discussion of India.

"My marriage was prearranged when I was thirteen," Jane said between bites of an almond cookie. "Since my parents never reported the dozens of rapes I endured as a small child, it wasn't a far stretch to have them basically sell me to a rich family. I was married at thirteen to Vihaan Singh, who at the time was fifty-four."

"What?" That got her. Sarah almost spit the crumbs out of her mouth.

"By your response, I can tell you're not versed in some of the customs of the Indian way of life. It's not all bad, but this is the sad part. My husband was rich and tired of me by the time I was twenty. You see, I wasn't young enough for him anymore."

"I don't know how much more I can take without hitting

the next man I see."

"I know how you feel. India as a whole isn't this way. Not all men are this way, either. Some are kind and gentle. Wouldn't hurt a fly. I have spent my life without the pleasure of such a man, but alas, these are the cards I was dealt."

Sarah found it interesting that she would say not all men were like that, yet she wanted to kill a batch of Indian men at a conference that had nothing directly to do with her pain. Some of those men may be the kind and gentle men she had just referred to. What if they had wives and daughters back home who they protected with their wealth and status? And what about her son, Blair? Wasn't he a kind and gentle soul? How could she say she didn't enjoy being around such a man when she lived with one right downstairs?

"My husband had human traffickers bring him young girls. I call them traffickers because who else deals in the flesh of the young? I was banished to my part of our house in India when he had his visits. But I knew what was going on. Two of the maids on staff told me everything I needed to know." She paused to drink from her tea. Sarah had forgotten all about hers. "When my husband fell ill, we had to come to the States for treatment. He died in Los Angeles."

Nothing in Jane's face evoked sadness. If she was ever affected by her husband's death, she was completely over it now.

"Once he was buried, everything became mine. I sold off his textile business, liquidated everything, and moved here where expenses are low, and I could live in peace, surrounded by men still, but men who were paid to protect me, not violate me."

Sarah wondered how she had remained sane through her

ordeal, then reminded herself she was talking to a sociopath, a woman made psycho by her environment in formidable years.

Jane got to her feet and walked to the dresser, where a paperback novel sat. She flipped through the pages.

"You ever read Greg Iles?" she asked.

"A couple of them."

"This is my favorite. *Sleep No More.*"

"Haven't read that one."

"If you get the chance, do it. You'll love it." She set the book down and faced Sarah, her eyes glistening. "You said you'd help me earlier. Is that still your intention?"

Sarah got to her feet, much steadier now as she'd eaten and had a few caffeine-filled beverages.

"I will help you get the device and then place it to detonate and take as many Indian men to hell, as you put it, as we can. That is what I will do." She stared at Jane, her eyes unwavering.

She had to convince her she was telling the truth. Otherwise, Jane wouldn't take her to the deal in Vegas. Without Sarah being at the deal, she couldn't stop Jane from killing so many innocent people.

Sarah was in this house, in this family's life, to stop a terrorist act on American soil. She knew that now and a part of her thanked Vivian for not telling her the whole story in this case. Getting to Jane, and having her trust Sarah through the withdrawal process, allowed Sarah to be a part of the team. She was hard-pressed to see another way to be in this exact spot in time, with this window of opportunity closing quickly if Vivian hadn't done it the way she had.

"Good," Jane said as she started for the door. "Our plane

leaves in the morning. We fly to Las Vegas, make the deal with the Bulgarians, and plant the bomb." She stopped by the door and placed a hand on it. "I have a booth reserved in the heart of the Sands Expo. We will set up our law enforcement booth. The bomb will be placed under the front table. I will tell you more as it becomes available."

Sarah was grateful for the break in the speech. Leaving her to rest and maybe talk to Vivian would allow her to prepare a plan. She needed more to go on, and she needed to know she would come out of this in one piece.

The door clicked without Jane asking for it to open. The lanky black-belt-looking guy stepped in and nearly bumped into Jane.

"Emergency. We need to leave. I have the pilot in the chopper. He's getting it warmed up."

Jane took a step back. "What emergency?"

"Four Mexican police officers were found slaughtered earlier today. The authorities are hunting a man named Parkman and Aaron Stevens," he pointed at Sarah, "her boyfriend. A third man was at the scene, but his name hasn't been released yet."

"What's this got to do with Sarah?" Jane asked, looking from Sarah to Lanky, then back to Sarah. "She's been here for days." Her voice took on an incredulous tone. "Sarah would've had nothing to do with it."

"Our contact at the police station just called. At least twenty officers are coming here to take Sarah back into custody. They think she knows where Aaron and Parkman might be hiding. If they take Sarah alive, that'll be the last anyone sees of her."

Jane gestured wildly with her hand. "C'mon, c'mon,

Sarah. We have to go. He's right. Downstairs to the chopper." She turned to Lanky. "Get my son on that chopper downstairs. He comes with us. Then call the airport. Get the jet ready. We are flying to Vegas now. No delays. Gather your men and meet me on the chopper. Go. Now."

Lanky jumped back through the door. She heard him say from around the corner, "The jet is at the airport, fueled and waiting for our arrival."

As Sarah ran down the hallway with Jane, happy to get out of that guest room for good, Jane shouted over her shoulder, "See, Sarah, not all men are useless. Some of them actually think."

She barely registered what Jane said while processing Lanky's words. Four Mexican police officers were slaughtered. Manhunt for Parkman and Aaron. A third man? Who? Drake Bellamy? And why would they kill cops? What had happened while she was lying in that bed in that ugly guest room?

Had the world gone mad?

Sarah got into the chopper along with Blair and three other men, and they lifted off. From a hundred feet up, she witnessed a long line of cars as they kicked up road dust en route to Jane's mansion.

Sarah shuddered at how close she came to being taken by the Mexican authorities. Vivian must've foreseen this too. Saw that Sarah's only way out of Mexico was with Jane Turner and her family. Saw that Sarah's life depended on just living it with Vivian steering things occasionally.

Maybe the arrangement they had for so many years did work. It didn't mean Sarah couldn't get pissed about it at times, though.

But Vivian understood her sister better than Sarah understood herself. Didn't she?

The helicopter stayed close to the ground as it raced toward the airfield while Sarah's thoughts turned to Aaron and Parkman.

Make it out alive, guys. I don't know what I'd do without you two.

She shut her eyes and whispered a prayer for their safety.

Whether God heard it or not, she was sure Vivian was listening.

Vivian was always listening.

Chapter 47

Ten blocks from the American embassy, Whitman turned the corner of the street that led to the casino where the accident happened on the night Sarah and Aaron checked into the hotel. He had made it out the back of the embassy in the chaos that ensued. The authorities at the embassy had ordered all personnel out of the building while they checked for a fire. While all available personnel searched the inside of the embassy, the rest were outside guarding the fence and gate. The Mexican authorities weren't stupid enough to attack the embassy.

It allowed Whitman to slip by the guard who had just been replaced at the gate. To enter the embassy, an ID was required. Security vetted all visitors. But to leave, you just needed to walk through the turnstile, like at most subway stations.

Whitman was out and walking briskly away from the

embassy long before they learned it was a false alarm. Parkman would be angry, as would that Casper guy. How the hell did a man as powerful as Casper get a name like that?

He slowed as he neared the hotel. A uniformed Mexican police officer stepped from behind a bush by the front entrance of the hotel and casino. They didn't have his description yet unless they traced him to the car rental. That could take several hours. Could he gamble on them, not knowing his face? How much of a risk was it? Could they have traced the car already and his picture distributed to the officers ahead?

Another cop came into view twenty feet ahead. Whitman stopped to pretend to read something on his phone. He waited a few seconds, then looked up as if lost and scanned the street, looking for a street sign. He counted seven uniformed officers and at least three other men who could pass as cops in civilian clothing standing within a block radius of the hotel.

Shit. Now what?

If Spencer was inside, Whitman couldn't risk meeting up with him now. He looked down at his phone and called Spencer's number. It rang until his voicemail picked up.

Shit.

This was trouble. He had thought he could meet with Spencer, fill him in, and decide what to do. Maybe Jane Turner would let him in to see Sarah as he was a friend. He was sure Sarah would want to see him. Then they could decide on how to extract her from Jane's clutches if that's what it took.

But with this many cops, something else was brewing, and meeting with Spencer was off the table. But without him,

Whitman was aimless. What now? Rent another car? They'd see that and track him. Buy a plane ticket out of Mexico? Leave without Aaron or Sarah?

This was bad and getting worse.

He slipped the phone into his pocket and turned back the way he'd come. Two men walked toward him. They came with the physical confidence of police officers. Arms moving at their sides, long, wide strides, purpose-driven. There was nothing he could do but continue walking toward them. Any evasive move now would alert them, not to mention the dozen or so men standing around a block behind him.

They drew closer. He kept his cool and tried not to think about how he was walking. He tried not to look suspicious, even though he felt like he was walking guilty like he'd just stolen a candy bar, and they would see that written all over his face.

The man on the right pulled out a wallet and flipped it open.

"Police," he said from ten feet away. "We need to see your ID."

They moved closer. He kept walking. There was no play here. He alone had murdered those officers. The authorities were hunting him for killing those men. He wouldn't last an hour in police custody. There was no play here. Nothing left but to hurt these men and run.

Run for his life. Something he'd done before. Running was familiar.

"Yeah, sure," Whitman said as he reached into his pocket. "Is there some problem?"

The cops stopped in front of him. "No problem. Just checking ID."

A car's engine revved behind him. It had to be reinforcements. He was doomed if he didn't get out of this now. His stomach flipped, and his knees wobbled, threatening to buckle.

Come on, Whitman. Just do this and move on with life.

He brought his left hand out of his pants pocket and held it up as high as his face, out to the left, staring at it. As he expected, both men looked at his empty hand.

"Look at that," Whitman said. "No ID."

While their attention was diverted, he drove his right fist —a sucker punch—into the guy standing closest. It connected below the jaw on the side of his neck, enough to make him drop to the pavement but not enough to collapse his trachea.

The other guy was already swinging Whitman's way, but Whitman anticipated that reaction. The moment the other man fell, Whitman dropped to his knee and drove his left fist into the other man's groin. Two hits and both men were leveled, writhing in pain.

His knees hurt because he dropped too hard on them, but that was the least of his worries.

The car that had revved a moment ago screeched to a halt almost on top of him. A whistle blew. A man shouted for him to stop even as he clambered to his feet.

"Get in!" the voice yelled.

Spencer.

Whitman hadn't planned on turning around. He had planned on running until he made the corner where he would disappear inside one of the other hotels. But when he heard Spencer's voice, he dove over the car's hood, landed on the other side, and hopped in the passenger seat as at least ten men ran up the block toward them.

"Go!" Whitman shouted.

Over the squeal of car tires, the back window blew out in a shower of glass. Spencer ducked sideways when Whitman lay out on the seat, banging their heads together.

"For fuck's sake," Whitman shouted.

Spencer managed to keep the car on the road even as bullets punched the back bumper and punctured the trunk. Then they were around the corner, and the gunfire stopped. They sat up at the same time.

Whitman rubbed his scalp where it had smacked Spencer's.

"We can't leave Mexico," Whitman said. "Not without Sarah."

"The fuck we can't." Spencer turned to glare at him with bloodshot eyes rimmed in dark circles. "You've fucked a lot of people over, Whitman. Your cover is blown. You're going to need a new name, a new life." Spencer smacked the steering wheel. "Fuck!"

"Wow, great to see you, too. Thanks for the welcome home."

"You've set Mexican and Canadian relations back a century, not to mention the Americans."

"Then don't."

"Don't what?" Spencer shouted.

"Don't mention the Americans."

"Oh, my fuck."

They rode in silence for a moment. Then Whitman said, "Drop me off anywhere. I'll find Aaron and Sarah on my own."

"Oh, no, you won't."

"I'll jump out at the next light then." It was his turn to glare at Spencer. "You don't seem to understand how important this is to me. I am not leaving Mexico without Aaron and Sarah."

"Aaron is a Canadian citizen, isn't he?"

"What's that got to do with anything?"

"When he left your little motel this morning, he came to the casino, too. We picked him up before the Mexicans could get to him. If you weren't so thick-headed, you would let me fill you in on these developments."

Chastised, Whitman turned in his seat and stared out the front windshield, his skull throbbing. "Go on then."

"We have a military flight booked for you and Aaron. You're both going to Las Vegas in about," he pulled his left hand off the steering wheel to glance at his watch, "forty minutes. I am trying to save your life. His too."

"Look, I appreciate what you're doing to save my life. But I don't need saving. Sarah does. So, take Aaron. Get out of Mexico, but I'm staying to find Sarah. A woman named Jane—"

"Turner," Spencer finished for him. "Blah, blah, blah, yeah, yeah, yeah, we know all about Jane Turner and how she bailed Sarah out of the holding cell. Well, guess what? If you want to help Sarah, then you'll be on that plane with Aaron heading to Vegas."

"How is that going to help Sarah?" Whitman almost screamed.

"Because our intel discovered that Jane Turner has a private jet booked to fly out of here in the morning. They've filed a flight plan that takes them to Las Vegas. It is believed that Jane is bringing Sarah to Vegas." Spencer smacked

Whitman in the arm. "You fucker. You should've never come down here. But now we're in this, and if you want to finish it, get on that plane to Vegas, and let's help Sarah stay alive with whatever she's doing."

"How accurate is this intel?" Whitman asked.

"Fuck off, Whitman. You think I'm feeding you a line? After all these years? Really? Fuck off, Whitman. How's that for accurate?"

Whitman remained silent until they got to the airport. He boarded the large Canadian Globemaster without protest. He decided that asking why such a huge Canadian military plane was in Mexico waiting to transport no more than seven people, plus the crew, would only cause Spencer to blow an artery.

Aaron was already on board, seated and waiting for them to take off.

They didn't talk to each other the entire flight to Vegas.

Spencer made himself scarce during the flight.

Whitman surmised it was so he didn't hit him again. When Spencer got this mad, he talked with his fists. It was something new he had started to do over the previous few years.

As Spencer always said to him, *new name, new game*, or some shit like that.

Chapter 48

A FIRE ALARM HAD awakened Parkman. Once the alarm was deemed false and things calmed down, he settled in again, only to be awakened by Casper shaking him.

"What?" Parkman asked. "What's up? I'm trying to sleep here."

"Whitman's gone."

Parkman sat up. "What? You let him go?"

"No. The alarm was his ruse to escape. He took off."

Parkman was awake now. "Then he's as good as dead."

"You're telling me."

"Send someone. Do what you do best. Find him. But let me sleep. I need at least two hours." He dropped back on the mattress and covered his eyes with his forearm.

"You can't sleep," Casper said. He flicked the lights on in the room. "Wake up. Coffee's on."

Parkman stayed where he was, forearm across the bridge

of his nose. "And why the shit can I not sleep?"

"Because we're leaving Mexico."

"And we can't leave in two hours?"

"No."

"Oh, for shit's sake." He swung his legs off the bed and pivoted as he sat up. "Why the hell do we have to leave so soon?" He rubbed his eyes and winced when his wounded arm protested.

"Because Sarah is on the move."

He stopped rubbing his eyes and met Casper's gaze, blinking sleep away. "What?"

Casper walked to the door and stepped into the corridor. "We understand she will be on a private jet heading to Vegas in the morning. We'd like to be there when she lands."

"What about Aaron? Whitman?"

"A Canadian problem. But one I'm pretty sure they're able to handle. Before I came in here, I got a courtesy call from them that they picked up Aaron."

"What? Really?" Parkman closed his eyes and covered his mouth with his hand as relief coursed through him. He opened his eyes and looked heavenward. Sarah was leaving Mexico. Aaron was safe with the Canadians. Maybe things would turn out okay after all. Casper would get him out of Mexico, and Whitman would turn up somewhere. This could all be coming to an end.

"Get ready, Parkman. We're to meet Aaron in Vegas along with two Federal agents running a case we've stepped in the middle of. They're quite angry up there in Vegas, but I can smooth that out. Once Sarah lands in Vegas at seven tomorrow morning, all this trouble goes away, and she and Aaron can finish their vacation on American soil. We will have to offer an official answer to the Mexicans, but once we write everything up, they'll see their men were at fault."

"I hope so."

Casper's footfalls echoed down the corridor as he shouted back, "Five minutes."

"I need toothpicks," Parkman shouted back. "For the plane."

A door closed somewhere down the hall, then silence descended.

Parkman yawned, stretched, and winced at his arm again.

It was a relief to have this all ending so nicely. Maybe they could stay calm for a while and take it easy. Maybe Sarah would actually take a vacation.

She may need a break, but he needed one for sure.

Hanging out with Aaron was dangerous. He was just happy Aaron was a terrible shot with that gun.

Or a good shot, depending on how he looked at it.

Chapter 49

THEY HAD TAKEN OFF without incident. Sarah felt like herself again as Jane Turner's private jet soared above the clouds en route to Vegas. Blair sat in a separate part of the plane as ordered by his mother.

In the brief moment Sarah saw Blair, he looked sick. His face appeared gaunt. The shallow expression, lack of smile, and pale complexion looked like he had some kind of disease. But Jane assured Sarah her forlorn son was sad because a *friend* of his—she had used air quotes when referring to Hank Olsen—was still in the hospital and would be for at least another month. In Blair's presence, Jane had said the word "men" sarcastically and then rolled her eyes. Sarah wanted to peck out those eyes with needle-nose pliers for the pain she caused her son. There should be parenting courses for people like Jane to educate them on the virtues of self-esteem and confidence building.

Once the jet had leveled off at thirty-thousand feet, Jane wanted to talk. In her words, she wanted to bring Sarah up to speed. Although this talk took on more of the planning stages and details of the device's purchase, she was now calling a radiological dispersal device or an RDD.

"What's the difference between that and a dirty bomb?" Sarah asked, not out of interest alone. She needed to know as much as she could about it so she could be able to handle the device, if it were radioactive, with limited exposure to herself.

A woman dressed as a flight attendant had served them wine five minutes ago. A smooth Chilean Syrah with a dark berry aftertaste. Sarah cleansed her palate quickly to calm her shaking hands. This job was much more delicate and nerve-wracking than a bunch of men with guns. This job could get her killed or, worse, poisoned with radiation.

"Since I can't get my hands on enriched uranium or plutonium, using a conventional explosive with radioactive materials is the next best thing. So, yes, an RDD is essentially a dirty bomb." Jane spoke of these chemicals like she might discuss a rare mushroom or tomato she was adding to a salad.

Sarah blinked a couple of times. She tugged at an earlobe, then dropped her hand to her pants and wiped the palm to rid it of sweat. What were the odds that she would be in this rich woman's presence discussing the illegal arms deal of former Soviet Union weaponry?

Am I in over my head, Vivian?

The small private jet shook with turbulence. It dropped a few feet, then shook again. By the sound of the engines, the pilot increased their speed.

"Seatbelts, please," came over the small speakers above their heads.

Sarah held her wine glass tight so nothing spilled. Jane wasn't so lucky. She hadn't touched hers since it was delivered, and red wine leaked over the rim of the glass and onto the small tray in front of her.

All the color had left Jane's face when the plane dropped and shook. She had grabbed the armrests and dug her nails in. Her bottom lip trembled, a red oasis on an otherwise ashen face.

It wasn't just a fear of flying. Sarah gathered Jane Turner had an extreme fear of death. Maybe even an irrational fear, like a phobia.

"You okay?" Sarah asked.

"Yes," Jane stammered.

"Fear of flying?"

"Not really. I fly quite a bit. When things are smooth, I could fly all day. It's more a fear of crashing." Her smile was clipped, then it waned to tight lips, pulled back by anxiety.

Deathly afraid of death. Jane wasn't going to Las Vegas to die. She was going to Las Vegas to live. Once she dealt this blow to the Indian community, Jane would feel better, and her load lightened some.

So who was set to deliver the bomb, then?

Jane giggled to herself. "You know what I find quite amusing?"

"No." Sarah turned her attention to the blue sky outside the window to think. Or wait for Vivian to offer answers. "Can't say that I do."

"They actually call this kind of weapon a WMD."

Sarah looked at Jane, her mouth hanging open until she

found the words. "A Weapon of Mass Destruction?"

"No. A Weapon of Mass *Disruption*. Isn't that hilarious?"

The white blanket of clouds crawled by below the plane when Sarah peered outside to avoid looking at Jane. "Yes, hilarious. A ball of utter laughter."

"I've arranged to purchase this thing from a former military intelligence colonel out of Sliven, Bulgaria."

"How would you meet someone like that?"

"Money. Status. The right questions. The right people. I've traveled to Bulgaria a few times. Set things up. Money's sitting in Britain to pay for it. A quick transfer, and it's all mine."

"Clever."

"The man hid these devices in various places. The one I'm buying was actually hidden in his mother's garden. Imagine that. Right beside her, potatoes or cabbage. Funny, eh?"

Sarah took a large gulp of wine as she contemplated the fate of mankind if there were people out there willing to steal and sell these kinds of bombs to the highest bidder. Money controlled the world, and that was the bottom line. Because Jane had money, she was able to purchase this device and cause her little piece of mayhem. Sarah had recently read somewhere that one percent of the world owned and controlled about half of the world's wealth.

The scales had steeped too high in one direction, and now there were people like Jane. Not a woman who came into money, but a *deranged* woman who came into money. Sure, Sarah would help her buy the bomb so it wouldn't disappear into the hands of some other lunatic. But she wouldn't help her detonate it. Sarah planned on taking off with the device and the money. Jane thought Sarah was a willing member of her security team. But Sarah, for the greater good, had no problem being a Judas.

"Why a weapon of mass disruption?" Sarah asked. She held her glass up to discover it was empty. Jane rang a button, and the flight attendant entered their part of the plane.

"More wine," Jane ordered.

The woman nodded and backed out of the door she had just emerged from.

"Disruption because of the economic ramifications. The social unrest and the widespread fear. It disrupts a lot of people, their lives, and kind of fucks with their good day. Before I came along, the Indian lawmakers were happy people. They'll be happy *shiny* people when I'm done with them."

Sarah caught Jane looking at her. She offered Jane a smile.

Jane continued, "These devices are meant to contaminate the area where they are detonated. Almost like chemical warfare does. Radiation poisoning is especially scary because you can't see or feel it."

"Will this device have a lot of radiation?"

"I'm led to believe it will. Oozing out from its very core."

"How about getting close to it? Dangerous? I mean, aren't we supposed to be setting up a booth at the conference right on top of this thing?"

"It's only dangerous for those who don't die once it's detonated. I won't care either way." Jane shrugged and stared into her wine glass. Her eyes moved up, then down, before she took another sip.

What was she thinking? Her last line, *I won't care, either way* didn't sound authentic. Did she have a plan to detonate the device remotely? Or send someone else in with the bomb? Blair? Her only son? One of her security guards?

Hey, sis, I could use some help here.

Nothing was forthcoming.

Jane pulled her iPad from the table beside her and turned it on.

"I have a quote to read from former Attorney General John Ashcroft." She touched an icon and opened a page. "He said on June 10, 2002, and I quote, 'A radioactive dirty bomb spreads radioactive material that is highly toxic to humans and can cause mass death and injury.' End quote. That's something." Jane shook her head as if she was amazed at Ashcroft's wisdom. She met Sarah's eyes and stared into her. "I wanted another Pripyat but can't have something that big after all."

"Pripyat?"

"The town near the Chernobyl reactor in northern Ukraine. You know, just before it was evacuated, fifty-thousand people lived there. Now the city's abandoned, empty, dead."

That happened in April 1986, three years before Sarah was born. Sarah's school had covered it. The media talked about it. The accident. The fallout. She had forgotten the name of the nearby city, but Jane hadn't. In fact, Jane Turner wanted to recreate that event. Sarah was sure Jane wanted to recreate that event *without* the evacuation of the residents. And she wanted to do it on Indian soil.

It occurred to her that this was a trial run, a test. What happened in Vegas stayed in Vegas, but something told Sarah that Jane Turner would run with the information and make a play against India itself soon. She had the money, the desire, and the cunning insanity.

A question rose in Sarah's mind. One she had asked herself in the past. Would she have killed Hitler knowing what he was going to do? Her answer was always a resounding yes. That's who she was, what she was all about. Stopping the villain before the villain hurt or maimed the innocent.

Should she kill Jane right now? End this here? Stop the detonation at the source?

The answer was no in this case. Or, more appropriately, not yet.

Sarah needed to be a part of the purchase of the weapon. Then she could take action against Jane and call in the proper authorities to deal with the sellers and the weapon, too.

She would be everyone's Judas. Only no one would ever suspect her because she was only along for the ride. She was supposed to be Jane's spirit guide, her protector, the one assigned to keep her alive. Wouldn't Jane be surprised when she discovered that Sarah was the one who was most likely to kill her? What was one death, Jane's, compared to dozens or even hundreds?

The flight attendant returned with a cart on wheels and a bottle of red wine. She poured them each a glass and retreated through the door to the area where Blair was. How much did he know? Was he privy to what his mother was doing?

The captain came over the speakers to announce he was starting their descent into Vegas. They would be landing within twenty minutes. Local time was 20:00hrs.

"We're twelve hours early," Jane said. "That'll give us a chance to gamble a little and get a good night's sleep. I have us booked into a motel off the strip tonight, but we check into the Venetian ahead of the conference tomorrow afternoon." She tapped Sarah's leg. "Right after we buy ourselves a little disruption device."

The glint in Jane's eye revealed a madness heretofore unseen by Sarah. A shiver oozed down her back. Jane's eyes widened briefly before she drank the rest of her wine in one go.

Definitely insane. That made her unpredictable.

Unpredictable to Sarah, but not Vivian.

Right, sis? You're still with me, right?

There was no answer.

Chapter 50

Las Vegas's SAC for the FBI, Samantha Puig, had summoned Agents King and Fitzgerald to her office for 07:00hrs. Rested, filled with coffee, and ready for the challenging day ahead, King led the way down the hall to Puig's office and shoved the door open without knocking.

The office was filled with people. At first, she thought she had entered the wrong room as she had only been here once before, yesterday when they first arrived in Vegas. Her partner, Fitzgerald, came in behind her and whispered this was the right place. She had to have read the confusion on King's face.

"Good morning," Agent Puig stepped out from behind her desk. "Agents King, Fitzgerald, I'd like you to meet Special Agent Buck Schaffer. He's running point on this operation."

King counted eight people in the crowded office and

instantly thought there were too many cooks in the kitchen. Aaron, Sarah Roberts's boyfriend, and Parkman were both here.

How come they're here? In the SAC's office? In Las Vegas?

King couldn't make sense of any of this.

A tall, well-built man with white hair stepped forward, his hand extended. "Call me Casper. Everyone does." He shook King's hand, then Fitzgerald's.

"What is this all about?" Fitzgerald asked.

"First, I'll go around the room and introduce everyone and explain why they're here." Puig moved into the center of the office as the crowd parted for her. "It'll give you both a better understanding of what's going on."

Fitzgerald nodded. King followed suit.

"I think you've met Aaron and Parkman." Puig glanced back at King. "In Mexico. Correct?"

"Yes. The police station."

"This man's name is John Whitman. He has known Sarah Roberts for several years and knows how she thinks." Puig moved on, using her hand to gesture at each person in turn. "This is Detective Spencer of the Toronto Police Department, Whitman's handler. Next, the man by the window is Detective Bruce Collins of the Las Vegas Police Department and his partner, Detective Mara Munro. They both worked on a loan shark case with Sarah Roberts a few years back in Vegas. They established a working trust, a bond. If she won't listen to Whitman or Aaron or Parkman, Collins here has a thing or two to say that'll make Sarah listen. He's the father of her dead cousin, Russell Anderson."

"Wow," was all King could utter.

"In this room, we have the most amount of people we could get on short notice that could bring this deal with the Bulgarians to a close and bring Sarah in."

"You said something about running point," Fitzgerald said. "I thought this was our case."

"Not anymore. Your files were given to Agent Schaffer when he arrived. He knows Sarah as well as anyone, having worked with her in Toronto, Amsterdam, Athens, and just recently in Mexico to destroy the Enzo Cartel. I'm not sure anyone else is needed between Schaffer, Aaron, and Parkman. Although when I sent the Written Memoranda of Understanding to the Las Vegas Police Department for their cooperation in this matter, Detective Collins and Munro came up in the system as having worked with Sarah. That's why they're here. In an observation capacity." Puig moved in front of King, glanced over her shoulder at Fitzgerald, then met King's eyes. "We aren't going to have a problem with any of this, are we?"

"No," King said. She wanted to offer a few expletives but thought it better to hold her tongue.

"Of course not," Fitzgerald added.

Puig turned away and moved behind her desk, where she took a seat. "The FBI Joint Terrorism Task Force is already at the airport waiting for Jane Turner's plane to land in forty-five minutes." She nodded at Agent Schaffer. "Get whoever you're taking and get out there as soon as possible. We are to take Jane Turner and Sarah Roberts into custody immediately. I want to know everything we can get on who they're meeting, when and where, and what Jane intends on purchasing with the money she transferred to Britain."

Everyone filed out of the office, walking past King's

stunned face. What the hell just happened? Her whole case, everything they had worked on, was being handed over to the motley crew in front of her. In all her time as an FBI agent, this had never happened.

"Agent King," the man named after a ghost shouted from behind her. "Coming?"

King blinked and looked around. The office had emptied except for Agent Puig, who sat behind her desk writing something down. The man with the white hair gestured for her to follow.

She put one foot in front of the other because that was her job. She had to see this through until the end. It would be a pleasure to arrest Turner and Roberts. She had been worried Sarah would fuck things up, but now she could arrest her. Stop her in her tracks. Maybe they'd even lay a few charges Sarah's way. Teach her to not fuck with FBI investigations.

That was the answer. In a world gone mad, where FBI cases were handed out to civilians, and local cops were offered ride-a-longs, making a charge stick to Sarah Roberts would make things right again.

At least for Agent King, it would.

Chapter 51

Sarah woke and felt more rested than she had felt in weeks. Ever since the Enzo Cartel debacle, she had been going non-stop. Her thoughts turned to Aaron. The time away had allowed her to heal, get rested, and think about their relationship. Perhaps she could look at the time at Jane's house as her mini vacation. Time off from running Vivian's errands.

Aaron had been there since the Rapturites had come after Sarah in Toronto all those years ago. His unwavering support was only equaled by Parkman's, who had been her confidante for much longer. Since the Armond Stuart days. Budapest and Italy. Had it really been five years since she met Parkman, the cop who idolized her, tracked her through the media, and trusted her when other cops wouldn't? She never had a problem with Parkman. Never had to worry if she lied to him to get him out of trouble or steer him in a direction he needed to go. He just trusted her. Believed in her.

With Aaron, that was a different story. He was more sensitive than Parkman and attached to her at a different emotional level. A more intimate one. She figured that meant a different level of trust, too.

Maybe she needed a truce with Aaron. Perhaps a pact. Something similar to what others would call a commitment, but theirs would be different in nature. Theirs would be part relationship, part arrangement. When this was all over, she would sit him down, and they would discuss it, navigate the pitfalls of their *arrangement* and make sure it was good for the both of them.

Just when he thought he was losing her, she would return with a pact and strengthen their relationship. She smiled as she stared at the ceiling of her Vegas motel room. Aaron would love it. Something he could sink his teeth into.

Someone knocked on her door.

"Time to move," a man's voice said. "You ready?"

"No."

"Ten minutes. No more." Jane's guard stomped away.

"Fuck you and your horse."

Last night, after checking in, Jane had sent her guards shopping with a list while wine was sent to her room. Jane had a room of her own with her guards, and Blair was in another room. Blair and Sarah had not said one word to each other this entire trip, mostly because they hadn't had a chance and partly because he looked like a bag of walking depression.

The guards had ripped the motel's phone from the wall, and Jane had left one man at Sarah's door. Had she wanted to, there were ways to escape, but she didn't want to. This had become a mission. A mission she was prepared to see through to the end because there was no way she could ever allow Jane to use that dirty bomb in the convention center.

After shopping last night, the guards returned with clothes that fit her. Tight black pants and a black T-shirt. Over that, Jane told Sarah to wear the Kevlar vest she had sent over to her room half an hour ago. The guard stated that Jane wouldn't stand to have anything happen to Sarah, so the vest was mandatory.

Where they got such a heavy-duty vest on such short notice amazed her. It was probably prearranged. And it was Vegas. With the right amount of money, many things could be had. Evidently, even weapons of mass disruption.

Sarah was to carry no weapons. No guns, no knives. She was a spiritual advisor only. According to Jane, if Sarah were going to die, her sister would stop it, thereby stopping Jane's death as they would be together. Again, that intense fear of death reared its ugly Reaper's head. The guards would handle the weapons and security side of things. Sarah was fine with that, but she had yet to devise a plan to secure the weapon once it was purchased from the Bulgarians and delivered. And how would she detain Jane Turner for the authorities?

With or without a plan, she needed to move forward. Walking away now was not an option.

She dressed, slid the Kevlar over her T-shirt, then slipped a light sweater over the bullet-proof vest. The Kevlar was much heavier than she expected. On each side, she clamped the base of the Kevlar vest together with electronic clips of some kind. A red light blinked, then changed to green.

She was ready.

Before leaving the room, she looked back at the bedside

table's clock. The red digits said it was almost eight in the morning. They were supposed to meet the Bulgarians at nine, check into the Venetian hotel by noon and start setting up the booth at the Expo center soon after that, with a detonation time set for four that afternoon just when the conference hall began to fill for the first evening's guests.

Sarah would have no part in any of that. She planned to make the nine o'clock meeting with the Bulgarians. Then the device, Jane Turner, and, if possible, the Bulgarians would be delivered to the Las Vegas Police Department. Her job would be done. Nice and easy.

Maybe Detective Collins was still in Vegas. They could go for dinner. She could offer her sympathy for the loss of his son, Russell, who gave his life to Sarah on top of that hotel in Toronto many years ago.

So many years, so many people dead. And what of Drake Bellamy, back from the dead? Where was he? In Mexico still?

Sarah held the doorknob and wondered how her life had gotten so messed up. How many people had come and gone? Was it all worth it? Could she add up the lives she saved and justify her actions?

The guard knocked on the door. Her hand was clenched on the knob. She let out a small shriek and jumped at least two feet back.

"Shitty asses," she bellowed before she could stop herself.

"Let's go," the guard shouted through the cheap wooden door.

"Coming," she shouted back. "Fuck," she added under her breath.

Lives saved? Add them up? Yes, she could because the ones that died deserved to die. Something she used to say years ago came back to her. 'Some people *should* die.' It made the world a better place.

Jane Turner's death? The Bulgarian's death? Or innocent lives at the trade show later today?

Easy answer.

She tightened her grip on the door to the motel room, ripped the door open, and stepped out into Las Vegas's morning sun a new woman. Revitalized, rejuvenated, rested, and ready. Sarah Roberts was prepared to fight. Even if stopping Jane meant losing her own life, it would be a noble end. Jane had to be stopped at all costs. It was the way of things. The order of things. It seemed death was a way of life for Sarah, and one more would make her life easier.

Sarah slammed the door behind her. She didn't look back as she crossed the broken pavement on her way to the waiting SUV. She didn't look back because she didn't want to give extra attention to the room.

Inside her room, hidden under the bedsheets, was a note for the person assigned to clean the room. A note for that person to contact the police. Call Detective Collins with the Las Vegas Police Department with a message.

Sarah Roberts is in town and would love to see him later at the International Lawmakers Conference at the Venetian Hotel, Sands Expo. The note said to bring his friends but to be there before four in the afternoon.

It was a matter of life and death.

Chapter 52

CASPER STOOD IN FRONT of the twelve men and women who made up the tactical team of the FBI's Joint Terrorist Task Force near a gate of the McCarran Airport. Jane Turner's plane was supposed to pull in and deplane twenty feet from its current position. Neither pilot nor passenger would see them as all team members were assembled behind a large food service truck.

Parkman stood at the back of the team and observed as Casper gave them orders. Jane was expected to have armed security guards with her. She did not currently pose a threat. Neither did the woman, Sarah Roberts, who was reportedly traveling with her.

Casper continued talking to his assembled team as Parkman scanned the faces of each member. They were strong, lean, armed to the teeth, and ready to storm the plane upon its arrival. All he wanted was Sarah to be back safe.

Then they could walk away from this and let the authorities handle it.

The latest development obviously perturbed the original two detectives he had met in Mexico. The case they had worked so hard on slipped through their fingers, and they were forced to be bystanders at their own show. King and Fitzgerald had been added to the JTTF team but were not to take the lead on the raid. Both agents were here to come in last to identify Jane Turner and her son, Blair Turner.

Aaron, Detective Collins, and his partner, Munro, Whitman, and Spencer, were one level above with the SAC, Samantha Puig, watching from an observation deck where they could see the entire gate and the team hidden behind the service vehicle.

Casper looked at his watch. He spoke into a lapel mic that relayed everything he said to the team, Parkman included.

"Has the tower picked them up yet? It's almost eight."

"Nothing yet," Puig said from somewhere above them.

"Okay, team. Be ready. Spread out. No deadly force unless they initiate. Jane Turner, her son, Blair Turner, and Sarah Roberts will be taken into custody unharmed." He stopped to meet their eyes. "Get into position and hold there. Wait for further instructions."

The team slipped away to take prearranged hiding positions. Casper moved closer to Parkman. He unclipped his mic so only Parkman could hear him.

"I got a bad feeling about this."

"Me too," Parkman said.

"What if the FBI were wrong, and Sarah's still in Mexico? We can't help her from here."

"I know. I thought of that."

Parkman turned his gaze skyward as the morning sun crept higher. A WestJet passenger airline was coming in for a landing. Lined up behind it was another one, lights blinking upon approach. No sign of a smaller private jet.

"What now?" Parkman asked.

Casper checked his watch again. "It's a minute to eight." He clipped his mic back on. "Agent Puig?"

"Here."

"Anything?"

"Nothing."

"Okay, either they're not coming, already here, or late."

"I'll look into it."

Casper unclipped his mic. "Parkman, I don't like this at all. Something tells me they're already here."

Parkman watched as the WestJet touched down. His mind wandered to Sarah. Wherever she was, she had to be on the job. For Jane Turner to garner this much FBI attention and to have Sarah reportedly with her on a private jet sounded like Sarah was back to work. Lying to Aaron back at their hotel wasn't about buying drugs as much as it was about not telling him what she was up to.

"She lied to Aaron," he said.

Casper fiddled with something on his JTTF uniform. "Sarah did?"

"Yeah. Back at the Mexican hotel. So she could leave the building without him knowing about it, she had him buy Advil from the hotel's little store. We haven't seen her since."

"And?"

"In my opinion, I suspect she did that because if she told him she was working something for Vivian that included the kind of people Jane Turner had gotten herself mixed up with, he would have strongly fought against it. Or asked to help her. It seems Sarah needed to do this one on her own."

"Okay. I'm listening. What's next for Sarah? Where is she going with this? Based on that, is she still in Mexico or already here?"

Parkman faced him. "The deal is to take place in Vegas, right?"

Casper nodded.

"Then where do you think she is?"

His eyes gave him away. He knew she was already in Vegas. He also knew that wasn't good. Without surveillance of any kind, Sarah was on her own with highly trained professional smugglers of illegal arms.

He clipped his mic back in, but before he could say anything, Agent Puig came in loud and clear to all the earpieces on the ground.

"I've just been informed that Jane Turner's private jet landed last night at twenty-hundred hours. That's 8:00 p.m. and not 8:00 a.m." She paused for a moment. "Everyone leave your post and meet me at the FBI vehicles on the south side."

Casper ripped his earpiece out. "It was either a mistake with their intel, which I will look into, or Turner had the flight plan filed for arrival this morning and came in last night in case someone was waiting for her." He grabbed Parkman's shoulders. "I'm afraid for Sarah. If this Turner woman is good enough to thwart the FBI and whoever else is watching her, then Sarah is in trouble."

"That's what I'm afraid of." Parkman started for the FBI vehicles. "That's what I'm afraid of, Casper."

Chapter 53

THEY DROVE NORTH OF the city in a stretch SUV, Sarah and Jane in the rear, Blair and Jane's guards in the seats near the front. The back was separated by a Plexiglas partition leaving Sarah and Jane alone.

"Aren't you afraid this vehicle will attract too much attention?" Sarah asked.

Jane sneered. "This is Vegas, Sarah. Stretch SUVs are everywhere. We can get in and out without trouble in this thing. And there's lots of room for my little device."

Sarah rested her head back and looked out the window. Her stomach, weighted down with dread, hadn't induced any thoughts of eating yet today. Everyone had their bulletproof vests on. Everyone was ready for whatever happened, but she wasn't.

No one could know she had left Mexico, so no one knew where she was. She could only imagine the kind of people they were headed to meet. Ex-Russian military types. Black market arms dealers. Smugglers. She'd never met these kinds of men. And she was sure Jane had no idea of the kind of men she was doing business with. Without Vivian—who was staying quiet—Sarah was lost.

"How much longer?" Jane asked the driver through a slot in the smoked-out Plexiglas partition.

Lanky opened his mouth to the small opening and said, "Five minutes."

Jane leaned back in her seat and adjusted her vest under her blouse. For some reason, her Kevlar vest looked smaller than Sarah's.

"What do you want me to do?" Sarah asked.

"You've done enough. Just being here reassures me I'm going to survive this. And don't worry. Your money is in the trunk of this vehicle. All one million in cash. When we're done, you walk away with the suitcase." A sly smile crossed her lips. "I changed my mind about half the money upfront and half later since it all ends today."

Ignoring her reference to the money, Sarah asked, "What about the meeting? You want me to wait in the SUV?"

Jane snapped her head to look at Sarah. "Are you kidding? For one million dollars? I want you up front and center."

"Front and center?"

"Right beside me. Attached at my hip. I believe in you, Sarah. If bullets are to fly, Vivian will stop this somehow."

If you only knew.

"Why are you going to this meeting? Why not send your men? You don't think this is too dangerous for you?"

"Sending my men was the original plan. But Boris

refused. He met me in Europe and will only deal with me."

Something sounded off. "*Only* you? Meaning, come alone? Was that what he instructed?"

"Yeah. But that doesn't matter. He knows me. I have security. I'm sure he does, too. He's a reasonable man."

The SUV slowed to pull off the two-lane highway. "How many times did you go to Bulgaria?"

"Just a couple. Why?" Jane's hands were shaking, and she had an uncontrollable twitch under her right eye.

"And you know this Boris that well?"

"It's not that I *know* him, but more I know the kind of man he is."

Oh shit.

"We're pulling in now," Lanky shouted back.

From the front of the vehicle, the sound of ejected magazines, guns checked, and ammo confirmed floated back to them.

"Don't worry so much, Sarah. I've got three extremely well-trained men in this vehicle. They know the score, and if things get bad, they'll settle it."

"It's not them I'm worried about," she muttered.

The SUV slowed as the driver eased close to a white building. Sarah dropped lower in her seat to look out the window on Jane's side of the vehicle.

A broken down, faded-white church, weathered by the sun, entire chunks of siding missing, sat in the middle of nowhere. A flat area to the left offered a glimpse of the parking lot, now covered in weeds and broken bits of concrete. It didn't look like anyone had come here to worship since the 1970s, at least.

The SUV stopped. Thick tire tracks had recently made a

path in the dry sandy dirt, heading toward the back of the church.

"Lanky, you stay in the vehicle. Protect the driver. Leave it running if we need to leave quickly. The rest of you, stay with me as we walk to the back of the church. Keep your weapons as well hidden as possible. Understood." There were nods up front. "Remember, I'm supposed to be alone, and there aren't supposed to be any weapons. Just stay alert."

Something wasn't right. Why park up here? Why not drive around the church, and meet Boris on the other side where he was? This looked too much like they were going to sneak up on Boris.

And why did she call her guard Lanky?

Jane reached for the door, but Sarah grabbed her forearm.

"Lanky? That's his name?"

Jane frowned. "We don't use their given names. He's tall and lanky, so that's what we call him."

Sarah let go of her arm. Jane opened her door. "You coming, Sarah?"

Sarah hopped out into the baking desert sun. It hit her like a wall of heat.

Lanky?

She couldn't believe the name she had been using internally was his name all along. Unless Vivian had something to do with that. Could Sarah just know things now? Intuitively?

She walked around the vehicle in a bit of a daze. The two guards separated, one standing in front, one taking up the rear.

This looked ridiculous. Professional military men would pick these guys off as soon as they saw they were armed.

They would take out the driver, kill Blair and Sarah, wait for Jane to transfer the funds, and then kill her and disappear back to Bulgaria or wherever they came from. Jane was walking in blind, and so was Sarah.

Unless that was what Jane wanted. Was this meant as a slaughter? These men knew her plan. Once it was done and the device had been detonated in the conference hall, these men would be loose ends. Maybe that's what this was all about after all.

Was that thought intuitive? Could she trust it as psychic?

No, this was a deal, and she was being paranoid. Her paranoia was fueled by fear as she had no weapon and no idea the kind of men they were about to meet.

With Jane in the middle and Sarah and Blair flanking her, the five of them moved along the left side of the church, their feet crunching the dusty gravel underfoot. The building probably served a lot of the faithful over the years, but it was abandoned long ago, gone to weed. The siding was withered and broken in spots. In one section, the roof sagged and appeared ready to collapse.

They continued along the side of the church to the rear of the building as Vivian swooped into her consciousness. It was so sudden Sarah jerked and ducked down but stayed upright.

"You okay?" Jane asked. "Something troubling you?"

The men surrounding them had slowed at Jane's voice.

"No. Nothing."

Sarah, Vivian whispered.

Sarah waited for more.

Drop to your knees.

Sarah dropped, kicking up small plumes of dust from

under her kneecaps. Jane stopped walking and looked back. Understanding dawned on her face, and she dropped.

"What is it?" Jane whispered.

Blair started to get down. The guards brought their weapons out from hiding and aimed them at nothing.

Sarah shrugged. "Don't know. My sister told me to get down—"

A weapon fired. Jane jerked and shrieked, her hands going to cover her mouth.

The man who guarded their rear teetered on his feet, then fell, his throat a red mess of tissue where part of his spine showed through.

Jane wrapped an arm around Sarah's shoulders and trembled beside her. Blair lay out flat on the dirt floor and covered his head with his hands.

The guard at the front of their group bent at the waist and ran for the wall for cover but was shot before he made it. Jane let out a yip at the sound of the bullet impacting bone.

The guard's jaw dislocated as the bullet hit him and entered his head. Blood shot from the exit wound. His glassy eyes stared off into space as he dropped to his knees, let go of his gun, then fell face-first into the gravel. In a grotesque manner, something out of a horror movie, the guard's dislocated jaw was forced sideways from the pressure of his face hitting the ground. Now his bottom teeth glistened with saliva in the sun where his cheek would normally have been.

"Don't look," Sarah whispered, feeling every bit the girl she had been before the heroin. She might die today, but she finally felt good again. This was where she felt at home. The adrenaline rush a BASE jumper got was akin to the rush she encountered when dealing with situations like these.

She had to think. She had to deal with it. Feel the rush. Ride that wave. All the while knowing she wouldn't die because she had Vivian. It was like an unfair advantage, but one she wasn't willing to part with.

Tentatively, she got to her feet. Something was running on the other side of the church. A pitter-patter of paws from some kind of animal. Whatever it was, it didn't sound human.

Seconds later, her suspicions were confirmed as a huge King Shepherd came into view, its fangs bared, a low guttural growl emitting from its throat.

More pattering as another dog came around the front of the church. In moments, they were surrounded by two huge dogs that looked like they hadn't eaten in days.

"What's happening?" Jane yelled.

Sarah hushed her as she watched the dogs. Testing their resolve, she took a step back toward the fallen guard. He had an unused weapon. She needed something to defend herself with if either of the dogs decided they wanted a meal.

When she was two steps from the guard's weapon, the horn from their SUV sounded. Sarah looked that way. A man stepped into view behind the shepherd.

"Boris?" Jane whispered. It was like she couldn't find her voice. She lowered her head, cleared her throat, then looked back up and tried again. "Boris?" This time it was much louder.

"Miss Turner," Boris said, his Russian accent evident. "What are you doing on the ground?"

"You shot my men—"

There was something unfamiliar in Jane's voice. She wasn't shocked. She was *acting* shocked. This was set up to remove her men, as Sarah had suspected. Was she set to be killed, too?

"Correction, Jane. You killed your men. I told you to come alone. That I would kill anyone who carried a weapon."

Bullshit excuse.

She wanted to kick Jane until she was a broken pile of pulp. Make her bleed for what she did to the men who were paid to protect her.

Boris stepped closer. "You changed the deal by coming with your own security. I don't like when the deal's changed. Means you're nervous. Means you might talk to the authorities."

"No, no," Jane pleaded as she tried to get to her feet.

"With this performance, you should audition for Broadway," Sarah whispered.

Blair looked up but put his head back down like he wanted to bury his head in the dirt. Jane's face didn't register that Sarah had spoken.

"Please, no." Jane wobbled on her feet but stayed up. "I need this deal to go through."

"I had a feeling you'd say that."

The dog behind them barked. Sarah looked over her shoulder, the heat making it hard to breathe with the thick vest covering her chest. Four heavily armed men now stood behind that dog. Thankfully they had put a leash on the dog's collar.

If only they had a muzzle.

"Come, join me." Boris beckoned with a wave of his hand. "All three of you."

Sarah waited until Blair got to his feet. Then as a trio, they started back the way they had just come, leaving the two guards to rot in the Nevada sun. Blair didn't look good. He was so white, his eyes half-lidded, that he looked like he was about to pass out at any moment. Jane seemed to be doing better than Blair. This was routine. This was her plan. Everything was working out fabulously for Jane.

Sarah wished she was in a thousand different places than by this abandoned church, about to be killed because Jane was an insane lunatic.

As their stretch SUV came into sight, so did Lanky's body. Jane stopped walking when she saw Lanky. From twenty feet away, Lanky's throat was visible. It had been cut. And not just cut, sliced open. An entire chunk was missing. His eyes were wide open like he tried to scream through them as his life ebbed from the wound in his neck. A cloth dangled from his mouth to keep him quiet while he died. The driver had suffered a similar fate; only his neck wound wasn't as macabre. All of the SUV's doors were wide open, like an invitation to jump in and drive away, although that probably wasn't what would happen.

What was the Bulgarian's play here? Kill everyone and not make a deal? Weren't they trying to sell something? Make money from that sale? Or were they only interested in killing people? Was this mercenary even the Bulgarian, or just a hitman?

Boris waited for a few feet to their left. Two men stood slightly behind him. Sarah counted seven men and two dogs in total.

"Jane, Jane, Jane, why did you do this?" Boris said.

Jane seemed speechless while they all waited in silence. Without turning around, the footfalls of the men from the rear moved closer.

Hope they still have that leash on the dog.

"You thought you could better me?" Boris said.

The fact that Boris was working so hard to show this wasn't Jane's idea in the first place made Sarah feel she would walk away from this to die another day.

Hopefully.

Or maybe it was for Blair's credit. So he'd never know his mother murdered her own men.

Jane moved in jerks and spasms. Her acting job made her appear delirious. How could Boris ever think to sell such a device to such an unstable woman like Jane? Was he really only after the money and damn the consequences?

Boris looked like he was trying to decide something. A breeze kicked up a swirl of dust between them. One of the dogs growled at it.

"Do you have the money?" Boris asked.

Jane nodded violently, her chin hitting her chest twice in the process.

"And your delivery system is in place?"

She nodded again.

Boris looked at Sarah. Then at Blair. "I am sorry it has come to this. For both of you." Boris reached behind him and opened his palm. For a brief moment, Sarah thought he would be handed a gun to shoot them with, but the man behind Boris placed a manila envelope in Boris's hand instead. Boris opened it and rifled through the documents. "It's all in here. The transfer was completed this morning on time. We will be leaving now. You will wait fifteen minutes. Then you will get in your SUV and"—Boris paused, again looking from Sarah to Blair, then pointed at Sarah—"she will drive. She seems the most together at the moment." He focused on Jane. "Are we clear?"

Jane nodded.

"I need to hear it."

"Yes, yes, we're clear. Sarah drives."

Boris stepped forward, handed the envelope to Jane, then retook his place.

"My remote detonator will be active for one more hour. Then it transfers to your detonator. If I detect a tail, the police, or anything I do not like, I will blow you all to hell and worry nothing, as the only witnesses to this transaction will be dead." He spread his arms. "I was never here." Boris kicked his heel into the dirt and walked away briskly. The two men behind him followed.

After a moment, a vehicle's engine turned on from the other side of the church.

Blair dropped back to the dirt on one knee, then vomited. Jane tilted sideways, dragged down by her son.

Sarah looked over her shoulder as two large SUVs picked up the dog and the men behind them. The Russians were leaving, and they had left them alive.

For now.

Whatever just happened between Jane and Boris seemed to satisfy him. But where was the bomb? What was that about a detonator?

I'm sorry, Sarah. Vivian hovered in her head.

"Sorry about what?" Sarah asked out loud, her mouth suddenly as dry as sun-bleached sand.

She stumbled away from Jane. At the SUV, she checked the rear, but no device could be seen. The suitcase with her money was still there, untouched.

She looked in each area of the large vehicle but failed to find the device. With each passing second, sweating profusely, hands shaking, she grew more and more afraid.

"Jane?" Sarah shouted as she stepped around the vehicle. Her heart was in her throat. She thought of the worst-case scenario and dismissed it as lunacy. There was no way. It couldn't be.

Jane was on her knees in the dirt beside her son, rubbing his back as he vomited again.

"What's wrong with Blair?" Sarah asked. "Are those nerves, or does he know something I don't?"

Jane slowly turned until their eyes met. After placing a hand on her knee, she forced herself to stand.

"I'm sorry, Sarah."

"About what? Why are you sorry?" Sarah fought the urge to run at Jane and pound the answers out of her lunatic mouth. "Where's the bomb that Boris said he had the detonator for?"

"I paid him this morning. The rule was I go alone. So I did."

"Then why are we here?" Sarah moved closer. Something told her she wouldn't like the answer, and she wanted to be close to Jane to break at least one bone.

"We came—" something caught in Jane's throat. She swallowed. "We came to pick this up." She raised the manila envelope. "In here are our passes to the Expo. Our booth number. Everything we need to go and set up."

"Then why kill the guards?" Sarah stomped her foot and threw her hands up. "You're lying! Something doesn't add up."

"The vest you're wearing."

Sarah looked down at the vest. She recalled how it was thicker than other vests she'd seen before. The red light turned green when it clicked on. Sarah stared at Jane as she remembered even Jane's vest appeared smaller somehow.

"There are two bombs," Jane said. "Two dirty bombs. They are radioactive and are set to explode at four this afternoon. Boris holds the detonator for one more hour. After that, I can detonate with mine. We can do nothing else except continue with the plan."

Sarah suspected she knew exactly where the bombs were but had to ask anyway.

"Where. Are. The. Fucking. Bombs?" She ground her teeth together and waited for her death sentence to be voiced out loud.

"You are wearing one. It's the vest. A little light turned green when you put it on and clicked it in place. That turned the bomb on." Jane held an arm up to ward off the sun. "Blair is wearing the other one. That's why he's sick. He has known the plan since this morning when my guards forced him to put the vest on." She looked down at Blair. "That's why he's throwing up. The radiation is already working through his system." She turned back at Sarah. "Sorry, but I just don't know why your sister didn't tell you not to click the vest this morning. It can't be taken off. Any attempt at removing the vest activates the device. Any attempt at cutting wires activates the device. Take it off, and you blow yourself to hell."

Halfway through her little speech, Sarah had stopped listening to the rantings of a mad woman. She turned inward and reflected on why Vivian had deserted her at her weakest moment. The drugs were gone out of her system. She had beaten heroin. She was out of the Mexican danger now and into the arms of a terrorist mad woman.

Radiation. A silent enemy. Working through her body. Killing her. It was over. It was truly over. There was nothing she could do to come back from this.

Blair vomited clear bile, his stomach empty now.

The pit of Sarah's stomach clenched, and her knees lost their ability to function properly. Careful not to bang the vest bomb she wore, Sarah dropped gingerly to her knees and wept, thoughts of Aaron and Parkman on her mind. Thoughts of what could have been. Thoughts of regrets and lost time.

"I'm so sorry, baby," she whispered to Aaron as she balled up her fists full of Nevada dirt and coughed out a cry that unleashed the pain of a lifetime spent missing out on love and kindness.

Sarah Roberts cried in the dirt that she was about to join by the day's end as she had no doubt that Vivian had truly deserted her.

Jane Turner had executed everyone who knew who she was and what she was up to. Sarah was as good as dead but still breathing.

It was over. The Sarah Roberts that anyone knew was gone. She had lost herself along the way, and now Aaron would lose her.

She cried harder, whispering Aaron's name through the mucus mixed with tears that dripped from her face.

"Aaron, Aaron, Aaron …"

Chapter 54

AFTER MEETING AT THE airport briefly, Agent Puig sent her field agents out to locate Jane Turner and Sarah Roberts. The rest were invited back to her office, where they were served an early lunch while waiting for news. Somewhere along the line, the investigation got away from them, and Agent Puig appeared to be the last person the blame was going to fall on.

Parkman sat in one of the chairs at the back of her office and sipped from a cup of coffee. Whitman and Spencer were lounging in various positions while researching the Turner woman on computers. Since losing the plane at the airport, nothing new had turned up. They knew Jane Turner had come to Vegas with Sarah to purchase a bomb. Where she would use that device was still a mystery.

Aaron sat across from Parkman, looking up conferences going on in Vegas, as Vegas was a city known for trade shows and huge conferences.

Airport security cameras showed Jane Turner, Sarah Roberts, Blair Turner, and several of Jane's security detail had entered the United States via the McCarran Airport the previous evening. Finding them now in Sin City was going to be a nightmare. Finding them before Jane did anything rash was what worried Puig.

Parkman drank more coffee while he watched Aaron typing on the laptop Puig had loaned him.

"Find anything interesting?" he asked.

Aaron looked up, shaking his head. "Nothing, really. A soap trade show is in town. They can make roses, books, and cool things with soap."

"Is that getting us any closer to finding Sarah?"

Aaron's face tightened. "Parkman, I have no idea. What I'm searching for is a target. Something that might induce Jane Turner to use her weapon. Bombers usually target where people are together in groups, and conferences offer that. With what little I know of her, I just thought I'd look for places in Vegas where a large number of people would be gathering."

"I know. I'm sorry. But a large number of people are gathering almost anywhere in Vegas. Check every casino. Concerts are happening every day. The Blue Man Group, Phantom of the Opera, and The Cirque de Soleil show. Without locating Turner, it might be hard to narrow just one location as her potential ground zero. Just saying."

"Wow, you really know how to make a guy feel useful."

"Aaron, don't be so sensitive."

"Parkman, I don't know all this investigative stuff. I've never been a cop. I'm killing time until something comes up. And what if I hit on something? Then what?"

"Exactly." Parkman pointed a finger at him with his free hand and drank more coffee with the other. After swallowing, he said, "And that's why you should keep doing it."

Aaron glanced down at his screen. "Like this trade show at the Venetian. Ironic that it's an International Lawmakers Trade show, right?" He looked up. "During a time like this, the crisis we're going through?" He cocked his head to the side. "Wasn't Jane living in India for a while?"

Parkman nodded. "She was married to an Indian man."

"Right. Well, at this conference, there's a large Indian presence presenting their take on the legal issues facing India."

"I highly doubt Jane Turner would want to kill a bunch of old lawmakers from the country that gave her the wealth she currently enjoys."

"Got it." Aaron looked down at the laptop. "Just saying."

Parkman smiled to himself. Aaron had to have the last word. After what they went through in Mexico, that was fine with him. It was probably the last time Parkman or Aaron should ever go to Mexico again if they wanted to stay alive. And even then, they'd be smart to keep a watchful eye on their backs and sleep with one eye open and a hand cannon under their pillows.

He drained the rest of his coffee and set the cup down as Puig's office door opened, and Detective Collins and his partner Munro entered.

"Anything?" Collins asked.

Puig shook her head. "I haven't heard back from any agents in the field. How about you? Has the LVPD found anything?"

Collins adjusted his shirt, tucking it in his pants to look

neater. "No hotels have them registered. No names on a manifest coming or going. Nothing we can trace like a Visa or debit card transaction. Absolutely nothing. They entered Vegas and disappeared. At our end, it's like they were never here in the first place. If we didn't have proof that the plane landed last night, I wouldn't believe they were here at all."

"Then where are they staying? A rented house? An apartment?"

Detective Munro stepped forward. "We checked that. There's no real estate with Turner's name on it in Vegas. We even checked her married name, Singh. Got a few hits there, but nothing leading back to her late husband or her."

"That leaves us in a tight spot." Puig rose from her chair, pushing it away with the backs of her knees. She walked to the window and looked out at Las Vegas. "If we don't find them in time, we'll learn of their whereabouts when Jane Turner detonates her device."

"If she plans on using it in Vegas," Collins added.

Parkman wondered what his point was. Why buy it in Vegas, then take the risk of transporting such a device? Turner would want to minimize the time it was in her hands, use the device, and escape the city, or country, whatever she planned on doing afterward.

"What are you saying?" Puig asked without turning away from the window.

Collins's cell phone rang. "Just a second," he said to Puig before answering it. "Collins here." He stared at the floor. "Yeah. Okay. Go ahead. Just tell me." His eyes widened. "Repeat that," he snapped. He looked up at Puig, who had turned around at the change in his voice. Parkman sat up, then got to his feet. Aaron did the same. "When was this?"

Collins asked. "Log the note in as evidence. Then text it to my phone. I want a copy on me." He clicked the call off.

"You won't believe this," he said, his tone tight, clipped. "Sarah Roberts left me a message. Makes sense since she wouldn't be privy to the FBI mobilized in their effort to locate her. And since she worked with me and trusts me from years before—"

"What message?" Aaron snapped.

Puig had been about to say something, her mouth still agape, but Aaron's voice stopped anyone from speaking.

Collins turned to face him. "I can see what she likes in you."

Detective Munro smacked his arm. "What was the call about?"

"A maid at the Red Mist Motel on the outskirts of Vegas found a note in room 2A, along with damage to their hotel phone."

"This note," Puig said. "Tell us."

"The note said that Sarah Roberts was in town and would love to meet me later at the International Lawmakers Conference at the Venetian Hotel, Sands Expo. The note said to bring my," he used air quotes for the next word, "*friends*, but to be there before four in the afternoon. That must be where the bomb is set to go off." Collins was clearly proud or honored that Sarah chose him as the one to get a hold of during this crisis. "The last line of the note said it was a matter of life and death."

"Why do you look so happy?" Aaron asked.

"Because Sarah is family to me. My son, Russell, is Sarah's cousin. I'm her uncle."

Aaron took a step back. "Wow. I did not know that." He

frowned. "Or maybe she told me when I met her, but that was years ago. I might've forgotten."

"There's a lot you don't know," Collins added. "It was mentioned earlier. You must've missed it."

Munro slapped his arm again.

Puig walked to the middle of her large office. "Are we done with the little family get-together? Can we get back to work?"

Collins faced her. "We might want to attend this conference and seal it off. It's almost noon. We've got time."

Puig momentarily hesitated in front of Collins, then walked behind her desk and picked up the phone.

Aaron headed for the door.

"Where are you going?" Puig shouted, the phone in her hand, the other hand hovering over the digits.

"A conference. I'm a free man. I'm on my way to pick up my girlfriend." As he walked by Parkman, he said, "See. That's the conference I was just talking about. I was doing something useful after all, wasn't I?"

"Is this a pissing contest, or are we judging dick sizes next?" Parkman asked him before he was out of earshot.

Aaron didn't laugh or reply. He just kept on walking.

"Wait, Aaron." Parkman stepped out of the office behind him and stopped in the doorway. "You need to let the pros handle this."

"Not this time."

He was too far for Parkman to grab him. How would he hold Aaron down anyway? It was no use.

Behind Parkman in the office, Puig's voice could be heard loud and clear.

"Security. I have a male Caucasian named Aaron Stevens

coming your way from my office. Make sure he doesn't leave the building."

Chapter 55

Sarah forced herself up off the dirt by sheer willpower. Her body shook with unused adrenaline, and her muscles were weak. Why fight it? Strapped to a bomb she couldn't defuse or take off, she was dead. Without any help from Vivian, this situation was hopeless.

"Sarah?" Jane used a motherly tone. "We have to go. Come. Get in the car."

"Fuck you," Sarah spit out. "I ain't going anywhere with you," she yelled.

"We had a deal." Jane sounded incredulous, like she couldn't believe Sarah's stance on this matter.

"Fuck your deal."

Sarah took in the scene. The guards lying dead. The vest wrapping her vital organs with death. Blair on his hands and knees, crawling in the dirt. Jane watched over the carnage she had caused with impunity as if nothing could touch her.

Within a couple of quick steps, Sarah grabbed Jane's collar, drew Jane close, and drove the hard part of her forehead onto the top of Jane's nose. Something cracked. A piece of cartilage.

Jane yanked herself away, screaming and grabbing at her face.

Sarah rushed her again, driving fist after fist into the flesh until she fell to the ground, exhausted, panting like she'd run a race. It felt good to let out all that rage. It didn't solve anything, but it felt good.

Blair was moaning something. She stopped pummeling Jane to take a breath.

"What?" Sarah shouted at him. "Stand up. Tell me what you think, Blair. What's on your mind?"

The macabre scene around Sarah was ridiculous. She was fighting a woman who couldn't defend herself. Sarah was never a bully. She fought those that deserved it.

"Yes, Jane Turner, you deserved that."

Jane had dropped to her knees by her son, her eyes a deep red and swelling where the bridge of her nose had been damaged. Her right cheek was bleeding, and her lower lip was already swelling and bleeding.

Disgusted with how far this had all gone, Sarah walked over to the building and leaned against the wall in the shade to collect her breath. Her eyes puffy, nose still running from when she cried for Aaron, she stared at nothing for a moment.

"Tell me how to take this thing off," Sarah said. "If not for me, save your son's life."

"I can't." Jane's nasally voice was hard to hear. "Once it's on, there's no taking it off. Had it built that way."

Puzzled, Sarah asked, "I thought you said this dirty bomb thing was from an old Russian military arms dump or something like that? But yet, you're having the bombs built for you? Doesn't make sense."

"The bomb itself is old. Conventional bomb. Small, like a grenade. Modified to fit into the Kevlar. I was told it's something like a squib, a miniature explosive." Jane had used the sleeve of her shirt to dab at the blood from her nose. "Think of it like tiny sticks of dynamite wrapped in high levels of radiation."

"Great thought. Gee, thanks for that."

Jane got to her feet, wobbled, and stepped closer. "What about the million in cash? Don't you want it?"

"What a stupid question. How am I supposed to spend it if I'm dead?"

"What about your word, then?" Jane pleaded. "You said you'd help me. Well, here we are. Now's your chance. Help me. Get in that car and drive us to the conference. This isn't over yet. It has just begun."

Sarah blinked. With effort, she turned to look at Jane. "Can you hear yourself? I mean, just listen to yourself."

Blair was still on the ground. He had stopped vomiting. He had shielded his eyes from the sun as he watched them talk. He looked beaten, done, exhausted. There was no way his mother could come back from this with their relationship intact if he were to live through it. But somehow, Sarah was sure Jane didn't care much about that.

"I hear perfectly well." Jane put her hands on her hips. Her nose looked awful. Red and puffy, it resembled an odd-shaped pomegranate sitting between her eyes. "I thought you'd be behind this more, Sarah. Aren't you all about girl power? We need to stick together. Fight the power. Isn't that what you do traipsing around the world? Because if you're unwilling to see this through, you're letting rapists get away with their crimes."

"Oh man, you're more fucked than I thought." Sarah clenched her fists and turned toward Jane. "Are you asking for another thrashing? I'd be more than happy to oblige you."

"That makes you just like them." Jane stepped closer, her arms out as she pleaded. "Sarah, these men are the walking wounded. Let me have my coup de grace, and I'll give them peace in death. Then I can carpe noctem."

"Where the hell is all the Latin coming from? You're lucky I don't kick your ass seven ways to Sunday." She thought of something else and decided to ask. "Why did you have your own men killed?"

Jane moved inside the line of shade the church offered. Sarah looked at Blair. By the expression on his face, he clearly wasn't aware what had just happened here had been orchestrated by his mother.

"That was necessary," Jane said. Her tone had changed. Her mind was slipping. Sarah could see it in the woman's puffy eyes. "I did it," Jane kept talking, "and I'd do it again if given the chance. But people don't come back from the dead. So I guess I can't kill them twice."

"Consider yourself lucky. If the dead did come back after this vest kills me, I would return to kick your ass every day." Sarah touched the Kevlar bomb strapped to her chest. "I don't know why I'm not attacking you right now. If this thing goes off, at least I didn't have to wait out here until four in the afternoon to die."

"You won't be here until four. We leave within the hour."

"Yeah? How's that? You think I will let you take me back to Las Vegas to blow people up? No, when this baby goes, I'll be the only victim. Unless you want to stick around. On second thought, please do. We'll have a going away party. We'll call it Fuck Jane, Fuck Me, Fuck You, and Fuck Us All Party. How's that sound?"

Jane looked at her feet and started shaking her head back and forth, mumbling the word *no* over and over, like a quiet chant.

"Sarah?" Blair said.

"What?"

"I'm sorry I got you into this."

"I'm sorry I didn't get you out of this. If my sister had spoken up sooner, I might've been able to."

"I'm going to go to the vehicle now, Mommy. I will wait for you there so at least you and I can finish this."

Sarah frowned. What could he be up to? The gentle, loving soul that Blair was wouldn't do that. She didn't believe for a second that he would willingly go to Vegas to hurt people. It wasn't in him.

Blair got to his feet and started toward the vehicle with a loping gait. He stumbled, righted himself, and continued toward the SUV.

What the hell? Has everyone lost their shit?

Jane's chanting continued but was slowly getting louder.

"Shut up," Sarah said.

Jane didn't.

"Shut up!"

When Jane kept looking at the ground, saying *no* repeatedly, Sarah moved in.

"Can't say I didn't warn you."

She shot her fist out fast in a right jab to the tip of Jane's nose, then stepped back to the wall. Jane stumbled backward, her hands covering her nose, blood seeping out through her fingers harder and faster than before. Jane moaned and cried out. The chanting had stopped.

"What have you done?" Blair shouted from beside the SUV.

"I shut her up. She needed that. Hey, wait a second. Don't ask me what I've done. What the fuck have you done? It's your mother. You got me into this." Sarah leaned against the church's wall again, shaking her head. "Everything's fucked."

"No, Sarah. All you've done is piss her off. You don't know my mother. Pain motivates her. She's taunting you. You're adding lighter fluid to a raging fire."

"Oh, goody. Maybe I should do it again. Would love to see Miss Lunatic here really mad." Sarah widened her eyes and moaned like someone fresh out of bedlam. "Maybe even off her rocker." She changed her face back to anger. "You gotta be fucking kidding me." She pushed off the wall and stepped closer to Jane, who now had blood running down her chin as she cried. "I am going to kill you, Jane, with my bare hands before this vest gets me. You hear me?"

"You're not thinking this through," Jane said, her voice sounding like it was coming out of a tin can now. "If persuaded, I can take that vest off you. I know how."

"Bullshit. Why would I trust you? And even if you could take it off, what about the radiation? I'm as good as dead anyway."

"They've got pills for that sort of thing."

Blair was coming back from the SUV. In his hand was a

man's shirt. He had grabbed one of the dead men's shirts to help blot his mother's—his murderer's—nose.

He stepped up to her and stopped. Before dabbing her face, he dropped the shirt. Concealed under the shirt was a weapon from one of Jane's guards.

Jane gasped, looked down at the gun, then back up at Blair.

"What are you doing?" she asked, her voice hysterical.

Blair began to cry again.

"Oh my shit," Sarah said. "Just shut her up already."

His hand shook, the tip of the weapon rotating in spasmodic circles. This was one time when Sarah wasn't inspired to stop a man from shooting a woman. Jane deserved it for what she had done to her guards and what she had done to them.

"How would this end any other way out here?" Sarah asked. "We're in the middle of nowhere. Blair and I are strapped to Kevlar death, and it's your fault. There are guns lying around. You can't tell me you didn't, for one second, see this coming?" Jane moved away from Blair and closer to Sarah. "Shoot her, Blair. End her lunatic rantings. I don't fucking care anymore." She waved a hand. "Unless you have a way out of this, Jane? If so, you better start talking."

"Blair, honey," Jane pleaded. "Don't do this. You don't want to hurt your mother."

Blair raised the weapon as he stepped to close the distance between them, placed the gun's tip near Jane's forehead, and pulled the trigger.

The gun's report was loud, but it faded fast.

Nothing happened. Jane staggered back but kept her hands on her nose, using the top of her shirt to plug the wound.

Blair examined the weapon in his hand, aimed at his mother, and fired again.

"Blanks," Jane said. "I gave all the guards weapons with blanks. There was no way I could risk one of them getting a shot off at Boris's men. Boris would've killed me."

"Oh my fuck," Sarah whispered. "You *had* anticipated this."

Blair dropped to his knees, crying. "I've failed as a man. I can't even beat my mother when she wants to kill me. I'm useless. I'm a nobody."

"You're not a nobody, Blair," Jane said in a cooing voice. "Sarah's a nobody. At least you stood up to me. Sarah didn't. She's a nobody."

"Yeah, I'm a nobody," Sarah shouted. "No problem. Just watch how nobody kicks your ass."

Sarah lunged. Jane was quick. She had seen it coming, calling Sarah on from the start. Jane stepped sideways, feinted left, and as Sarah countered the move and lunged in with her arms open to tackle Jane to the dirt, Jane stuck her with something sharp. They fell in a heap of dust, hair flying in her face and a pain that spread fast in her deltoid area, near the base of her neck.

"What the—" Sarah tried to say, but her mouth tightened, and she stopped talking.

Quickly, Sarah's body went limp. Jane rolled her off and got to her feet. Whatever it was worked quickly. It had a calming effect, a dull throb. Things stopped working all over her body. Her hands ceased movement, but she could still feel them.

Okay, this sucks. Hey, sis, little help here.

Paralysis set in limb after limb as Jane walked over to Blair out of the corner of her eye and stabbed him, too, with whatever she had concealed in her palm. Blair fell over and lay spread eagle on the dirt, unable to move as well.

Only Sarah's eyes moved.

What did you do? Sarah tried to yell, but her mouth didn't respond.

"A very strong muscle relaxant," Jane said. "I had it tweaked to work extremely fast." She stepped into Sarah's view. "All your muscles are so relaxed. They won't respond to any commands for about two to three hours. If I start to notice you twitching, I'll dose you again." She smiled, and Sarah saw all the psychosis for what it was. Absolute madness flashed behind Jane's eyes. Whatever had hurt her in the past forever changed her into this new person. "Now, the tricky part. Getting you and Blair into the SUV by myself."

Jane went to work on yanking Blair across the dirt. Without the luxury of being able to move, Sarah could only listen to Jane's ministrations as she lumbered over her son's inert body.

Instead of allowing panic in, she calmed her mind by listening and waiting. Vivian had taken over her body in the past when a chemical or drug commandeered her limbs. All Sarah had to do was wait for Vivian to stop this.

When the dirty bomb strapped to her chest blew, Sarah would die, but Vivian would never let Jane load her into the SUV and drive her back to Las Vegas. That would be tantamount to mass murder. Better the three of them die here, by this abandoned church, than to be taken to Vegas where innocents could be included in the list of the dead.

After what felt like half an hour, Jane had worked tirelessly to clean up the scene and load Blair's body, leaving Sarah to roast in the sun as it had moved westward, placing her face out of the shadows.

I don't need a tan, Vivian. Any chance you're around?

Something pulled her. She tried to look down but couldn't. Then she was sliding along the dirt. Jane had a hold of her ankles. This had gone too far.

Vivian, you started this. Take over my body and end it. Here and now.

But there was no response.

Fine. You want an apology? You want me to say I need you? Is that what this is about? If so, fuck you because these are real lives we're talking about back in Vegas. You have to stop this. You can't let innocents die because you're upset with me.

The shadow cast by the SUV covered Sarah's face. Jane had done it. She was about to load Sarah's dead weight. In the time Sarah had waited in the sun, none of her fingers or toes had moved. She could do nothing as the muscle relaxant still held her body in its vice grip.

Jane wasn't kind in her manhandling. At first, Jane lifted Sarah's legs into the back seat, walked around to the other side, and climbed in. Then she pulled Sarah's legs as hard as she could, forcing Sarah to bend backward, her butt stuck on the lower edge of the door, her head going upside down and adding pressure to her neck.

Jane got out and walked back around to Sarah. She seized her under the shoulders, whispered a count of three to herself, then stood with Sarah, whose legs were still inside the SUV, and forced her to bend at the waist as she pushed her into the vehicle. Sarah clumped down onto her thighs and found breathing difficult. Something was obstructing her diaphragm. She gasped a breath. Then another.

Jane shut the car door behind her and could be heard walking around to the driver's side.

Sarah struggled to breathe. Her head lightened. She struggled and breathed again. Jane turned on the SUV.

One more breath. That was all she could get. Darkness clouded over her eyes, consuming the edges of her vision as raw panic set in.

Someone yelled.

Then she was shoved backward, and her airways opened. Instantly, she could breathe again. Her vision came back just as fast.

"Sorry about that," Jane said. "Didn't see you struggling there."

Sarah's back rested against the armrest of the SUV's door, her legs across the seat in front of her. Vivian hadn't stopped it. Vivian hadn't come to her rescue. There were no words of wisdom or hope. Only silence from the other side.

Jane drove away from the church with her new dirty bomb device intact. Jane got what she wanted. The bomb, the documents in the manila envelope to get her into the conference hall, and the perfect delivery system.

Someone once said something like a secret is a secret when three people know it as long as two of them are dead. Someone also once said: Hurt people, hurt people. Sarah should have considered that. Jane was smart. Jane was rich. But more importantly, Jane was hurting. And now dozens and dozens of people, if not hundreds, would hurt because Sarah went along for the ride and couldn't stop her.

This was Sarah's fault. She had wanted to buy drugs. She had turned her back on Vivian. And when Jane revealed her issues and what she wanted to do in Las Vegas, Sarah agreed to come along to stop it. She had good intentions, but someone also once said good intentions pave certain roads one shouldn't travel on.

She shouldered the pain, the blame. If she could go back, there were a hundred things she would do differently. But she couldn't go back. There was no tomorrow, only sorrow for the people left behind. Her loved ones, like Aaron, Parkman, and her parents. And all the loved ones of the soon-to-be dead at the convention in the Venetian.

Even if the maid from the motel contacted Detective Collins with the note she had left on the sheets of her messy bed, would he show up at the Venetian? Would he know how serious Jane was and what she intended to do? No, he wouldn't. He would be unprepared and probably die, too, because of Sarah.

Somewhere, deep down inside, as all hope was lost, Sarah felt a spark of life begging to be heard. An irrational voice in the darkness of her misery. There was still a way, the voice said. Focus, listen, observe, and take every opportunity to make this right, increasing the chances of success.

That little voice had to be insane. There was no way out of this. Even if she somehow got the vest off, stopped Jane, and saved the day, she would die of radiation poisoning.

But wasn't Sarah a fighter? the voice asked.

Sarah tried to nod her head but couldn't. Old habits.

Give me the chance. I'll fight.

Then be ready, the voice said. Just be ready.

Is that you, Vivian? Sarah asked.

There was no reply as Jane turned onto the main highway heading to Vegas with Blair in the back and Sarah sprawled out on the seat, waiting for the Grim Reaper's arms to take them.

Jane laughed to herself as she drove.

A moment later, she was laughing hysterically, the sheer volume of her voice raising goosebumps of anger in Sarah.

The laughter died as suddenly as it started, and Jane began mumbling to herself.

She mumbled until the neon lights of Vegas came into sight as they passed the windows Sarah could see through. It had to be around lunchtime. There were less than four hours until the bomb was to auto-detonate.

Only four hours to live. Or less.

She asked forgiveness for the people about to die and prayed for her soul as the SUV traveled deeper into the heart of Las Vegas, carrying death with it.

Chapter 56

Aaron watched as Detective Collins scanned the list of attendees for the International Lawmakers Conference, his finger stopping on anything that seemed remotely related to Jane Turner. Nothing significant had shown up. Special Agent in Charge Samantha Puig had printed photos of Sarah Roberts, Jane Turner, and Blair Turner distributed to all security staff at the Sands Expo. Detective Collins had done the same with the Las Vegas Police Department. As far as Aaron understood it, if Sarah or Jane were to come within a dozen meters of the Sands Expo, they would be stopped.

As a precaution, if this wasn't their final destination, every cop on the street—and every available FBI agent—was looking for them as directed by the FBI's Joint Terrorism Task Force.

Parkman assured Aaron that Sarah would be found and Jane would be stopped before anything happened. But Aaron wasn't willing to be so optimistic. Since the Enzo Cartel, things had gone from bad to worse.

Outside the convention center, car after car stopped and let people out. Four police cruisers sat parked along the side of the building. Aaron had mentioned a few times that the cruisers needed to be moved. If Jane Turner saw a large police presence, she might flee the area and disappear until she showed up somewhere else, too late for anyone to stop her.

A few hundred people were inside setting up their booths for the weekend-long show, but the FBI had forbidden Aaron from entering the building to look around. Agent Puig had made that very clear when she detained Aaron before he could leave the FBI building. This was an FBI investigation. He only knew as much as he did because of his connection to Sarah. Otherwise, he would be completely in the dark.

To Aaron's right, standing in the shade of the building, out of the direct sun, Spencer, Whitman, and Parkman talked in hushed tones.

"Collins?" Aaron said. "Anything?"

Detective Collins looked up from the conference guide and shrugged. "Nothing pops out at me. I have no idea if one of these booths is Jane's or if she's targeting one of them. We don't know enough about her to understand which one she'd be after or even what her interest is with this trade show."

"You'll let us know the second she shows up on your radar?"

"Of course. You guys'll be the first to know."

Aaron patted Collins's shoulder and thanked him, then backed away to join the Toronto men talking to Parkman.

"Anything?" Parkman asked.

Aaron shook his head. "They can't seem to narrow their focus on a point of interest for Jane. No one knows why she would pick this conference if she even picked it all. We're all here because a maid found a note in a motel. Jane could have written that particular note to throw the authorities off track. For all we know, she could be planning an attack on the Stratosphere as we sit here with our thumbs up our asses."

"Aaron, this is all we have to go on. So we go on it. Until something else comes up, this is all we have. That's how it works."

Aaron nodded and looked away, avoiding Parkman's gaze.

"I know you're frustrated, Aaron. I am, too. But we'll get through this. Most importantly, Sarah will get through this. She always does."

Aaron watched the vehicles coming and going. Men and women, some in uniforms, others just working the show, everyone with their trade show badge dangling from their necks.

Nothing whatsoever looked off. He had no hunches, no intuition, nothing telling him anything was wrong. It was just another Friday in Las Vegas as convention presenters prepared their booths and got ready to show the attendees their wares. This conference had everything from security systems to police training to K-9 units and even robotic security guards to booths covering police officer theory and philosophy. In the law enforcement industry, there was a vast array of objects, people, and ideas on how to do it better, and this show was about putting all that on display.

Maybe Jane had a problem with law enforcement. Perhaps she wanted to show the world that even the law enforcement convention could be attacked. Perhaps it was as simple as that.

"Aaron?" someone said.

He came out of his daze and turned to Parkman.

"I said your name a few times," Parkman said. "You doing okay?"

"Yeah, just thinking. You guys come up with anything?"

Whitman and Spencer both shook their heads.

Parkman stepped around Aaron and peered at the side doors. "We're thinking of spreading out around the entrances to the convention center and doing our own surveillance. Agent Puig won't like us too close, but we can stay out on the street." He turned back to Aaron. "You in?"

"Nothing better to do. Can't stand here all day."

"Spencer and I will enter the casino and watch from the side where people can access the Expo. You two want to watch these doors?"

Aaron nodded. Whitman nodded, too.

They separated, leaving Whitman standing too close to Aaron.

"You don't need to worry about me," Whitman said.

"I know." Aaron kept his eyes on Parkman and Spencer as they headed toward the front of the Venetian.

"I mean, I came to see Sarah to thank her for saving my life. Meet you, buy you guys dinner. Just chat. Reconnect. Then this happened."

"I didn't get a chance to thank you for what you did back at that shack in Mexico."

"No need to. You would've done the same for me." Whitman slapped Aaron on the back.

Aaron glanced at Whitman's hand, not used to people

touching him. Whitman took his hand back.

They stood together, watching cars come and go for five minutes without a word from either one.

"I've probably not been the most receptive since you showed up," Aaron said. "I just got suspicious. I mean, you were supposed to be dead."

"Yeah, there's that. I understand."

And that was about as close of an apology as Aaron wanted to offer at the moment.

After another dozen cars came and went, he faced Whitman and offered his hand.

"Friends," Aaron said, knowing Parkman had left them together to talk or beat the shit out of each other.

"Friends," Whitman said, taking Aaron's hand.

They shook. When he released Whitman's hand, a hearse pulled up to his left. It caught his eye because a woman was driving it. He usually didn't see women driving hearses.

Her hair was pulled up and stuffed under a chauffeur hat. She wore a white shirt and suit jacket. He wondered how a hearse contributed to a law enforcement conference as the driver parked and got out. A side glimpse of her face revealed a nose swollen to twice its normal size.

Standing by the open door of the hearse, the woman gazed at the four police cars, then at the entrance. After a long moment, she seemed to make up her mind and closed her door. It was a law enforcement conference, after all. Of course, there would be police officers.

In the second the woman looked their way, Aaron was sure he recognized her.

"Whitman, do you have one of those photo sheets Puig was handing out?"

"Yeah. Right here." He yanked it from his back pocket and unfolded it.

Aaron stared at the photo of Jane Turner. He studied her eyes, then glanced back at the hearse driver.

It was her. Jane Turner. No doubt about it.

Aaron dropped the photo sheet and stepped forward.

Jane was near the back of the hearse. She watched Aaron, still forty feet away from under the lip of her driver's hat. He felt her eyes on him like laser pointers.

Without waiting a second more, he broke into a run, Whitman close on his heels.

The hearse driver scurried to the driver's door, ripped it open, hopped in, and slammed it shut before Aaron got halfway there.

The hearse's tires squealed as it shot out of its parking spot. The driver careened wildly off the front bumper of one of the parked police cars and shot out into an opening in the traffic, heading toward the Las Vegas Strip.

Chapter 57

By the time the SUV had come to a stop inside a small warehouse of some kind, one of Sarah's fingers had started to move slightly. With her shoes on, it was hard to tell if any toes had moved yet.

Jane exited the vehicle, opened the back hatch, and started doing something to Blair. From the little Sarah could see, this wasn't the conference building. They were in an oversized garage. A hearse was in her line of vision beside the SUV, but that was the only other vehicle she saw with her limited ability to move.

Jane mumbled something to Blair as she worked, breathing loudly through her ruined nose. It sounded like she was talking to him about her plans. She couldn't offer platitudes to her son because she didn't care enough. She hated him for being gay, and she hated him because he was a man. This was her way of dealing with all that. Her way to fix the mistake that childbirth had been for her.

Whatever she was doing sounded tough as she grunted and moaned between what she said to him. Something heavy dragged across the concrete floor. It stopped, and the interior light of the hearse turned on. She had put Blair into something and was placing that something into the other vehicle.

Why change vehicles? And why a hearse? That's going to stand out. People look at hearses. This didn't make any sense. Weren't these bombs supposed to be for a trade show? How would she smuggle them in with a hearse?

Sarah tried to move her finger again. It curled in nicely. She unfolded it. It wouldn't be long before Jane learned the error of her ways.

After a moment, something moved inside the hearse, shaking the vehicle slightly. Looking as far to the left as she could, Sarah barely made out the corner of something wooden through the small side window in the hearse.

A coffin?

Was Jane putting them in coffins?

No fucking way, Vivian!

The door opened behind Sarah, and she instantly dropped out backward as her back rested against the door handle. Jane caught her and eased her out the rest of the way, her feet falling lazily to the concrete floor. When the door opened, both her arms jerked as a reflex to catch herself, but Jane had missed the movement. The drug was wearing off. It was only a matter of time before she would be able to stop this. But then what? Where were they? How close to civilization? How many people would be hurt if Sarah tried to drive out of the city before four in the afternoon?

"I want to tell you a few things, Sarah," Jane said in her deeply nasal voice. "First, I appreciate your sacrifice. You could've stayed in Mexico. You could've refused my offer of one million dollars. But you didn't. You chose the money over liberty." Jane left her on the cold concrete while she moved out of eyesight to do something. "You fought me on this. You wanted to stop me." Her voice echoed in the garage. "I know your type, Sarah. You only fight for personal gain." She moved closer, dragging something. "You tried to beat me up and steal my million dollars. I know that now."

A loud thunk resounded throughout the building as Jane dropped whatever she was dragging. Then she knelt over Sarah, looking down at her through the space between her bent knees.

"So because of that, you selfish cow, I want to explain a few things as I load you up for your last car ride." Jane placed her hands under Sarah's shoulders and lifted.

Sometimes the insane possess strength the rest of us don't have.

As she placed her down, Jane said, "You and Blair will be my models." Jane moved around to lift Sarah's legs in. "On display, at the conference, in these plush-lined coffins. Only your eyes will move, freaking people out." Jane straightened Sarah's legs and pants. The feeling in certain areas of her legs was coming back. They tingled when Jane moved her. "My conference booth is all about the shooting of law enforcement officers across the States lately. Even with Kevlar vests, people will see more dead cops if tensions aren't lowered." She raised her hands. "You see, you and Blair in these coffins works. Wearing your vests and unable to move until BOOM!" she yelled that last word.

Sarah jolted under her skin but kept her hands still.

Jane slid a strap across Sarah's chest as these coffins had no lids. "This'll hold you in place until I set you up at my booth."

From the little she saw of the belt, it looked like a regular strap. Jane wasn't concerned with tying her in as Sarah couldn't escape without the use of her limbs.

Once the strap was tightened, Jane raised her hand and brought it down across Sarah's face. Without being able to move away or defend herself, her cheek took the whole bite of the slap. It stung like a dozen bees had attacked her.

Jane raised her hand from the other way and slapped her other cheek.

"How's that feel?" Jane asked. "It hurt my hand, so I can only imagine your pain."

Sarah tried to scream, but nothing worked yet except her one hand.

Jane worked to take her shoe off and raised it above Sarah's face.

"I don't want to hurt my hand anymore."

Oh shit.

Everything in her mind told her to bring her arms up and move her face away, but the defiance in her limbs and muscles continued as the heel of the dress shoe Jane wore connected with Sarah's cheek, breaking the skin.

Fuck!

Then again, from the other side as Jane emitted a maniacal laugh.

The shoe came down another time, then another, and all Sarah could do was lie there and watch it happen, blinking each time to protect her eyes. Blood painted the bottom of

Jane's shoe as she lifted it for the sixth time. The pain was maddening, making her want to crawl out and away from her skin.

Jane's laughter stopped abruptly. The shoe lowered, and she slipped it back on her foot. Sarah's eyes leaked tears at the pain. She couldn't scream; she couldn't fight. There was nothing she could do with the madness around her but endure.

"Sorry about that. A little payback for earlier, out by the church." She leaned in the coffin and wiped the dirt and small pebbles from Sarah's cheeks. One pebble stuck in the skin made Jane dig at it with her nail. Sarah wondered if this was a version of insanity. Something patients dealt with when being worked on by a Nazi doctor.

"You're the model who scuffled with the bad guy before being shot."

Jane got up and began to drag the coffin toward the hearse.

"Inside your vest are two electrical leads," Jane said. "A plug with a small bridge wire separates them. Open the vest, break the bridge wire, and the squib ignites. Cut the wire, either one, the vest blows." She set the coffin down by the back of the hearse. "Are you listening to me?" She yelled.

Sarah squirmed on the inside as the pain in her cheeks had gone to a dull, numbing ache. Blood rolled down past her ears, cool and wet.

Jane lifted the end of the coffin and placed it on the back of the hearse, then walked around and lifted the other end before she shoved. The coffin slid in easily until it clunked to a stop. Blair's coffin was beside hers. The plush pillow her head rested on afforded a peripheral view of Blair's coffin.

Neither had a lid, which Sarah was grateful for. She breathed deeply, focusing on something other than the pain. Ignore the pain. There were more important things than pain. Like getting her muscles working again.

"I knew you weren't listening to me, you stupid bitch. Sarah Roberts. The hero. Fuck you, Sarah. Fuck you and die."

The back of the hearse slammed shut.

Jane entered the front, turned the vehicle on, and backed out of the garage. As she did, Sarah caught a glimpse of the sign on the wall. Darnell's Car Repair.

In minutes, they were back on the Vegas strip and heading to the Venetian Hotel, where Sarah hoped Detective Collins was with an army of cops. It could go either way. Jane saw the cops and panicked, detonated the bombs in the hearse in the middle of a crowd. Or Collins was smart, stayed out of sight, and arrested Jane without incident.

If she could be so lucky.

Her hand twitched and moved enough to raise it off the satin of the coffin. Her mouth opened a little at the prompting of her jaw. The muscle relaxant was wearing off quickly now. She had to do something as soon as she was able to.

It wasn't her life she was worried about anymore but the innocent people who would die when Jane detonated the vests in a crowd.

"It's been a while since I jabbed you with that paralysis drug," Jane said from the front seat. "Don't worry. I'm watching the clock. You will get one more jab when I pull in to unload the coffins. That'll keep you paralyzed until the fireworks. How's that sound?"

Jane shrieked with laughter.

Sarah struggled to get her other hand to respond, but nothing happened. It was no use. She wasn't able to move enough to fight Jane off yet.

Her only hope was Collins.

Who would've thought Sarah was hoping for police intervention after all the years of not working with the police and, at times, even shunning them?

Humbled in that knowledge, the hearse drove on through Vegas, taking Sarah in the coffin to her final task as a living, breathing woman.

Sarah fought on the inside and cried on the outside.

Chapter 58

"WE'RE HERE," JANE TRILLED. "In a few moments, we'll be inside, and my booth will begin to come to life, so to speak."

Sarah's right arm was back, but her left was just starting to move below the wrist. The toes on both feet were definitely working now. She needed ten minutes, maybe twenty, and she'd be mostly herself again.

The hearse stopped. Jane hesitated in the front seat. Sarah listened. What was wrong? Why wasn't she doing something?

"Is that Aaron?" Jane asked. "It's impossible. He's back in Mexico, looking for you. There's no way."

She opened her door and got out, the hearse adjusting slightly with her movement. Sarah fought to move more body parts before Jane jabbed her with the drug again.

The back door opened a crack. This was it. The final moment.

"I don't like this," Jane said to herself. "He's staring at me. He's looking at a paper of some kind. Who is that man with him?" Sarah struggled to move her limbs if Jane tried to jab her. "Not good," Jane shouted between clenched teeth, then slammed the door shut.

Sarah let out a breath of relief. She still had time to break the drug's hold on her limbs.

The hearse shook when Jane jumped back in the front. The second the car was on, it jerked forward, squealing its tires.

Could it really be Aaron? Here in Vegas? How did they follow her? Was all this Collins's doing?

The coffin smacked the side, then wobbled the other way as Jane took a corner too sharply.

She cursed in the front seat and shouted something about detonating the bombs early. Sarah didn't listen. She struggled to bend her arm high enough to undo the strap that tied her to the coffin.

The hearse swerved to miss something, jostling the coffins back and forth.

Her hand touched the strap. She began working it through the loop as the hearse jerked again and violently shot sideways as it rammed into something.

Chapter 59

AARON WATCHED AS THE hearse peeled out of the loading and unloading area. The closest vehicle was a police car. He ran for it, hoping they had left the keys inside. Who would steal a cop car?

The second cruiser had the keys in the ignition. Aaron slid behind the wheel, cranked the engine, and took off with Whitman yelling something at him. None of that mattered. Jane Turner drove that hearse, and Jane had Sarah. Whitman could stay behind and let everyone else know where he had gone.

Jane was heading for Las Vegas Boulevard. Up ahead, he watched as she swerved to miss a yellow cab turning right, kept the hearse moving left, and crossed the center of the intersection on a red light.

By the time he had switched three buttons on the dash, Aaron had the police lights going, the siren blaring. At the same intersection, cars slowed, allowing him to drive straight through.

He dropped the pedal to the floor and raced after the hearse, hoping this wasn't symbolic. Chasing a hearse, chasing Sarah as if she was dead already. It couldn't be. He wouldn't allow it.

As Jane tried to make it through the next intersection, a dump truck clipped the back end of the hearse, sending it sideways. It hit another car, righted, and continued forward.

Aaron had caught up and swerved around the stopped dump truck as the hearse sped away, screaming pedestrians who were trying to walk with the light diving away from the hearse. Aaron came around from the left, aimed at ramming the corner taillight of the hearse, and jammed his foot down again.

Just as the hearse was about to take off on him, the cruiser's grill smashed into the back corner. The hearse fishtailed back and forth until the wheels caught, and it shot forward again.

But it wasn't lined up with the road. When it shot forward, the hearse jumped onto the sidewalk, smashed through and over the railing, and took to the air as it tumbled upside down.

It came to rest on its roof in the Fountains of Bellagio's large pool of water. The tires continued to spin.

Another cruiser sped by and slammed to a stop into the wall beside where the hearse had broken through.

Before Aaron could get out and run to the hearse, Whitman was out of the other cruiser and jumping over the edge and into the water.

Chapter 60

After righting itself, Sarah had successfully taken the strap off her chest. The hearse jerked again, smashed into something, and landed on all four tires once more.

Over fifty percent of her body was back, listening to the will of her mind. She hoped it wasn't too late.

The hearse shot forward. Sarah placed an arm on either side of the coffin's rim and lifted. She forced her neck around at the sound of police sirens and saw something incredible. Aaron was driving the Las Vegas Police Department cruiser.

"What the?" she whispered with half her tongue still dead.

Aaron raced at the corner of the hearse, rammed it, and forced it sideways. Jane couldn't handle the hit, swerving back and forth. Sarah dropped back in the coffin just as the hearse smashed into something and took air, tilting sideways.

A second later, the hearse stopped, coming to rest upside

down. Sarah's forehead, chest, and knees smacked into the upended roof of the hearse, the coffin falling on top of her. She tried to get herself up but didn't have enough strength yet. Water seeped in from somewhere.

Water? A river?

The water rushed in, soaking her legs, the Kevlar vest, and her face. It was cool and calming, but she knew how deadly it could be. If she didn't get herself up and out of the water, she would drown, and so would Blair, who was probably buried under his coffin as well.

Jane shouted a primal scream from the front seat, then said, "I'll just detonate now, then."

Sarah was sure she had heard those words. An icy chill that had nothing to do with the water coursed through her. Aaron would die, too.

She pushed up with her hands, calling for all her strength, tilted her back sideways, and pushed the coffin— light for its size—off her back. She slipped her fingers under the rising water and then under the lip of Blair's coffin and lifted. In seconds, he crawled out from under his and came up gasping for air. Blair moved until he was propped up against the inside wall of the hearse.

At the front, Jane struggled against the door, kicking at it. Metal screeched as the door opened and water rushed in.

Sarah watched as Jane crawled out. Through that door was freedom. Sarah mumbled her intentions to Blair and started that way, trying to keep her head above water. It got easier as she went because she didn't have to support all her body weight in the water. She dog-paddled as she passed the top of the front seat and turned for the open door.

Blair was close behind her. They were going to make it.

A tiny sliver of hope made her think they'd clear the hearse and, with a stroke of luck, be able to take the vests off before four in the afternoon. But reality set in, and if everything Jane said were true, that would never happen.

Escape the car if they wanted, but she still acted like a zombie—a dead woman crawling out of her coffin.

She held her breath, ducked her head under the water, and came up beside the spinning front tire on the other side. A second after, Blair surfaced behind her.

Jane had something small and black in her hand. Aaron and Drake stood five feet from her, their hands up, pleading.

"Don't do it," Aaron said. "It's over."

More sirens wailed in the distance. Others were coming. Aaron was here. Drake was here. Maybe the police would bring a bomb technician with them.

Jane spun around and glared at Sarah. Before Aaron or Drake could reach Jane, she dove backward to land between Sarah and Blair.

"Stand back," Jane shouted. "Or I'll blow them up. Both vests are wired to blow." She looked at Blair. "What do you say? You want to die together, son?"

He tried to push her away but didn't have the strength to be effective.

"Look at that," Jane shouted. "Even in his final moments, he's trying to save his mother."

She cast a pained glance at Sarah. "You caused all this. Somehow, and I don't know how you made this happen."

From the corner of her eye, Sarah detected Aaron and Drake moving closer. Cars screeched to a halt twenty feet away on the road.

"For that, we die together." Jane held the detonator high

and looked at Aaron. "Say goodbye."

Sarah met Aaron's gaze. She blew him a kiss and mouthed *I will always love you.*

Jane pushed the button on the detonator.

Chapter 61

NOTHING HAPPENED.

Sarah raised her hands and looked at each one. Aaron and Drake had turned to protect their faces. Blair had dove into the water and came up unharmed.

Jane looked at the detonator and frowned. She pushed the button again and again, her thumb pounding it. A loud moan escaped her lips with each push, her eyes taking on a frantic look as madness overran what sanity she had left.

Aaron moved toward Sarah.

Drake sloshed through the water toward Jane, hands extended before him.

Jane tossed the detonator aside and came up with a gun.

Sarah wondered where that came from while Jane screamed something unintelligible and aimed at Sarah. Without hesitation, Jane squeezed her finger on the trigger.

In a flash, Drake dove and smashed into her.

So close, the weapon's report was deafening. In that briefest of moments, Sarah tried to jerk away, but the water limited movement to slow motion.

Drake and Jane went under the water.

A moment later, Aaron flew by her, landing in the same spot as Drake did a moment before him. Then all three were submerged. Sarah edged away as the water swirled above the submerged fight.

Panic swelled in her at the thought that either Drake or Aaron would get shot, but she didn't want to help or get close to them because of the radiation emitted from the vest.

The muscle relaxant was almost all gone. Movement wasn't as limited anymore. Blair was swimming away from them toward the emergency vehicles near the fence the hearse had broken through.

Half a dozen men in uniforms jumped in the Bellagio fountains and waded toward them.

Sarah dipped under the water and opened her eyes, but it was too murky to see what was happening. Her facial wounds from Jane's shoe stung in the water. When she brought her face above the surface, two cops lifted her up and away from the scene.

"Guys," she said. "Careful. The vest is an explosive."

They instantly dropped her and stepped away. The cop on her left reached for his weapon.

"Take it easy," Sarah said. "Not my explosive." She pointed toward the hearse. "That woman's."

Aaron surfaced. A moment later, Drake emerged, dragging Jane with him. She was unconscious, her head hanging to the right by her shoulder.

If she's dead, the world will be better off.

Medical personnel took over and ushered everyone to the sidewalk, where they took Jane away in an ambulance, sirens wailing with an FBI escort.

Aaron hugged Sarah close as Parkman moved in behind them.

"Aaron, you have to let go and stay clear of me. Jane said these vests are radioactive. Blair was showing signs of radiation poisoning."

Aaron waited a heartbeat, then released his arms and moved away. She could see it pained him to do so.

She watched as her friends formed a semi-circle around her in support. Casper was there. Detective Collins nodded at her. His partner Mara was behind him. Drake and Spencer stood by Parkman, a bandage on his arm.

A woman moved through the group.

"I'm Special Agent King." She pointed at a man with several pieces of gear and electrical devices strapped to his person. "This man will examine the vest for radiation and remove it if he can."

"You can't remove it," Sarah said. "Jane had it rigged to blow if it's taken off."

"Joel here is an expert. Let's at least hear what he has to say."

"Go ahead. Do your worst. Offer me hope. I'm not above that."

Joel started with a small handheld device, running it over the vest, front and back, like a wand at airport security.

"What's that?" she asked.

"Radiation detector."

"Anything?"

"Minor amounts. Nothing unsafe."

Euphoria swept over her. "What? Really? How's that possible?"

Joel moved around her waving his wand. "Not sure I understand the question."

"Jane bought these things specially built for her. She would've checked the radiation levels."

"There might have been more at one point. I can't be sure. Even my device is registering a reading. But it's way below safety levels."

"Then why was Blair throwing up?"

Parkman and Drake moved apart, and Blair stepped inside the grouping. He wasn't wearing the vest anymore.

"I was vomiting because of what my mother did to her men at church. Made me sick. Literally. When she said the vests were radioactive, how would I know any different? Joel just did the test on my vest. It's clean. They took it off."

"Then take mine off."

"Working on it," Joel said.

He replaced his radiation device and took out something that appeared to examine the vest's wires.

"Dead," he mumbled.

"Dead?"

"The vest is dead. Whoever made it did a fine job, but they didn't make it waterproof. The electrical leads are soaked. It shorted the vest out. When you and Blair went swimming, the vest died. The water effectively cut off the ability to send the detonation signal."

Sarah went to grab the clip to undo it, but Joel beat her to it.

"Easy." He looked at her. "Let me."

"It's your gig. Just do it already. I need out of this thing."

Joel unclipped the vest, eased it off, and returned to the emergency vehicles with it held high. Spectators parted to let him through like a parting of the sea.

Sarah shuddered with relief. "I thought I was done for in that thing." Aaron moved close and wrapped an arm around her. "So good to be back. What happened to Parkman's arm?"

"I shot him," Aaron said. "Long story."

She frowned and turned to Parkman.

He shrugged. "To save my life, he needed to shoot me. Whitman saved our asses."

"Who's Whitman?"

"That's me," Drake said. "New identity after what happened in Toronto."

"New name, new game," Spencer said, then shrugged.

"You're going to fill me in, right?"

"As much as I can." Whitman and Spencer exchanged a harsh look.

"You saved Aaron and Parkman?" she asked Whitman. "And just saved me when you jumped on Jane as she shot at me." Sarah let go of Aaron and stepped to Whitman to hug him.

"I owed you after Toronto," he said. "I'd be dead if it wasn't for you. When I heard you were in trouble in Mexico, I just had to come."

Sarah pulled away and looked into his eyes. "Was that you who followed us from the border to the hotel in Rosarito?"

"Yup."

"Fucker."

He shrugged.

"Thought you were an enemy," Sarah said.

"I would've too. Just didn't want to approach until I had you alone, like in the lobby. I mean, you thought I was dead. There might be a certain level of confusion."

"And there was." Sarah eased away from him in the water, nodded at Detective Collins, and examined them all.

"So good to see you all together. Collins, thanks for taking my message seriously and bringing everyone to the Venetian. I know you did a lot of good here, too, Casper."

He winked at her. "But we need a break, okay? No more fucking around. I've exhausted a lot of favors."

"I agree. No more favors." She gave him a wry smile, then touched Parkman's bandage gently. "What the hell were you guys doing while I was away?"

"Long story," Aaron said. "What happened to your face?"

"The heel of Jane's shoe."

Detective Collins edged closer. "Sarah, the FBI's here. They will want you examined at a local hospital and then take a statement from you."

"Aaron will take me to the hospital. I want Drake to come, too. And Parkman. Right now, I need to be surrounded by them."

Collins nodded his understanding. "I'll let them know." He moved away to talk to Agent King.

They had done it. Lived through another nightmare. Where had Vivian been in all this, though? Maybe she was trying to show Sarah that she could do it on her own.

They piled into an SUV provided by the FBI with Special Agent King driving.

"There's a warehouse we need to stop at before we go to

the hospital. There's a bag of mine I have to pick up."

"Sorry, Sarah," King said. "Straight to the hospital. I have my orders."

"Change them. It's Darnell's Car Repair, or I get out here."

"Warehouse," Aaron said.

"Warehouse," Parkman added.

"Warehouse," Drake said.

King slapped the steering wheel and pulled away from the curb.

"Fine. Where's this warehouse of yours?"

Chapter 62

AFTER BEING CHECKED OUT in the hospital, her wounds tended to with only a few bandages, Sarah was driven to the FBI building, where she gave her statement. She covered everything from Blair's love for Hank Olsen to Jane buying the devices made into Kevlar vests and how Sarah was tricked into putting it on. She described Boris and his men as best as she could.

As the day waned, she was told the FBI might have more questions tomorrow. In the event they did, they offered to put her up in a Vegas hotel for the night. She accepted their offer and told them she wanted to stay at Caesar's Palace with Aaron. After some cajoling, Caesar's Palace was approved for two nights.

She waited in a sitting area with Aaron, just outside the interview rooms where she had given her statement. Agent King had asked them to wait as a dirty bomb specialist was eager to explain a few things to Sarah.

On the ride to the FBI building, Vivian finally appeared. Before Sarah could shun her or try to disengage Vivian from her head, her sister had explained her stance. Within seconds, Sarah understood everything. It made so much sense. Sarah wondered how she couldn't have seen it before.

Then Vivian was gone again.

Parkman had left with a toothpick in his mouth, and the spares in his pocket headed back to Santa Rosa. He'd done his time in Mexico and Vegas and needed to return to work.

Sarah rested her head against the wall and said, "We're going to get a vacation after all, Aaron. But there's something I need to do first. Is Blair still here?"

"As far as I know, he is. I'll ask."

Aaron got up and crossed the waiting room toward an office, where he motioned for Agent King's attention. She had been talking to Casper. King and Aaron chatted briefly, then Aaron headed back toward Sarah.

"Blair's in interview room three. He should be out soon."

"We can't leave without seeing him."

"Okay," Aaron said, his tone revealing he didn't know why but wasn't about to ask.

Whitman and Spencer said they'd stay the night and talk to Aaron and Sarah tomorrow when they were clear of the FBI building. There was so much catching up to do, and Sarah wanted to learn more about the new man Drake had become.

A door opened at the end of the corridor, and an odd-looking man walked down the hallway. His pants were too high, his shirt pinstriped, and his glasses had the nerdy, stereotypical tape between the lenses. He walked side to side, his shoulders thin and bony.

Agent King stepped out of her office and met him in the hall. They approached Sarah together.

"Sarah," King started. "This is Carl Wingerton. He's our resident expert on all things that glow in the dark. Think Reed from Criminal Minds."

Carl laughed like he was hiccupping. Then stopped abruptly.

"He has a few things to tell you," King added. "To put your mind at ease about the vest."

"I'm all ears. I'd love to hear more."

Carl fumbled with a pen in his pocket.

"It was from smoke detectors," Carl said, punctuating each word with a whirl of the pen.

"Smoke detectors? I don't think I'm following you."

"All smoke detectors come with a radioactive isotope, americium-241. It's a small amount. Exempted from regulations applied to larger sources." The pen made Sarah think of a conductor at a concerto. "It produces radiation outside the device. Collect enough smoke detectors and add the radioactive isotope to the vest, it'll read as if it's radioactive, but it really isn't dangerous. At least not like a nuke or something." The pen didn't stop bobbing.

"Who knows this stuff?" Sarah asked, her mouth agape. "Is that common knowledge?"

"It's all over the internet," Carl said, almost losing the pen on the last word. "Some European countries have banned smoke detectors for this reason."

"Because it could be used in dirty bombs?"

"No." He suddenly appeared upset, like she wasn't following his logic fast enough. "Radiation."

"Right."

"I think that's enough," King said as she turned to go. When Carl didn't move, she turned back. "Carl?"

"It's okay," Sarah said, looking at King. She turned her gaze to Carl. "I'm interested in what he has to say."

"Me too," Aaron chimed in.

"Old clocks, too," Carl said.

"Old clocks are interested in you?" Casper asked from the side. He had come out of the room where he'd been waiting for King to return.

Carl didn't look his way. He kept his eyes on Sarah.

"Old clocks, before the 1960s, were painted with radioactive luminous paint. Basically radium. Highly radioactive, with a half-life of 1600 years. Even if the dials aren't luminous anymore, that's not the radium." He smiled when he said that, almost like he was enjoying his chemistry lesson because he held an audience rapt. "It's because the radiation of the radium has worn out the fluorescence of the zinc sulfide medium."

"Wow," Sarah said, genuinely surprised by what Carl was saying. "That's crazy. So I can guess they discovered how dangerous radium was and stopped using it on clocks?"

Carl shook his head with vigor, then stopped. "They have used radium in toothpaste, hair creams, and even several food products, but that got stopped when it was deemed dangerous. Radium was used in cancer treatment, but it causes cancer. The human body responds to radium like it would calcium. It deposits it into the bones, destroying cells and mutating them, causing cancer. Radium can also—"

"Okay," King stepped in front of him. "I think that's enough. Sarah's vest wasn't radioactive. We're good now,

Carl."

"Thanks for the lesson, Carl," Sarah said.

It took a little persuading, but Agent King got Carl to follow her down the hall and out the far door.

"That was something else," Casper said. "Out of my league."

"Mine too," Sarah added. "But I got the gist of what he was saying. Casper, can you give us a few moments."

"Sure." Casper headed back to the office he'd been in, then stopped. "Just one more thing. Aaron, there's news for you."

"What's that?"

"The manhunt for you, Parkman, and Whitman has been canceled in Mexico."

"Really?"

"What manhunt?" Sarah asked.

"Long story."

"Stop saying long story," Sarah muttered. "I hope you'll tell me all these long stories soon."

Aaron nodded her way but stayed focused on Casper. "How did that happen?"

"Someone left an iPhone recording at the scene of a rundown shack. It was found among some rocks, the battery dead. Once it was charged, they found a video. It's all over the news down there how several cops had tried to kill you guys. The use of deadly force to escape, even leaving one cop alive, was quite evident on the camera, even though the video was taken at night. Whoever did that was brilliant. Saved your asses. Just thought you should know."

"Wow. Thanks."

"iPhone?" Sarah asked. "Was that you?"

"No," Aaron looked down at the floor as he thought about it. "Must've been Whitman."

"If it was, he saved all of you. Twice."

"So true, Sarah. So true."

Aaron and Sarah waited another five minutes before Blair exited the interview room. He looked better and less frazzled, even though his mother was being brought up on terrorist charges that looked like all her properties and assets would be seized. Blair would have nothing to start his life on unless he returned to the drug business.

"Blair. Come over here a minute."

Sarah introduced him to Aaron and got him to sit with them.

"What's your next move?" Sarah asked.

"Not sure." He looked at his lap and fiddled with his fingers. "I won't speak to my mother. Or see her ever again after what she did." He looked up into her eyes. "As soon as I'm allowed to leave, I'm going to see Hank in the hospital back in Rosarito. Maybe now we can start our new life together."

Sarah reached under her seat and withdrew the bag that contained the million dollars Jane had promised her. She had Agent King drive them all to Darnell's Car Repair garage to get it in the back of the SUV, claiming she had left some of her things there. Nothing had been touched in her absence.

"Take this. It'll help you get started. It's yours. One million in unmarked bills. No one can trace it."

His eyes widened briefly. He placed a hand on the bag.

"Why, Sarah? Why don't you keep it? You earned it."

"It's not mine to keep. It came from your family. Since everything your mom's name is on will be government property soon enough, this is something they can't get to. Just take it. Go, live your life now. You deserve it."

He started to cry. "I can't thank you enough for all that you did."

Sarah moved around the bag to hug him.

"We did it together. It's over. Let it out."

Blair's tears even brought a couple to Sarah's face. They cried for several moments until Agent King came to inform them that they were free to leave the building but stay in Vegas for a few more days.

After saying their goodbyes to Blair, Sarah, and Aaron took a taxi to Caesar's Palace and settled into their room on the fifth floor. Sarah ran for the bed, dove, and landed on it, bouncing once. She gestured for Aaron to join her.

"We need time for ourselves," she said.

He lay down beside her, the expression on his face distant.

"What's wrong, Aaron?"

"I'm afraid to ask."

"Really? Don't piss me off with shit like that. Just ask."

"How's your withdrawal?"

"Oh, that? It's over. Done with. Jane hired some guy named Dr. Wesson to fix me up. I was doing that in Mexico before she flew me up here." Sarah leaned away from him to look into his face. "Is that what you were afraid to ask?"

He nodded. "In case reminding you would trigger the urge."

"It's nothing. Forget about it now. That part of my life was temporary, and it's over."

"You lied to me, Sarah. Back at the hotel."

Sarah stared at the ceiling, a hand behind her head

squished into the pillow. "You know I had to. You were too close. I needed to meet Blair, per Vivian. To stop Jane. The condition I was in, you wouldn't have allowed it."

"You're right. I wouldn't have." Two minutes went by before he spoke again. "Is this something I am to expect in the future?"

"That depends."

"On what?"

"You."

"How so?"

She turned toward him. "If you trust me, believe in me. I will tell you anything and everything. But you have to trust me. Even if what I have to do looks dangerous or insane. If I have to do it, you can't stop me."

"I do trust you. I believe in you. But that's a tough proposal, letting you do something insane."

"See, there's the problem. You said, *letting* me do something. It's never been about *letting* me. It's about you letting go." She took in a deep breath. "Aaron, people teach you how to treat them, how to manage them. You've taught me to manage you by not giving you the whole truth because you can't handle the truth. Unteach that, and I'll open up with whatever it is I'm doing."

He seemed to have to think about things for a moment. Then he said, "Fair enough. That's a valid point. You start an open secret policy, and I'll be there for you as much as I can, and soon you'll learn what to keep and not to keep from me. But I suspect you'll see that I can handle the truth." He tried to emulate her voice in the last few words.

She smacked his arm. "Don't mimic me."

He laughed. "No one can mimic you, Sarah."

"Vivian told me I should share something with you."

"What's that?"

"She gave me a piece of wisdom on the way to the FBI building. Because she's in my head, I understand her in a way that's hard to verbalize, but I'll try." Sarah cleared her throat. "I had asked for more of the big picture. I told Vivian that you lost a finger, I got addicted to heroin, and that, basically, she had gone too far. If I knew the big picture, maybe there'd be a way to manage what she wants me to do without so much pain and injuries. Especially to the people I love."

"How did she take that?"

"She explained that she couldn't offer the big picture and gave me a list of examples. One was the radioactive vest that wasn't radioactive. If she had told me what it was before I put it on, an entire series of events would've changed. For starters, I would've been shot and killed by Boris's men because there was no way I would've put the vest on. Had I not gone to the meet in the first place, I wouldn't have been with Jane all the way to the end. Vivian knew the future. She knew the water would defuse the bomb and that the amount of radiation was harmless, but if she had told me that, I wouldn't have acted as afraid and angry as I did, which kept me authentic. Almost like method acting."

"Wow, that's a lot to take in."

"There's more, but we can save it for another time." Sarah rolled over and held out her hand. Aaron took it. "Suffice it to say; I have to learn to trust the process. She's got my back. Just do what she needs and keep my wits about me, and it'll all work out. Now, with you, let's shake on it. Let's make a pact, a deal. We will work together and be together without the added shit. If I need to meet a drug dealer to buy heroin and I'm suffering from withdrawal, you will have to let me go. Vivian sees and knows things we aren't privy to. If she says meet the dealer, I meet the dealer. You must agree, too, or it'll never work between us. Deal?"

"Saying it that way sucks. It's like we have a third person in our relationship, but I understand." He shook her hand. "I'll agree to the deal because there's the deal and Sarah, or no deal and no Sarah. Can't live without my Sarah." He pumped her hand. "We now have a pact."

The phone rang beside the bed. They looked at each other.

"Who knows we're here?" Sarah asked.

"As far as I know, just the FBI."

Sarah rolled away from him and grabbed the phone.

"Hello," she said in a gruff voice.

"Sarah?" It was her father.

"Dad?" she said, glancing at Aaron. "How did you find me?"

"Called Parkman. He told me you were at Caesar's. I called and got your room number."

"It was that easy?"

"Yup."

"Is everything okay?"

"When are you coming back to Santa Rosa? Anytime soon?"

"It wasn't in the plans right away. The FBI needs me here for two more days."

"When you're done with them, come as soon as possible, Sarah. It's important."

"What?" A thought struck her. "Is it Mom?"

"No, nothing like that."

"Then what?"

"It's your sister. Vivian."

For a moment, Sarah couldn't work her mouth. She got up off the bed and walked to the room's window.

"She's been in touch with us, Sarah," her father added.

"How?" She swallowed, a sense of shock coming over her. "How is that possible?"

"A time capsule. We were to open it after twenty-five years. Well, we're almost at twenty-five years, and your mom and I couldn't wait. Sarah, the whole thing is for you."

"For me?"

"Your sister wrote a note for you before she died. It's a pact she wants you to read. A pact between you and Vivian. If you can, come alone. I don't think Aaron should be here for this."

"Okay." Her mind was stuck on one and two-word answers. She couldn't think to get it unstuck. None of what her dad had said was computing.

"A pact?" she mumbled.

"Yes, Sarah. You need to do what this note says, and you can't tell anybody. We shouldn't even know, but we read it anyway. I'm sorry, Sarah, but get home as soon as you can."

"Okay. Two days."

"Sarah, there's something you should know."

"What?"

"Your sister was psychic when she was alive. She helped people. We didn't know. She was so young when she died. While on Earth, she talked to the dead. Now dead, she talks to the living. What she has to say, Sarah is not something I can repeat over the phone. Just come home. Hurry."

"Two days."

"Okay, Sarah. Glad you and Aaron are okay after that cartel business."

Her mind was unstuck when she turned to face Aaron. How would she tell him he needed to stay behind or go home to Toronto because she had to go see what Vivian had left for her after the deal they had just made minutes before the phone call? They had even called their deal a pact, too.

"You don't know the half of it, Dad. I'll fill you in when I get there."

"See you soon, honey. Be safe."

She hung up and set the phone down, her stomach full of dread.

Now what?

Shit cake with lemons. This was going to be sour.

"Aaron, we need to talk."

Afterword

Dear Reader,

Many years ago, back in my youth, I was raised in a family that didn't read for the most part. I learned at an early age what the written word meant to me. Before I attended school, at a very early age, my older sister would come home from her classes, and I would ask to see her school books. I couldn't read them yet but was fascinated by all the words littered across the page, all lined up and in order.

The question I recall asking my sister over and over was could she read those words. She would always reply in the affirmative and then watch *General Hospital* or whatever the show was after school. (Years later, for me, it was *Gilligan's Island*.)

One day, I got caught. I was reading—pretending to—with her school books. I had a blank notebook out, and I was writing, word for word, in the blank notebook, every line, every paragraph of a novel my sister had to read for a book report. This goes back some time, but that's how I remember it.

She commented that if I loved writing that much, I would love school because I'd have to write report after report and essays. Well, in short, she was wrong. I did not like essays one bit. I just loved words. I loved writing. Something I still do to this day—yeah, I know. That part is obvious. I wrote this book. Self-evident. Hang in there. I'm going somewhere with this. Soon enough, school taught me how to read. And I couldn't stop. Book after book from the library. Oh, the adventures I went on sitting in a chair as the snow fell around my school.

But there was one problem. I only read books with pictures. Not comics. Just books like Peter Rabbit and Dr. Seuss.

Then I met Jerry—not his real name—and he asked me why I only read books with pictures.

"Is there any other kind?" I responded. "The rest are all textbooks or too hard for me. I just started reading not too long ago."

"Here." He handed me a Hardy Boys book. *The House on the Cliff.* "Try this. It's not that hard to read."

I loved the cover and the feel of the book. Then I opened it and saw chapter after chapter of words—just text.

"Looks interesting," I said, handing the book back. "But not for me. I prefer pictures."

He didn't take the book. Just pushed it gently toward me.

"This book does have pictures."

He must be crazy. I had just looked. To humor him, I

flipped through the pages again, and when I got to the end of the book, I held it up.

"No pictures."

"Sure there is," he said.

I remember thinking about how stubborn he was.

"The pictures are hiding."

Now he had my attention. I looked down at the book in my hand.

He continued, "The pictures are *inside* the words."

"What?" Now I was confused. (Remember, I was quite young.)

"Read the first page. Maybe the second. You'll see." He nodded at the book. "The pictures will rise out of the page and into your head. Don't worry. Your eyes will form the pics from the words."

He started to lose me at that young age, but I did what he said. I opened the book to chapter one and started reading.

And I gasped.

A picture formed instantly. He was right. Frank and Joe Hardy were on a mystery, and I was sold. I saw everything with my mind's eye, and reading became as much a part of me as breathing. I'm forever grateful to Jerry for that moment in time, and I will never be able to thank him for what he did for me because I have no idea where he is or what his real name is. It's been a lifetime since that day.

So I write in pictures, just as I read.

And I read newspapers because I need to stay current with world affairs. I started reading newspapers when I was fourteen and became addicted. Today, I read at least five papers a day, all online, sometimes more. Newspapers serve as inspiration as the world is a terrible place to live sometimes.

Having said that, the statistics and supporting data in this novel regarding India and rape are all true. I did the research, and an easy search online can substantiate what I wrote here.

In addition, the selling of dirty bombs still goes on today. Moldovan police have arrested and stopped black market smugglers of nuclear material to extremist groups four times in the last five years, and that's just the Moldovan police. Sliven and Russian arms dumps are real, and sales routinely happen on the black market.

Having said that, I enjoy delivering what I see in the news through Sarah's eyes. I also enjoy bringing these people down fictitiously. It's a wild ride of words and pictures for me.

I'm having fun. I hope you are, too.

Lastly, I'd like to add a few plugs. The TV show *Ray Donovan* was mentioned in the novel. It's an unbelievable show. Watch it. Amazing.

Band of the Hand, a movie by Michael Mann, was also mentioned. When Agent King said she rewound the VCR and re-watched the entire movie, that was me circa 1986. To this day, wherever I travel around the globe, I have that movie on DVD. Still my favorite of all time. It's the 1980s in that movie, and it's an eighties movie completely. Get past the hairdos and the clothes and just watch the movie.

Finally, I talked about Greg Iles. I've loved every one of his novels. Loved *Sleep No More* and *Dead Sleep*. So good. Check him out. You won't regret it.

Credits:

Samantha Puig: I appreciate you letting me use your name for the FBI special agent in charge in Las Vegas. Get caught reading!

Stacy King: Again, thanks for the use of your name. I loved you as an antsy agent in the field, hating stakeouts and wanting to deal with Jane Turner firsthand. You've got guts, Agent King!

Mary Fitzgerald: Using your name as the lead agent on the Jane Turner case was great. Thanks! I loved your quiet demeanor and by-the-book attitude.

Tracy Martin: Thanks for the use of your name—Detective Tracy Martin—for the bit part of being in Toronto when Parkman called through. Many thanks to you!

And to all the readers out there, I am eternally grateful to you. I can't do this without you and, in the immortal words of Whitney Houston (I know, Dolly Parton, but I only knew the Whitney version, so I'm quoting her here), "I Will Always Love You."

Now, as is my ritual when I finish writing a novel, I'll have a tall glass of my favorite whiskey. It's Sarah's favorite, too.

This is me, raising my glass to Sarah because I'd be lost without her.

See you all in *The Pact*, book seventeen, for a crazy time on the wild ride of the written word.

Until next time, get caught reading.

All mistakes found in this novel are mine and mine alone. If you've ever done heroin or dealt with withdrawal (or know someone who has), I apologize if I got some of the facts wrong. You have my sympathy and my love. May you be Sarah, be strong, and stay on the solid path of being clean.

Yours truly, with warmest regards to you and yours …
Jonas Saul

About Jonas Saul

Jonas Saul is the bestselling author of the Sarah Roberts Series—more than two million sold!—and has written and published over sixty thrillers. After acquiring an agent, he signed several deals in Los Angeles, with MadRiver Pictures optioning his Sarah Roberts Series— over forty books!—(currently in development).

Jonas has often outranked Stephen King and Dean

Koontz on Amazon over the past decade. He's regularly invited to be a guest speaker, teacher, or workshop presenter at international writing conferences and film festivals worldwide. He hosts an annual writer's retreat in Greece, where he currently lives. He focuses his teaching on how to get tension and emotion in every scene, on every page, how he made it as a creator/writer, the path to success in this business, and the pitfalls to avoid. He also hosts a reading retreat in Greece with guest authors, yoga retreats, and hiking retreats. Visit the Imagine Greece Retreats website at www.imaginegreeceretreats.com, or email him directly to discuss an opportunity to join one of the retreats at jonas@imaginegreeceretreats.com.

Jonas is also a professional freelance editor. He works for several publishers and does private editing for clients, with many testimonials on his website at www.imaginepress.org, which details each author's response to Jonas's editing skills. Email Jonas directly for an editing quote at editor@imaginepress.org.

To book Jonas for a speaking engagement at a writer's conference/festival, to have him on your jury at a film festival, or even to say hello, email Jonas directly at jonassaul@icloud.com.

For updates on releases, hit the "Follow" button on Amazon or Bookbub, and join Jonas on Facebook, where he's most active.

Contact Jonas Saul

Linktree: Find me here

Email: jonassaul@icloud.com